THE SPLENDID CITY

OTHER BOOKS BY TERENCE CLARKE

Novels
My Father in the Night
The King of Rumah Nadai
A Kiss for Señor Guevara
The Notorious Dream of Jesús Lázaro
La espléndida ciudad (Spanish language edition)
When Clara Was Twelve
The Moment Before

—

Short story collections
The Day Nothing Happened
Little Bridget and The Flames of Hell
New York
San Francisco

—

Non-fiction books
Fathers, Sons, and Seizures
The Sea Lion and The Sculptor
An Arena of Truth: Conflict in Black and White

THE SPLENDID CITY

A NOVEL

TERENCE CLARKE

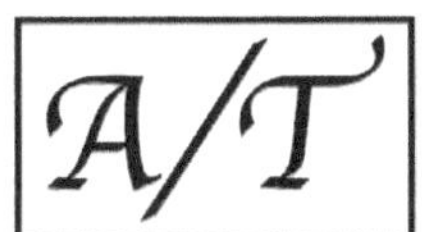

For Beatrice Bowles

*Hundí la mano turbulenta y dulce
en lo más genital de lo terrestre.*

*I sank my turbulent, tender hand
in the furthest genitals of the earth.*
Pablo Neruda

CONTENTS

1
PROLOGUE

Pablo Neruda stood at a podium, having just received the Nobel Prize. He looked down at the gold medallion in his hand, possessed by so few. The likeness was a kindly rendition of the man who had invented dynamite.

The audience's applause had proven as respectful of Pablo as could be. They had dressed conservatively and well. They represented the world of letters at its best and had just given him the most prestigious award that any person of letters could ever receive. The hall rose up above them grand, august and formal, lit in such a way as to emphasize the serious congratulation that his work had garnered for him.

Pablo fidgeted nervously about his words. He would speak of his poetry, of course, his cherished verse. And the politics, to be sure, his troublesome Communism. But now in 1971 (so late in life) and here in Stockholm (so far away), he wished really to speak about something else, of which these people knew nothing, and of which he knew…well, everything. *I'll tell them what they've come to hear,* he thought. *But now…just now—*

"My speech will be a long journey." He touched the lapel of his coat, glancing down at the boutonniere, smoothing the lapel a moment as he rehearsed one last time the story he wished to give to them. "A voyage I once took through faraway, antipodean regions, for that reason not much different from the landscape and solitudes here of the North."

The rhythms were coming to him. *Yes. The escape.*

"I speak of the extreme south of my country." *The far south, yes*, he thought. *But even more, the nearer east, the Andes cordillera with its terrifying mountains…loving, ghostly mountains…so brutal…splendid but beyond difficult…merciless.*

"We who live in Chile must go so far to touch the South Pole with our boundaries, that it seems to us very like the geography here of Sweden, whose head brushes against the snowy north of the planet." Pablo smiled, enjoying the playful metaphor he had just made. His breathing began to hurry, though. Suddenly he was in danger, there, again. "Down there, in those far reaches of my country…" He felt his voice grasping for the occasion, his wish to tell the story. "Where events, that are now themselves quite forgotten, once took me, one must cross …" He laid a hand on his chest. "And I had to cross …" He took in a breath, still astonished by his having survived. "The Andes mountains."

2
PABLO SEALS HIS FATE

Things were looking up. The war in the Pacific was over. The Japanese had been pushed back and defeated. The English and Australians in Malaya, the New Zealanders as well, Indians from the sub-continent, Gurkhas from Nepal—and, yes, Pablo had to admit it—even the United States, had all prevailed. Fascism in Europe had been ground under by Comrade Stalin and the glorious Soviet victors, with a bit of minor help from the English and—here, too, he had to be fair—from the United States.

And now in Chile, the Left led in the election polls, and its leader had summoned Pablo to a meeting. In Pablo's opinion Gabriel González Videla stood knocking at the door to greatness as a statesman and politician, his hand on the very doorknob itself. The only thing needed was victory in the 1946 election, which was about to take place. Here, now, the man himself gestured to Pablo to sit down in a large leather chair on the other side of an oak desk. The Chilean flag hung from a standard behind Gabriel. He would soon be president of the nation, and he had just made Pablo a remarkable offer.

"I know you're a Communist."

"Not yet."

"Yes." Gabriel looked aside, clearing his throat. "Good old Uncle Joe…"

Pablo grinned. After the Spanish Civil War and now, after Hitler, he felt that Communism had proven to be the only real defense against Fascism, so why wouldn't Joseph Stalin deserve congratulation? He had beaten the German back from the gates of Stalingrad. He had taken the fight into Berlin itself, destroyed the place and murdered Hitler in his bunker. Altogether memorable.

"I need the Communists, Pablo. Without them, I don't have the votes."

"I know."

"And having you in our camp, the finest poet on this continent, and a Communist to boot…"

Pablo had grown used to praise. His friend Pablo Picasso had declared that Pablo Neruda was the greatest poet of the 20th century, in any language. He had been elected to the Chilean Senate two years earlier. He was famous, in and out of his own country.

But this was special.

"I want you to be my head of information and campaign manager… and, of course, to keep your own much-deserved office as senator." Gabriel sat back, gathered his hands together on his stomach, and studied Pablo's response. A devoted leftist, Gabriel González Videla was the best man in all of Chile to take the reins of government. He was honest, forthright, and truthful in every respect…and he needed the Communists. "You'll be one of the most important men in this country." He placed his hands on the desktop and searched Pablo's eyes. "I need you, Pablo. The country needs you."

Gabriel was a formal man, not a lot of fun, not really to Pablo's tastes. He didn't seem to like cocktail parties much, which to Pablo was a minus. Gabriel's education had been spotty. He spoke with slovenly diction. He didn't know a lot about the imagination. *Maybe nothing about it,* Pablo thought. He dressed dully and stiffly, in gray or black suits and gray or black ties. Pablo had never had a meal with him, but he imagined that, if Gabriel's eating were anything like his speeches, he had the same things for breakfast, lunch and dinner every day. Toast, no butter, water…

"We've come a long way, haven't we, Gabriel?"

"We have indeed."

"I remember just a few years ago, up in the desert, when I was running for the Senate." Pablo's voice wandered into silence.

"Pretty rough up there, isn't it?"

"Has been forever." Pablo looked out the window, suddenly in a reverie of the battle tank that had come to listen to his poetry. "Very good people, though."

—

Pablo held his hands out to the wood stove. Cold filled the shack, and speaking to these men was difficult. They were attentive, but they seemed impatient, even stolidly disdainful, as though Pablo's voice were just another shovelful of management indifference, the usual sort of shit—they could be heard to mumble—that comes from anyone who runs the show.

That offended him, since he had had to argue loudly with the manager of the mine for the right just to speak with these men.

Pablo admired miners, especially one whom he had met just today...the kid Josecito. An *atacameño* Indian from the far northern desert, he now sat with the others, wrapped in a wool poncho against the cold, weakened by the crisis through which he had gone several hours earlier.

What miners did was one of the most difficult tasks any worker could be given. Indeed, they often died doing it. Pablo was also, always, mindful of the fact that the United States owned the copper operations in Chile, that companies with names like Braden and Kennecott had paid a few high Chilean officials, the president and such, a couple million dollars each. It was a fortune for them, but essentially nothing for the Chilean people. The companies had then extracted the ore and sent it off—summarily—to the U.S.

Pablo imagined that, in the chambers of government in Santiago, champagne glasses had been raised high. Miners' rights? What miners?

Working down there could be disaster enough, in such harrowingly dark, claustrophobic tunnels where movement itself was of necessity cramped and painful. Then from time to time miners perished, so thoroughly trapped that even their prayers were choked into black submission.

Here in this northern region, in the Atacama Desert, it rained less than a tenth of an inch a year. So, above ground, it was almost as bad as below ground. There were few people, but those there were—the men working the mines, and their families—were a major voting block. The candidate Pablo, who was on his very first campaign swing for senator, who had almost never traveled in the Atacama and who had never been down a mine, felt that he should be aware of the dangers these men faced. So, he had just this morning descended into the Braden Paraiso #1 mine. The manager, an idiot from Santiago dressed in slacks, a shirt and a tie, whose name Pablo could not remember—he actually did not wish to remember it—had told him that it was against regulations for a non-employee to go down into the mine. Pablo, in front of a group of miners just then walking toward the entrance to begin their shift, had objected.

"*Amigo*, if I'm to represent these men in Congress, I must understand what they do." The miners had stopped shuffling toward the entrance, pickaxes and shovels resting on their shoulders. They were watching. "And besides, I checked when I was in Santiago. They said they'd contact the bosses in New York and ask, and that we'd get a response in a couple months, probably...maybe…sometime after the election." A rumble of understanding emerged from the miners. "But in the meantime, I know for a fact that there is no such regulation, since my opponent was here last week paying a visit."

A larger rumble, this one of approval—of laughter actually—came from the miners. As one of them handed Pablo a helmet with a lantern on it, Pablo thanked the manager, clapped the miner on the back, and headed with the group to the entrance.

The mine closed in on Pablo like death. This was his first time ever in such a place, and his blood felt to have been thickened in its progress through his heart by the heat of the mine as they descended. He knew this was just an illusion. *But what an illusion!* he thought. With the rising temperature in the mine, his blood would slowly turn to hot red sludge, its wet oiliness racing down any passageway. *What would that actually feel like?* he wondered as he and the miners descended in an iron wagon on a pair of rails. He looked ahead, down the narrow tunnel the walls and ceiling of which were held up by hand-hewn wooden beams. The beams were thick and ruggedly tied to one another by black rope. Yet, as the wagon proceeded down the steep tunnel into the darkness, the beams appeared so fragile that Pablo saw himself and the miners lost forever were they to collapse, as they appeared—to him, at least—ready to do.

He imagined that he was a single drop of blood, the vital molecules of which grew more and more slippery as the temperature moved higher and higher. Finally, in his last living movement, his entire body decomposed and burbled into separate puddles and blurts, a tropic mess, quite dead.

"Don't be scared, *amigo*," one of the miners said, touching his shoulder.

"I am."

"That's all right. We all are."

They went down and farther down, finally passing the point at which Pablo felt he was as frightened as he could ever be. But he became even more frightened. He sensed his heart, the only thing that by now he could really feel, banging in him as though it were being struck by a hammer. The car continued descending. The air was so close that it could hardly be breathed, as, finally, the car arrived at the end of the rail line. Sweat careened from Pablo everywhere. An air hammer, manned by a very small person bent over by the closeness of the conical chamber in which he was working beyond the end of the rail tracks, was battering the stone. As Pablo stepped from the car, a cloud of rock dust burst from the hole, and he fainted.

A few miners gathered around him, and as he came to, he fought them off. "I'm all right. Leave me alone."

"But *don* Pablo—"

"I want to see this. Leave me be!"

After a moment, Pablo crawled up the hole a few feet, to get as close as he could to the air hammer, despite the thickness and smell of the dust that was blowing from the hole. Like all the others so close to the actual mining, he had placed a folded cloth mask over his nose and mouth. One of the miners had handed him a pair of goggles, like those the American fighter pilots wore in World War II movies, of which Pablo was a fan. He could barely see through them.

The hammer-operator's entire body shook with the force of the machine. His clothing was as black as the dust swirling from the hole in the rock. His hands, the back of his neck, the helmet he wore...all black, as, Pablo imagined, he himself must now be. Wet blackness clung to him like glue. The noise of the hammer buffeted the very center of the poet's hearing. He placed his hands over his ears and attempted looking over the miner's shoulder. The hammer's bit slashed at the rock, and the miner worked it in and out of the crevices in the wall. After another few moments of ratcheting noise and distress, the miner turned off the hammer, motioned to Pablo and the others that he was coming out of the hole, and backed away from the wall.

The fellow had panicked. He coughed, choking, although when others tried helping him, he pushed them away, grasping at the cloth over his mouth and nose. He pulled it from his face, and black spittle, then hot black vomit, tumbled from his mouth. He threw his own goggles to the dirt, and then went down to his knees. Two other miners knelt next to him, pounding him on the back. His coughing came in liquid growling hacks, a dog drowning. He suddenly collapsed, writhing, until the others were able to roll him over on his back and minister to him.

"Josecito," one of them shouted. "José!"

Josecito held his hands over his chest, his legs kicking back and forth as he tried to get control of his breathing. Finally, after several minutes, he calmed, acquiescing to the embrace of the other miner, like a child in the arms of his father.

The hammer remained behind in the hole. Pablo looked back at it, the rubber hose connected to its stock, leading back up the tunnel to some source of forced, cool air. It was constant air, too, of the sort that had not been given to José. The machine lay on its side, as covered with dust as José had been. Black and gray, of a seemingly angry, metallic imperviousness, the hammer appeared wounded. More accurately, it had died. The steel protuberances, the trigger and the aggressive, pointed bit seemed to Pablo to have lost their souls. Without the miner to give it breath, it was just a lot of metal, organized for force that had now been angrily abandoned. The machine had served as a slave to indentured servants, therefore, as a slave's slave.

Pablo discovered that Josecito was a child.

"*Gracias, tio* Mateo," he said to the miner holding him. His high voice had not yet changed. "Don't tell my mother...."

—

"You cannot speak with these men, *señor* Neruda."

The manager had summoned Pablo to his office, in a wooden building near the mine operation entrance. Pablo, his coveralls and shirt so remarkably soiled from his descent into the mine, felt like a piece of versifying filth. He tried wiping the still damp mine dust from his face, but his fingers were so soiled that the black goo on them simply exchanged itself with the goo on his lips.

"Why not?"

"I told you not to go down into the mine. And there are other restrictions. For example, here..." The manager pointed with an index figure at the typed sheet of paper on a clipboard. "I have clear orders from Santiago that the men are not allowed to be approached by political candidates."

"What about my opponent?"

The manager held tight to the clipboard.

"Wasn't he here last week?"

The manager looked down his nose at the clipboard as though it were a piece of excrement. He was an educated man, Chilean, with an advanced degree in mining from the Universidad Nacional de San Juan in Argentina. Well-groomed, his hair precisely cut, his slacks pressed, as were his white shirt and dark blue tie, he stood his ground. "But he is approved by the company."

"And I am not."

"That's right."

"So how will these men know for whom to vote?"

"They know who to vote for, *señor*."

"My opponent, I would imagine."

The manager glanced again at the clipboard. "We'll have to wait and see, won't we, Comrade, until after the election?"

—

That evening, in the miners' dining hall, a large unpainted wooden shack with screen doors at either end that held three long hand-hewn wood tables with wood benches on either side, Pablo spoke to them. It was the stump speech he always gave to unions, in which he bludgeoned the current oligarch regime and made a stirring call to the workers to take up the twin weapons of The Right To Organize and The Right To Vote. His voice rose and fell as the justice of his message came from him in its full fury, demurred a bit to a more thoughtful presentation of a few economic facts here and there—the manner in which the government was screwing the miners, etc.—and then rose back to its previous histrionics. He approached the catch phrase, the one that the International Workers of The World in the United States used. It was a shout so compelling, so engendering of rumbles of support and demands for a change in government…. It was the unifying cry that Pablo was sure would usher him ultimately in triumph into Congress. He was headed for that cry, as he eventually was at every union meeting. His voice rose. He was getting there. *It really is a terrific speech*, Pablo thought. He himself was moved by it, every time.

"So, I say to you men, for the good of your families, for food on your table, for better working conditions, for higher wages and a boot in the ass to management, cast your vote for the workers! Vote Communist! Vote for me, Pablo Neruda, for senator! So that rich man and poor man, brown and white, electricity men, farm workers, factory workers, maids and miners alike can shout from the peaks of the Andes *cordillera* to the blue waters of Isla Negra, from the green forests of Araucania to the windy cold of Patagonia, from the great buildings of Santiago to the desert emptiness of Atacama…so that all working people from every town, each village and all cities can enter into the chambers of the government in Santiago shouting 'Workers of the world, unite!'"

With this, his clenched right fist raised well above his head, his eyes wild with patriotic intensity, Pablo awaited the rattle of noisy applause from those assembled before him.

There was none. He waited a moment longer until, embarrassed, he asked for questions. There weren't any of these either. The miners remained seated on the benches. They appeared to Pablo to have no recognition of what he had said. There was simply no interest in it. Their shoulders were slumped and dejected. Many of them were wearing sandals, and their black-nailed, gnarled feet shuffled a bit on the floor. They looked about at one another, their eyes wondering, scratching their heads with nervous embarrassment.

One of the men, Josecito's uncle Mateo, rose to his feet, raising a hand. He was a man made of chunks, of hard muscle and bulk and ravaged in the face. His shoulders sloped and weighed down even as he gathered the courage to speak.

"*Don* Pablo, we..." He looked down to his right, at his nephew. Josecito remained badly weakened and leaned against one of the other miners. The boy appeared to be about twelve years old.

"Josecito would like it if...we all would like it...if you would recite a few of your poems."

Pablo had brought along a stack of flyers, each of which contained the main points of his plan for returning the reins of government to the people. He had hoped to give these out. But just now he kept them in his hands. "Poems?" He put the papers on a wooden table at his side.

"We know many of them, maestro."

"You do?"

"Oh, yes. Often, when there's not much to do, when we're so tired at night, we recite them."

"Who to?"

"Each other. Our families."

Pablo sat down on the end of one of the benches, leaned forward and asked one of the miners which poem he would like to hear.

"The anti-tank one, *don* Pablo..."

"You have an accent."

"Yes, *señor*. Madrid."

"You're from there?"

"I was. My brother fought there, in the Civil War."

"And he survived, I hope?"

The miner lowered his head and did not respond. Pablo knew about the cruel madness of the Battle of Madrid during the Spanish Civil War in 1936.

"'*The anti-tank men,*'" Pablo said. "'*You have been in the dark-night mouth/of the war...*' That one, amigo?"

"Yeah. How does it go? '*Angels of fire, the terrible ones,/the pure sons of the earth*'"?

"That's it."

"'*You launched...you launched...*'". Distracted, the miner looked aside. "How does it go?"

"'*You launched not just the pure explosion of a fragment-bomb...*'"

"Yeah, '*...but also your deepest steaming heart,/a whip as...as...*'" He glanced up toward Pablo.

"'*Blue.*'"

"Yeah...'*as blue and destructive as powder.*'"

No one spoke. The miner, his mouth turning down with sadness, exhaled and sat back.

"That's how your brother died, Carlitos?" one of the other miners asked.

Carlitos remained silent.

Pablo looked further up the line of seated men. "Josecito?"

The boy coughed. He gathered the poncho around him and began, with shy hesitation, to speak. "'*Woman's body, hills of white, white muscles...*'"

His uncle, who had sat down to listen to the recitation, broke into gruff laughter. "José...you know about that?"

The other miners laughed, as did Josecito, for the first time in the evening.

"Yes, Uncle." He smiled, looking down. "Well, no."

Outside, not far away, the rattle of some kind of industrial mining machine, a giant steam shovel maybe, on treads, approached the hall. Josecito, frightened, looked toward the door, as did the other miners.

"Say on, boy," Pablo said.

The noise outside grew louder. The benches began shivering. The boy's voice had weakened. The miners, equally distracted by the approaching cacophony, strained nonetheless to listen to him.

Josecito gathered himself, turning back. "With your permission, maestro."

"Don't worry about that out there. Keep going." Pablo addressed the miners. "Comrades, José wishes to continue."

Most of the miners were clearly alarmed, yet turned their attention to the boy.

"*'But the vengeful moment falls away, and I love you.'*"

The steam shovel came to an abrupt halt just outside the hall. Its headlights flooded the room.

Pablo glanced at the door, at the glare of light. "Don't stop!"

"*'Body made of skin, made of moss, of covetous strong milk.'*"

The miners erupted in applause. Mateo, demanding silence, insisted that his nephew finish the sequence.

"*'Ah, the vessel of each breast! Ah, the absence in your eyes!'*"

Pablo, stunned, sat back and listened to the chaos of acknowledgment. The noise in the room, the joy of having listened to the parts of *don* Pablo's poems recited by their two friends, to have witnessed them reciting to the great poet himself, to hear others among the miners shouting out for other poems, for "Poem Three" from *Twenty Poems of Love* or "Old blind man, you weep" from *Crepusculario*, and many others, exclaiming how much this poem had meant to a particular girlfriend, how his wife had loved that one, how a cousin over there in Antafagosta, a lover in Peru, a mother or sister had enjoyed it…all of this fell over Pablo like crystalline, avalanching snow.

The screen door at one end of the shack sprung open, and the manager hurried into the hall.

"Okay, no more of this! Everybody out."

Pablo stood up. "No more of what?"

"Get out, Neruda! I told you that you couldn't do this!"

"The free exchange of ideas?"

"Out!"

"Democracy in action?"

"Get out!"

"Bravo." Pablo turned to the miners. "Come on, *amigos*. Follow me!"

The miners were reluctant to do so, until the manager ordered them out of the hall as well. The lights blinded Pablo and the others, and after a moment Pablo realized that it was no industrial machine that had brought the manager to the clandestine meeting. A tank rested several meters from the door, its turret gun aimed at the meeting hall.

"What is this?"

The manager folded his arms. "Company orders."

"Company orders! Fascist cowardice, you mean. Idiocy..." Pablo walked toward the tank. His gut boiled. He looked up, shielding his eyes against the tank's tremendous light. The gun turret, like a round, black iron castle, hovered before him. He could make out two other things: the cannon barrel itself and what was obviously the helmeted head of one of the tankers sticking out of the top door to the turret. "Hey! You up there!"

At first the tanker remained still.

"Come down from there, son of a bitch!"

Behind him, Pablo heard the appreciative, though guarded, laughter of the miners. It sounded like whispered grumblings beneath a blanket. The tanker, still for the moment motionless, appeared as immovable as the tank itself, as though he were a part of its steel structure, bolted into it. But suddenly, he jumped up from the tank door, hunkered a moment on the top of the turret, his hands on his bent knees. He looked to Pablo like the silhouette of an enraged ape, observing his enemy before attacking him.

"What was that you called me?"

"*¡Hijo de puta!*"

The tanker jumped down to the front platform of the tank, then to the ground, where he stopped before Pablo, his hands on his hips. He was backlit entirely in white light. Blinded, Pablo could not make out his face.

"I'm a son of a bitch, you say?"

"You are."

The soldier took Pablo by the arm.

"Don't touch me, *puto*."

"*Señor.*" The soldier nodded his head toward the miners, over Pablo's shoulder. "A word, privately..."

Pablo looked back. The miners had gathered outside the hall and stood rag-tag, unwashed and brilliant in the light from the tank. All of them appeared terrified.

"All right, come on."

They walked a few yards into the desert, it's very occasional cactus of no concern, its dry sands having been here in the north of Chile, unchanged, more or less, for twenty million years

"What's your name?"

"Lieutenant Ochoa."

"Chilean army?"

"Yes"

"So, what do you want?"

They stopped in the darkness, which was so complete that Pablo could barely see the soldier at all.

"*Señor*, you're endangering these men."

"I am not. It's that fool manager and his Yankee bosses."

"Perhaps so. But I hope you'll listen to me. I... I've..." Ochoa turned his head. The miners remained arrayed before the hall, lit like silvered targets for a firing squad. "What were you doing in there?"

"Reciting poetry."

"Poetry."

"Yes." Pablo lowered his head. "For Christ's sake, Lieutenant—"

"Was it yours?"

Pablo felt that he was in the company of a ghost, a phantasm of such destructive power that he could, in a moment, obliterate everything.

"Why do you ask?"

"Was it your poetry?"

Pablo grimaced. "Yes."

Suddenly, the phantasm let out a chuckle. "I've read your work, *don* Pablo."

"You?"

"Yes. I'm a fan, actually, and I would ask you this favor, please, for the sake of these men." Ochoa looked over his shoulder. "I mean you no harm."

"You? The lackey enforcer for this—"

"Listen, *hijo de puta*! My father's a miner. I mean them no harm. So, desist in this."

"Desist! From an act of free speech protected by your country's constitution?"

"No...no, *señor*." Ochoa looked back once again. He held up a hand, as though asking patience from Pablo. "Not that. But if you could just, for these men, *señor*, their families... If you could please just..." He sighed, "For the moment, stop, *señor*."

The miners had not moved.

"This *maldito* manager...I'm under orders to do what he says." Ochoa exhaled. "If he says so, I've got to take action."

The miners sulked in the blinding light.

They appeared to Pablo as fearful here as they had been in the mine. Pablo too sighed. In silence he considered the fate of these guys, possibly so much worse a fate—imprisoned by the company, possibly killed by it—then the one they faced down in the mine. Finally, he looked back at the soldier.

"Okay. But you should be ashamed of yourself, Lieutenant."

The soldier did not move. "I hope you'll find me to be less a son of a bitch, *maestro*..." He looked down at the ground. "Eventually."

"Things will change, I assure you."

"Yes, *señor*. Could be."

Pablo glanced at the tank, which like a blinding dog of hell sat in the darkness, the inexorable enforcer of the flames themselves. "All right, let's go."

—

Gabriel leaned over the desk and extended his hand.

"This will be an historic moment for Chile. And if you can deliver the Communist vote, Pablo, it will mean that your party will have real power."

Pablo shook Gabriel's hand with both of his. Moved by such a prospect and, he had to admit to himself, flattered that this future president was so sincere in his request for help, he vowed that he would do everything in his power to get him elected. Anything less would be a betrayal of his own convictions, Pablo thought, and especially of people like Josecito and his uncle Mateo.

3
THE FIESTA

1948 hadn't amounted to much, except for the glass of champagne in Pablo's hand, the little sandwich in the other hand, and the danger of being arrested. It had been just one safe house after the other, for months. "I'm bored, *mi amor*." Pablo caressed the back of the neck of his wife Delia, who sat at a desk writing a letter. He wanted to have a Christmas party, but his handlers wouldn't allow it, especially the young one, the kid Alvaro.

"Don't you realize, *maestro*, that they're after you?"

He was a good boy, Alvaro Jara, a history student, maybe a professor someday, but too serious. Just because Pablo had been relieved by the Supreme Court of his office in the Senate and hounded into secrecy and disappearance, he did not think that a good, riotous celebration wasn't possible. Parties justified life. They made it worth living. A party was like the moment in which a man and a woman, wound up in each other's arms, come with noisily exchanged orgasmic intensity. That's what a good party did for you. Wine. Food. It was all that and more. Laughter. Hors d'oeuvres. Champagne. That's what he wanted. Conversation. Kisses.

"That may be so, *joven*. But the Communist Party is protecting me."

Alvaro scratched his head, on the verge of breaking into laughter. He was indeed a "*joven*", a young man. But he was also, at least at this moment, wiser than the world-anointed poet that stood before him. His duties, which had after all been given to him by The Party, made him take a more serious tack. "The Party, *señor*, are like rabbits running in circles."

"You're speaking of the sons of Lenin himself?"

"Yes. You're on the run, and…"

Pablo waved a hand. "Don't remind me, Alvaro."

"And being on the run, and being…" Alvaro shrugged. "Forgive me, *maestro*, but your being a political pariah and a criminal makes having a Christmas party difficult." He turned his head away, tightening his lips as he laid out his thoughts. "Too much worry about arrests and imprisonment. For all of us. Too much the possibility for punishment. It's too much!"

Pablo realized why this was happening. It was that article he had written and then, worse, that speech he had made. You can't accuse The President of The Republic, on the floor of Congress, for God's sake, of self-obsessed, manipulative, and politically motivated murder, and expect there to be no reaction. *But this is always a problem with those kinds of people*, Pablo thought. Presidents often viewed themselves as unassailable simply because they have won a majority and, therefore, the presidency. For Pablo, a president was always assailable, even with one hundred percent of the vote (which occasionally happens in South American countries, although seldom, he reminded himself, in Chile), and especially when, once elected, that president refuses to do what he had promised to do. Or even worse, when he has done just the opposite. And that's what this fool González Videla had done.

It was an easy thing to describe. Gabriel González Videla, the candidate of the people, of whom Pablo had been an ardent supporter and for whom he had been propaganda chief!…. González Videla had promised that there would be nationalization of the banks once he was elected. Grand land redistributions in which the oligarchs would be reduced to the status of everyone else, and everyone else would be allowed ownership of some portion of the oligarchs' undeserved and, Pablo thought, artistically ridiculous holdings. All that French furniture? All those ersatz-English country *palacios*, polo ponies, and all that golf? North American corporations would be sent running. Presidents like this fellow Truman and the fellow that had preceded him, that Roosevelt fellow, would be snubbed. The people would reign. The miners. The railroad employees.

But then when González Videla had won, none of that had happened. The new president began to sound like the old president. He began to caution against moving too fast. The system was not ready to support such radical changes. The people had to be educated about how to use the land that they would be getting. ("Taking back!" was the better phrase, Pablo muttered.) The monetary system being changed so quickly would have grave international repercussions. The United States would be angry with us. Miners didn't really need a union.

El señor presidente became the trinket of the rich, and for Pablo that was the end of that. González Videla took on several traits of the rich as well, especially those that emerge when the rich are being threatened. Jail for the fools in the street parading around with their placards and complaints. Prison for those miners who felt that there really ought to be a union. The concentration camp at Pisagua for the really serious offenders, and there were many of those, most of them miners. Middle of the night raids in troublesome towns. Disappearances. Murder.

Pablo felt that this was not fair, especially since the majority of those who had voted for González Videla were now the ones who were being so rudely disenfranchised. So, to redress this, Pablo had written an article in a Venezuelan newspaper—*an even-handed piece*, he thought, *a simple stating of the truth*—in which he had observed that "the ideal of Señor González Videla's life can be summed up in one phrase: 'I *want* to be President!' In other American places, superficial, fickle politicians like him resort to intrigue and overthrow to gain power. But this is impossible in Chile, with its bedrock of democracy. So Señor González Videla has been obliged to don for himself the cloak of the demagogue."

The next day, Gabriel had asked the high court to throw Pablo out of office, and so they had.

Pablo appealed, and everything was up in the air when, on a summer January day in 1948, he stood up in the Congress and delivered a stirring speech, one of his best, he thought, in which he accused Gabriel of lying, hypocrisy and genocide against his own people. He detailed each of these allegations shockingly. He also read out loud each of the names of the 628 political prisoners who were being held without charges at the Pisagua concentration camp.

Two weeks later, someone set fire to Pablo's house in Santiago. There was a reward posted for information leading to his arrest, and he took refuge with his wife Delia in the Mexican embassy.

—

So, a party. By now, he and Delia had been hiding for almost a year, first with the Mexicans, then in the houses and apartments of poet friends, other writers, painters and musicians, sympathetic diplomats, in beach chalets and attics, back and forth to Valparaiso, Santiago, Viña del Mar, and who knew how many other places? And now it was Christmas.

They were staying in a large apartment owned by a man named Sergio Unsúnza and his wife Aída. They were both lawyers, not usually Pablo's choice for a profession for his friends. But they were extremely kind, and particularly friendly to union miners running from the government. Both the Unsúnzas were Communists, and Pablo often laughed with the recollection of their surprise when Alvaro, telling them that he had yet another couple of fugitives afraid for their lives, presented them with Pablo Neruda and his wife.

"We have to have a party," Pablo told Alvaro.

"Look, *don* Pablo, you can plan for a party—"

"With a tree, Alvaro."

"Which is okay because no one knows about it yet."

"With ornaments."

"But then when you hire the people who bring the flowers, who bring the wine, the food, the Christmas tree, for God's sake, then someone knows about it. And when you are of a certain political…fame, shall we say?" Alvaro said this with an ironic smile. "They'll raid your party and take you away."

Pablo was offended. It wasn't his fault that the president of the nation was a spineless nincompoop parading as a plucky dictator. Nor was it Pablo Neruda's fault that Gabriel González Videla was a liar and a sneak. Liars and sneaks should be taken to task in Congress, because they have no moral restrictions about lying or sneaking. Shouldn't they?

So, no. I'll have my Christmas party, Pablo decided. *And Alvaro, may little baby Jesus bless him, will simply have to accept the idea.*

He felt badly that he felt badly about Alvaro Jara. Really, he was a valuable person to have around. He was enamored of the ideals of freedom for all and a fair deal for everyone. *That's the essence of Communism, isn't it?* Pablo asked himself. At least for him it had always been. So, in the end Alvaro was okay. But he had also shown himself to be something of a fear monger. He pushed Pablo and Delia around and forced them to abandon one house for the next, sometimes with no advance notice. He could not be argued with, and this was the source of Pablo's dissatisfaction with him. Alvaro always seemed so worried that the police would arrest *don* Pablo and sequester him in some cave for all his days. Pablo understood that, but he still found Alvaro hard to take. The boy didn't know what it was like to have fun. Sure, he'd read a lot of poetry. He knew who Pablo Neruda was. He even knew who…who, say, William Butler Yeats was.

But you couldn't just sit down and have a talk with the kid. Skinny, nervous, always dressed in a slovenly manner in black pants and a black coat, he was forever too enthusiastic about Communist ideology and the beauty of Lenin's ideas. He was one of those fellows whose personality is so overtaken by the doctrinaire that he is incapable of conversation with someone of a more expansive vision. Theater. Painting. Comedy. *Chimichurri*, that delicious Argentine sauce so wonderful with beef. Alvaro barely knew what *chimichurri* was!

So, Alvaro was against having a party.

—

But Delia was for it. Delia. Willowy Delia. For eleven years, she had been Pablo's sweet love. She was Argentine, but really she was French, having been raised in Paris, and Pablo had always envied her friendship with artists like Leger, Picasso, Le Corbusier and others. He had also been jealous of her acquaintance with the poets Louis Aragon and Paul Eluard, the French firmament! But "jealousy" wasn't the right word. Rather it was admiration for the way Delia was able to engage the attention of such men.

Best of all, Delia was a Communist too.

When he had been thrown out of the Congress, Pablo had slunk home to their house in Santiago, nervously composing descriptions of what had happened.

"But what really happened, Pablo?" Delia had quickly grown impatient with his stumbling explanation.

When he finally did blurt it out, she embraced him. She hurried to the icebox for a bottle of champagne. She brought out a wedge of French *bris,* another of Spanish *manchego*, with some fine stout bread and a leafy salad. They drank the champagne, and then had a second bottle and a good portion of a third. Finally, the next morning they lay in bed, frowsy and exhausted by everything that had followed the champagne and the cheese.

Pablo sighed, caught between the luxurious dream of Delia's excited skin that, creamy and in ecstasy, she had offered to him, and the certainty that he would be punished, badly and soon, by the president of his country. 'What do we do now, *amor*?'"

Delia sat at her dressing table putting on the day's make-up. Her back was to him, and Pablo luxuriated a moment in the way her musculature made the silk of her slip move, a kind of languorous rippling. She was still so youthful, Pablo thought, smiling at him in the mirror, enjoying his study of her. Pablo had not yet risen from bed. His entire body felt liquid, spent of its musculature. Delia's sensuous energy, he grinned to himself, had defrocked him of all ability to move from the bed. Now, the way she so slowly applied her lipstick, a proud movement in her fingers that, she seemed to imply, was made even more proud by the illustrious action of her husband on the floor of Congress, re-energized in Pablo the spark of interest. Not interest, precisely, which was usually there, but ability. Pablo felt movement in his pubis.

She was twenty years older than he, and Pablo loved Delia as though the world, without her, would slow in its twirling. That the grand mass of peoples on the earth's surface would be unleashed as the world slowed, and would fly into space and oblivion inertially, centrifugally released as the world ground to its circular halt.

"You ask me what to do?" She replaced the cap on her lipstick tube. "You stand your ground, your index finger waving beneath Gabriel's nose."

She tossed the tube into a small basket that contained all her lipsticks. "And continue holding his betrayal up for everyone to see."

"Difficult to do, without my Senate seat."

"You're the greatest poet of your generation, Pablo."

"True." He did agree, although for the moment he felt less confident of himself.

"The moral compass. Chileans don't care about senators. But they love poets."

"Yes, my dear." Pablo turned over on his side, resting his head on the fleshy inside of his arm. "But I'm in trouble."

"I know you are, Pablo. I know. I'm worried."

"So, should we get out of here?" Pablo exhaled, turning over on his stomach. He puffed up the pillow, laying his head on it sideways. "Paris?"

"Just like that? We leave?"

"Gabriel won't let me appear on the streets of Santiago. He'll be after me, soon, within..."

"Days, *querido*. Hours."

And within days, the couple was indeed on the lamb. Friends shepherded them here and there. They barely missed being arrested on a number of occasions. They slipped away beneath the police's noses. They slept on cots in basements. The worst was that they learned how to be cloistered, to be silent, and not to be celebratory.

—

"How many?"

"I've gotten the list down to two hundred." Delia sipped from the glass of *pinot noir* before her. She loved *pinot noir* and was unhappy that the wines they made in Chile were not very good. The country lacked the French, she felt, and she often said so. She and Pablo had first lived together in Paris, in 1937, and the wines of France had astonished Pablo. He had become expert in many of the different regions (a kind of amateur expert; he simply drunk what he liked) and the variety of the wines, the numbing quantity of wineries and appellations in France had made him wish that things were different in Chile, where you could usually order only red or white. (Pablo imagined a faraway future for his country, in which, finally, great vintners would equal these French with Chilean wines of such refinement that it would be said of them that they were the most august and valorous wines in the world, the finest made anywhere. But that was in the future. In 1948, it was just red or white.)

Pablo had an acquaintance in Santiago, an importer named Huneeus, who brought in some French wines. The day before, Pablo had snuck out the back door of the apartment building in which he and Delia had been hiding the last few weeks. In his new beard, wearing a light beige suit, a white shirt, a country straw hat, and sunglasses, he had felt that no one would recognize him. But it disconcerted him that several people on the sidewalk had turned to watch him after he had passed, pondering who that man was, the big fellow in the straw hat, *I know I've seen him somewhere.* Many people.

"Two bottles of the *pinot noir*," he had asked of *señor* Huneeus, whom Pablo knew well and who, just now, maintained the illusion that he was not acquainted with the tall man in the straw hat and sunglasses at all. *Señor* Huneeus was also tall, a very slim man with a kind of courtly manner that hid an adventurous personality. He was funny, which, of course, was one of the reasons Pablo liked him so much. *Señor* Huneeus even knew how to fly an airplane, something that engendered a kind of comic jealousy in Pablo.

"There you are, *hermano*." *Señor* Huneeus handed the bottles across the counter, refusing to take anything for the wine. "A pressing like this… it's worthy of great verse." He laughed. "Wine is the color of the day…"

"And of night."

"Right! Purple feet. Topaz blood. It's the starry child of the earth! So I won't accept money for it."

Another customer entered the shop, and Pablo kept his back to him, not wanting to be recognized.

"Pablo, is that you?"

He glanced to his left. Victor Bianchi stood before him.

"It is!" Victor extended his hand. "It's wonderful to see you, Pablo."

Pablo looked furtively toward the door. Seeing that for the moment no one else was coming in, he embraced his friend.

"You're alive." Victor laughed.

"Yes, at least there's that."

An uncle of Victor had arranged for Pablo's first diplomatic assignment, to Rangoon twenty years earlier, and Pablo had been a friend of the family ever since. Victor was of special importance because he was a noted alpine mountain climber, an activity that Pablo admired for the bravery it took simply to undertake it. Indeed, Victor himself had almost died during an expedition on Argentina's Aconcagua, the highest mountain in the western world. He had survived, but most of the other climbers had perished. Victor's face bore the marks of his suffering. It was quite weathered, the cold and wind on that mountain having battered it. He looked much older than he was.

"And Delia?"

"Very well, despite the problems."

"Yes, I..." Victor took out a business card and handed it to Pablo. "I won't ask you where you're staying. But if you need anything, call me."

"I will, Victor."

On the way back to the apartment (Pablo had to hurry, because he knew that Alvaro would have discovered his disappearance and would be coming out to find him) Pablo felt revived, having seen his old, close friend. He fingered the card in his pocket, unnerved by the number of people who turned again to watch him flow by, wondering *¡Carajo! I know him!*

"That should be enough invitations." Delia placed the glass of *pinot* on the table and looked out the window. "But I don't know if we can even get two hundred people in here." She wore a white silk blouse with scalloped short sleeves, a calf-length light wool brown skirt, silk stockings and brown leather pumps. Delia's slim, crossed legs invaded Pablo's vision. Her light hair, long, with a natural curl, shielded the left side of her face as her large eyes, their lashes closing and opening like two flirtatious anemones, went down the list. They had had few disagreements about whom to invite. The one criterion that Delia and Pablo had for a party was to invite only those people whom they actively cared for. Both hated conversations with dullards, and surely there were enough of those in the world to go to other parties. So, there was no need to invite them to their parties. This policy ensured that Pablo and Delia's parties were always noisily chaotic.

"What about Alvaro?"

Delia checked off a name on the list with a pen. "He'll be here, because he'll be making sure you're remaining isolated and hidden."

"But do we tell him about it?"

"Of course not. He'll learn about the party when people begin arriving." Delia folded the list and put it in the small ledger book in which she kept her diary. "We'll make him answer the doorbell."

—

Alvaro had told him that morning that things were getting particularly dangerous. The Party felt that it would be best if Pablo left the country, and they had a plan for that, which was to commence in a month or so, January or February 1949.

Without Delia, though, such a journey would be one of pure darkness and lonely disaffection. The Party insisted that she stay behind, that having her join Pablo in the escape would possibly so complicate the thing that his safety could not be guaranteed.

"It can't be guaranteed in any case, *don* Pablo," Alvaro had told him. "But arrest is inevitable if you stay here."

He had placed an elbow on the kitchen table at which they were sitting. It was a warm day, and Alvaro's white shirt was rolled up at the sleeves. His hair had grown quite scruffy in the last months, so harried had he been in his determination to keep the poet safe. Pablo's complicated feelings for Alvaro, his resentment especially, was tempered by the kind of affection that comes, finally, from realizing that the difficult relative or sullen acquaintance cares for you really and would act differently toward you if he could. Often Pablo observed to himself how curmudgeonly exhaustion could actually be a sign of good humor, if it comes with the right glint in the eye. Alvaro did have that glint now and then, and Pablo had learned to seize upon it when it appeared.

"But I want Delia to come with me."

Alvaro's lips tightened. "No."

Pablo saw the glint just now, although this time it was filled with reluctance and sadness. As Alvaro glanced at Pablo and tapped the tabletop with an index finger, Pablo suddenly felt, for the first time, that something like a son of his was imploring him to be reasonable. "In fact, I insist."

"*Don* Pablo. We can't allow it."

"But—"

"It will be too dangerous."

"So? She's put up with such things herself. She saw the Spanish Civil War. She's a good Party member."

Alvaro lowered his head. His voice fell almost to a mutter. "*Don* Pablo, *señora* Delia has never had to put up with the kinds of things you'll find in the Andes."

"The Andes!"

"That's where we're going. And maybe on foot."

Pablo had an immediate vision of Delia, and of their freezing to death in each other's arms, cocooned in snow. The high peaks. The ice.

"Oh, Alvaro."

"That's right, *señor*. You understand, I see."

Pablo placed his head in the palms of his hands. He closed his eyes. "You didn't tell me, Alvaro."

—

"No." Comrade Saturno slumped on a couch before Pablo as though he were grieving. He had been called in by Alvaro, as a senior operative of the Chilean Communist Party, to set the poet straight. Saturno's entire body leaned to the left. His head was like a sack filled with wet sand.

Pablo crossed his legs. He noticed that Saturno was not wearing any socks. Also, the right cuff of his suit pants was frayed. "She has to come with me."

Saturno looked with a kind of rehearsed inattentiveness out the window. "No."

"Are you capable of other kinds of speech, Saturno?"

"Yes." Saturno shifted his weight in the chair, still looking away. *He would make an excellent corpse*, Pablo thought. "What else would you like me to say?"

"That my wife Delia will accompany me on this journey, that we will traverse the Andes together and arrive in Argentina on a Turkish magic carpet the way that Juan and Evita Perón do."

Saturno remained silent. Indeed, he appeared, except for the fact that he was discernibly breathing, to have died of annoyance. "No."

—

They lay in bed. Versions of several of his poems, hand-written and heavily edited, lay around them on the blankets. He had been writing steadily throughout their year in secrecy, a new book called *Canto General*. The radio was on, to the national news.

"The whereabouts of the disgraced senator Pablo Neruda remain unknown." This announcer's voice had the prideful insistence that the announcers on newsreels in the movie houses had, officialdom expressing itself. "He and his wife disappeared ten months ago, and the police and federal authorities have been tireless in their search for him. His capture is imminent. Asked this morning where he thought Neruda could possibly be, President González Videla said that Neruda is in the south of Chile. 'The only way we won't get him,' the president said, 'is if he's left the country altogether. But we're sure that no one would want to help such a man.'"

"Pablo, when will we see each other again?" Delia caressed his eyelid with the end of a little finger. Her lips were so close to his that he could only imagine, in this moment, pressing his into hers. Hers would fold into his like petals of one rose brushing against those of another. *It would be so easy to answer her question in that way*, Pablo thought, and so he did. A shudder of pleasure and the movement of blood went through Delia, and she passed both her arms around Pablo's neck, each hand opened and splayed across his upper back.

"In Paris." Pablo's answer was not quite a lie, because a lie depends upon knowing what the truth is, and Pablo had no idea. He knew that he could easily end up a black, leathery corpse in a snowy Andean ravine, his teeth yellowed, his lips petrified in a skeletal grimace, or a forgotten piece of dried flesh down some granite moraine. Disappeared in an alpine river, beneath a submerged boulder, his arms flailing about in drowning's watery clutch.

"You think so, *amor*? Paris?"

Pablo's heart broke. "Of course. Paris. Yes."

—

Victor Bianchi had found Pablo a Christmas tree, which he had cut down from the slope of a hill on the little *finca* he owned outside Santiago. He had sent an errand boy to the Unsúnza home after Pablo had called him, with a note telling Pablo that he could send "a messenger, *amigo,* or a Communist toady or somebody" to pick up the tree. Pablo, not willing to trust anyone with the secret, determined that he would pick it up himself.

Victor drove him back to the Unsunza's apartment, the tree tied to the roof of his car. It was Christmas Day, 1948. There was a crowd out front.

A noisy gathering, perhaps fifty people, all of them were well known to Pablo and Delia. They were waiting for the lift to go up and down, each trip carrying four or five guests up to the Unsúnza's apartment. There were wrapped gifts, flowers, frivolity, and laughter.

"Yes, pull up in front, would you, Victor?"

Victor slowly approached the curb.

"And you'll come up and join us, no?" Pablo smiled.

"Of course!"

Once Victor had untied the tree from the top of the car, Pablo hurriedly took it into his arms. He was wearing a black greatcoat, despite the heat of the day, a pair of sunglasses and a Spanish beret. At first, many in the crowd did not recognize him, hidden as he was behind his new beard and the large tree. He greeted them as he walked toward the door to the apartment building, admonishing them to remain quiet as long as they were out in the open, that they didn't know anything about this Christmas tree, and that as far as they knew the famous poet was dead. There was much more laughter and, his way through the crowd cleared by Victor, Pablo entered the lift and told Enrique, the daytime security man, to take him and Victor to the fourth floor.

"*Claro, maestro.*"

As they approached that floor, it became evident from the loud talk and music up above that maybe a hundred people had already entered the apartment. It sounded like the audience's enthused chatter and humorous exclamation after having watched a fine act in the circus. Enrique opened the elevator door, and Pablo, the tree still in his arms, preceded Victor up the hall, a finger out through the branches of the tree, to ring the bell to the apartment.

The door opened and Alvaro, a glass of red wine in his hand, in confused, offended mid-answer to what had obviously been a humorous question from one of the guests, beckoned the tree into the apartment, and it walked in accompanied by its two friends Victor Bianchi and Pablo Neruda.

4

SERGEANT URBINO

"It will be a Mercedes Benz, *don* Pablo."

Pablo sensed that Alvaro was impatient. When he had asked the question "What kind of car do we use for the escape?" Alvaro had sighed, looked away and thrown up his hands.

Why so angry? Pablo felt that it had been a reasonable question, coming from a senator of the Congress, after all. *Well,* he thought, *okay, a fired senator, but once the courts get around to it, to the challenge, to the public outrage, to the despicable government abrogation of the law,* still *a senator.* Pablo scratched the back of his neck. *And,* he thought, *a poet of inexplicable verbal and written grace, a lyric maestro—* "That's an unusual question?" *Doesn't such a man deserve the right to ask what kind of car he's going to get?*

"It wouldn't be, *don* Pablo, under more usual circumstances."

"And what would those be?"

Alvaro placed his hands in the pockets of his pants. "Going to the beach with *doña* Delia."

"Excellent!"

"Making love in a Paris apartment."

"¡Menos mal!" Even better!

"But the president, see, would like to put you away forever." Alvaro nodded, his eyes widened and quivering. "To have you rot."

Pablo remained silent a moment. "I recall that."

"So, I see all this, forgive me, this nattering about what kind of car we're going to put you in—"

"Yes?"

"I see it as, I'm sorry, foolish."

Pablo grimaced, surveying his shoes. "They're going to put me away for eternity, you say."

"Yes."

"So, it doesn't matter how I escape, as long as I do."

"As long as we get you out of here, it doesn't matter."

For a moment, Pablo considered the Spanish Inquisition. He had read about it extensively, its excesses reminding him of a good deal of South American history. Indeed, the Inquisition and that history had been one of the reasons for his often invoked and gleeful laughter at the Catholic Church. That dour, privilege-encrusted bureaucracy, he grumbled, intent upon aggrandizing itself, the rest of the world be damned. He imagined confessing that point of view to the Inquisition itself, and then being imprisoned for life in one of those iron cages, hanging from the damp stone ceiling of an obscure Madrid castle prison. His filthy hands would appear annealed to the bars of the cage. His hair would look like the branches of a dead oak tree. His eyes, uncomprehending, filled with despair, would contain only the slightest evidence of his long-ago cries for mercy.

Alvaro sat down on a stool a few feet from the poet. He said nothing else. He surveyed the fingernails of his left hand, his demeanor shot through with silent impatience.

Pablo was a large man, now at the age of forty-four noted for his very enormous, even commanding head, and the nose, like a fleshy eagle's beak, that graced it. He did not consider himself handsome, but he knew that when he entered a room, the weather in the room changed. Pablo garnered attention as a matter of course. So, an escape like this was not going to be easy.

Just now, his brown slacks were well pressed, his white shirt equally so. A long-sleeved black sweater was draped around his shoulders, the sleeves tied together in a loose knot down his chest. He wore brown loafers, his favorite kind of shoe, stylish but comfortable. He approached the balcony, which was on the fourth floor of a Santiago apartment building. The beard he had been growing in order to disguise himself was now thick, bushy and well kept. He reminded himself, now and then while trimming it, of Joseph Conrad. He stood a long while looking at the traffic in the street, savoring its clamor.

He would miss his country terribly. Here he was, the acknowledged troubadour of his people, the poet of the world, and they were chasing him out. The Araucanian forests. The azure, dark Pacific, font of all that fed him. The still, treeless north, so bleakly ruinous, home to all those miners who had elected him to the senate. The light, no matter where he was in the countryside, the rains in the south, the very feel of Chile itself, its heart… now all these pleasures surged through the chambers of his blood, intent upon his heart.

He mourned a moment for the Pacific Ocean, or at least the memories he had of it up and down the Chilean coast. How could so inexplicable a body of liquid, so inexorable in its movements, offer such delicacy of blue so constantly?

Could he just walk away from all that?

"A Mercedes Benz." he said.

"Yes, *señor*."

Pablo lowered his head. "Okay. Let's go."

—

The Chevrolet—"It's almost new." Alvaro muttered. "1946!"—was colored black. It was a two-door.

Pablo stared at it from the balcony.

"We had to make a change, *don* Pablo." Alvaro was bustling around so intently that Pablo sensed he was trying to avoid being asked any questions at all. He hurried Pablo's suitcase toward the apartment door. He went into the kitchen for the thermos of coffee and the cups. He had his own leather satchel that he moved from the couch to the door.

"Alvaro."

"We heard that the police were looking for a Mercedes Benz. That they knew about it and were getting closer."

"I don't believe you."

"That they may show up here at any moment."

"Come now. We've been here for two or three weeks, and they haven't shown up."

"That they may be out in the street even now."

Pablo looked down from the balcony. The Unsúnzas lived across the street from the Parque Forestal in Santiago, and Pablo had enjoyed the few walks that he and Delia had been allowed there by his Communist handlers. He had wished to view it in the full light of day. But that was not permitted. Too risky. So, they had only strolled in the park after dusk, when it was nonetheless so suggestive to Pablo of the Araucanian forests that had enchanted his childhood that he had pretended he was a youngster once more as they had strolled up and down the pathways. Just now, Pablo looked out over the large expanse of green and reveled a moment in the blanket-like folds and rolls of the tree canopy seen from above. But there was no Secret Service down below. Just a lot of pedestrians and automobiles.

Toddlers holding their mothers' hands in the park.

Maids going to market.

Alvaro became even more restless. "The others will be here in a minute."

The poet kept quiet, but allowed the intensity of his silence, coupled with his gaze, to follow Alvaro around. "Who's going with us?"

"Jorgelito Saenz."

"The miner?"

"Yes. The Party insists. But only until we get out of Santiago. The others, *señor* Unsúnza, *señora* Aída, they just want to make sure everything is arranged for you."

"And to say goodbye, I hope."

"That, too, I guess."

Sighing, hurt, Pablo put on his overcoat and hat. He had been told to bring these along as part of the disguise for the trip. He and Alvaro would be driving south for many hours, then heading east to the Andes *cordillera*, passing through several towns and villages, in any of which Pablo could be spotted. His false papers, with the quaint name of Antonio Ruiz Lagoretta, could do at least something to protect him. But Pablo was a very famous man, and a single wandering eye, a single suspicion on someone's part, that the bearded enormous fellow wearing large sunglasses, in the Stalinesque-looking greatcoat and black wool *gaucho* sombrero with the excessively wide brim, may be the poet himself…that could bring everything down disastrously.

He sat on a couch, slouching, and placed his hands in the pockets of the coat. A round object, crusted and rough feeling, secreted itself into his fingers. He pulled it out and smiled at it, resting in his hand like a jewel. A mollusk shell that Delia had given him. It was perfectly round, a small janissary turban in white, brown and gold.

It occurred to him that maybe his poems were colorful excretions, the way this shell was. When his flesh was no more, his poetry would remain, to be fondled by an appreciative hand and admired by loving eyes. He did not want to go to prison. But he didn't care, in the end, if they put him there. His poetry would tell them, with its very great quantity—not to mention all its inventiveness, its sophistication, and the rough-hewn finesse for which it was known—to fuck themselves.

Pablo chuckled, and then recalled that this shell had come from the beach in Isla Negra, during a walk there on vacation with Delia. It was a nice place, Isla Negra. They had bought a house. But they couldn't go there now, not to Isla Negra, not anywhere in Chile. He wished Delia could be with him on this journey, that it not be so dangerous for her in the Andes. But up there, the danger was real. The *cordillera* was, after all, the up-thrusting result of great earthen movements, where whole continents and oceans had collided and hardened into the grandest obstruction in the southern hemisphere.

He examined the shell. It was like that, too, in its ridges and ravines. Imagine what they were like to some molecular consciousness trying to make its way across them.

"All right." Alvaro took up his satchel. "It's time."

Pablo stood, buttoned the greatcoat, and moved toward the apartment door.

The two men paused a moment in the lobby. The security guard Enrique, about seventy, whose face looked like a many-times folded piece of brown paper with a set of eyes and a nose, held the door for them. He was in on the conspiracy and touched a pair of fingers to his forehead as Pablo nodded to him.

"*Suerte, maestro*." His eyes carried gentle regard for the poet. "Good luck."

"But Enrique, where's Sergio Unsúnza? He's supposed to be here, no?"

Alvaro spoke with Enrique a few moments, guarding the conversation from Pablo.

"He couldn't make it, *don* Pablo," Alvaro said.

"Then let's go back upstairs so that I can phone him."

"*Don* Pablo."

"I want to tell them where we're going."

"No!"

Quickly, Alvaro motioned to Enrique, and the two men hustled Pablo out of the lobby toward the car. Like a black sail in a wind, protesting, his sunglasses sparkling in the light, Pablo nonetheless bolted across the sidewalk past a few startled pedestrians and around the rear of the Chevrolet, headed for the front rider's seat. But there was someone there already, and, as Pablo opened the door, the fellow leaned forward, pulling the seat back with him so that Pablo could have access to the rear.

"I'll sit up here." Pablo waited for the man to vacate the front seat. He recognized him, Jorgelito Saenz, a Party functionary, a man who had survived the great Rancagua coal mine explosion of 1945. He lacked a right arm. He wore a black suit and a white shirt, no tie. His remaining hand was exceptionally large for so small a man, and it was quite grizzled and muscled, the same color as his graying hair.

"No, Comrade, you're in the back."

"Jorgelito, I'll sit where I want."

"You'll sit in the back, *maestro*. And don't argue. In fact, you'll lie down in the back."

"Lie down!"

"Under the coat."

Pablo saw that Alvaro was watching him across the car roof.

"Completely under the coat."

Pablo began a disruptive profanity, but Alvaro tightened his lips, fixing the poet with very stern disapprobation. Pablo glanced once more at Jorgelito, who was not going to budge. He recalled from his electioneering days that miners as a rule don't budge. Finally, sighing, Pablo leaned over and climbed into the back seat.

They had driven about a half hour, clearing the outskirts of Santiago, when Pablo pushed aside the collar of the coat, revealing just his eyes and nose. "When do I sit up, Alvaro?"

"When we get to the *cordillera.*"

"Many hours, then."

"That's right."

The car sped on.

"So…after Jorgelito, maybe," Pablo said.

Jorgelito had said almost nothing since they had left the apartment. Now he turned his head, placed his left arm across the seat back, and frowned. His face was a gathering of thick lines, between each of which were dark declivities and ravines, pouches of skin.

"After Jorgelito, what, Comrade?"

"I get to sit in front."

Jorgelito turned back toward the windshield, shaking his head. The car continued on.

They stopped momentarily in a small village, and Alvaro described it for Pablo, its three or four wooden structures, a water mill next to a stream and, at one end, an oak tree. Pablo pulled down the coat collar once more. Alvaro held a hand up, shushing any talk. Pablo, looking up out the back window, saw blue sky and two clouds, one of which resembled the foot of a chicken.

"Do you see anyone, Jorge?" Alvaro looked all around. "That barn over there?"

"Nobody."

"Behind the tree?"

"No."

"So, this is it, then."

"Yeah. *Suerte,* Comrades." Jorgelito looked once more out all the windows of the car, in every direction. He reached for the doorknob.

"Jorge," Pablo said.

Jorgelito paused, irritated. He kept his eyes on the doorknob.

"For what possible reason did you come with us?"

"To keep an eye on you, Comrade." He left the car, turning to close the door behind him.

Pablo lowered his hands to his stomach and gathered them together once more. Jorgelito looked in on him, his walnut-like head seemingly hanging in mid-air.

"I've been under this coat for an hour, *amigo*. How could you be sure that I was still here?" Pablo held out a hand. "I might have flown up to heaven."

Jorgelito smiled. "The Party knows everything."

"Even how to keep a poet buttoned up?"

"Beg your pardon?"

"Stalin knows how to do that?"

Jorgelito offered a brief salute, two fingers laid against one eyebrow. "He especially knows how to do that, *maestro*." He turned away, and Alvaro put the car in gear once more.

—

They drove south through the night.

The following morning, they passed through Temuco, the place that Pablo considered his hometown.

"I want to see it." Pablo moved to sit up.

"Too dangerous, *maestro*."

"But I was raised here."

"Get back down."

Pablo acquiesced. "Alvaro, I do so under protest. My poetry was born in this town. Between those hills and the river. The rain in Temuco is a voice. The forests here are the inception of my verse."

"Yeah, yeah, *don* Pablo, but—"

"You're making me betray my own soul, Alvaro."

Alvaro took his anger out on the accelerator pedal. "*Don* Pablo. Please." The car lurched ahead.

Pablo pulled the coat over his body. "I wish to weep." He remained silent for several moments.

"Have you finished weeping, *maestro*?" Alvaro said.

"I haven't begun yet."

"Then you'd better hold off a while longer, because we have a police checkpoint up ahead."

Pablo hurried the coat over himself and brought his feet up.

"Two hay bales on either side of the road." Alvaro slowed the car down. "Two lanes. Three policemen, and I wish you could see them. They all have that robot way, maestro. Not a thought. Savages."

"Police are always like that."

"I know."

"Like the United States." Pablo adjusted the coat once more. "Or the pope."

"I guess so."

Alvaro brought the car to a halt a hundred meters from the checkpoint. He feigned searching in his satchel for his papers while mumbling under his breath at Pablo, that he stay down under the coat, bring his knees up so no one could see his feet, try to breathe as little as possible, and keep quiet. Even though he was not looking at Pablo and would appear to the police ahead to be simply gathering himself together, Pablo himself felt that Alvaro was very frightened. Indeed, he knew he was because of the sheen of sweat on his forehead, his shallow breathing, and the rapidity with which his fingers worked the satchel.

Alvaro's terror heightened Pablo's own. This was where they would be caught.

—

"Let me see your papers."

In the darkness beneath the coat, his heart galloping, Pablo heard Alvaro's shuffling about once again, his hands in his satchel. Pablo's shirt stuck to his back. He was offended by the odor of his own sweat. There was a silence, then the sound of a passing transport truck.

"And you're going to...?"

"Lake Ranco, *señor*."

"Fishing, eh?"

"No. I sell school supplies."

"Ah, so you're going to the town of Futrono."

"Yes, among others."

Another silence, much longer. Pablo imagined the policeman thumbing through the few documents, considering what to say next.

"Paper? Pencils? That sort of thing?"

"Yes, *señor*."

Two more vehicles went by.

"And no one's with you?"

Pablo held the knuckle of his right thumb between his teeth. His left fist was clenched against his chest. He imagined the entire coat quivering.

"No, *señor*."

Pablo almost ceased breathing, hoping that the officer would not stick his head in the window to survey the back seat and then, to Pablo's ultimate horror, ask what was beneath the coat.

"My daughter likes those kinds of things," the policeman said.

Pablo heard more rustling in the satchel.

"Would she like these?"

"She would, yes. Very much."

"With my compliments."

"Thank you. You can continue."

Alvaro put the documents back into the satchel and engaged the car's gears.

"Stay on the main road."

Pablo, still frightened, exhaled, relief flooding his heart. The Chevrolet moved forward a few meters, until the policeman shouted out.

"Hey! Wait a minute."

The policeman's footsteps, accompanied by others, approached the car from behind. Surely, they had drawn their weapons. Pablo envisioned his arrival at the jail. The welcoming rats would be crawling over him by evening.

"Any room for a passenger?"

"*Señor?*"

"Yeah. Sergeant Urbino here needs a ride."

"*Hola, hermano.*" The voice was deep and raspy, the victim of years of cigarettes. "You got an extra space?"

"Yes, of course."

"Thanks." The rider's door opened, and someone got in.

"Sergeant Urbino, was it?"

"Yeah, but, eh! call me Gastón."

—

The Chevrolet hurried down the road. The conversation had been spirited, about the women in this part of the country, the crops, whether the new railroad spur that had been planned through here would actually be built. Pablo, listening, was interested.

"But even as the government says they'll do something..." The wind blew in through Gastón's open window. "They don't, right?"

"I don't have an opinion about that," Alvaro said.

"It's true, though. The police, we get that all the time."

An object fell on Pablo's head. He was still hiding. It was something light, something round. Suddenly, a hand pushed the object across the coat toward the armrest, as though to prop it up, and Pablo flinched.

"What's this?" Gastón pulled the coat aside. "Somebody's here?"

Pablo lay on the back seat. He was wearing his sunglasses. The *sombrero* covered his face. He didn't move. Gastón's hat lay next to him.

"Jesus, for a minute I thought it was a dead body." Gastón reached out and removed the hat. Pablo, unable to think of anything else, smiled and gestured. "Sergeant Urbino."

"Where'd you come from?"

"Santiago."

"No, I mean just now."

Pablo sat up and ran a hand through his hair. "I've been here the whole time."

Gastón turned toward Alvaro. "Why didn't you tell us about him?"

Alvaro continued steering with his right hand, the elbow of his left arm hanging out in the wind.

"You forgot about him?" Gastón fixed Alvaro with a dank stare. Gastón was dark-skinned with a thick black mustache. His nose resembled an apple long fallen to the ground. His hair was waxed, so that he had the air of one of those Latin lovers in the movies, Pablo thought, although he was nonetheless a startlingly ugly man.

"No, no, we—"

"He was dead and now he's alive?"

"No."

Gastón turned back toward Pablo. "Take off the sunglasses."

Pablo held up a moment, thinking to resist. But he realized that that would surely blow his cover, and he did what Gastón asked. Gastón stared at him, into his eyes, for a long moment, then looked over his whole face, the white shirt, and the beard.

"I should tell you who I am," Pablo said.

Gastón waited, and Pablo noticed that Alvaro's eyes were twitching, trying to dictate the scene to Pablo while still driving.

"I'm Antonio Ruiz Lagorreta." Pablo reached into his coat pocket for the false documents and brought them out along with Delia's mollusk shell. He handed over the papers.

"And what do you do for a living?"

Pablo demurred. Would this policeman know anyone with such a name? Was he supposed to be on the lookout for the person with that Ruiz name, knowing that the guy's real name was that of the seditious criminal ne'er-do-well Communist Pablo Neruda? Was Gastón on orders from President González Videla? Was he a member of a death squad?

"I'm a malacologist."

"A what?"

"*Bueno, amigo*, a—"

"That's a seashell there, isn't it?" Gastón pointed at Pablo's hand.

"Yes, it is. *Odontocymbiola magellanica.*"

"I wouldn't know any of that. We just call it a red snail, no?"

"Yes, we do, too." Pablo surveyed the shell. Dark brown-gold, it had an intricate surface that resembled lacquer. "A kind of little crown, isn't it?" He held the shell out to the policeman, who took it in both hands, turned toward the windshield, and investigated it.

"I used to hunt for these." Gastón held the shell up. "It's beautiful, isn't it?"

"Where?"

"Valparaiso, *amigo*." Gastón turned once more, a grin on his face. "You know it?"

"I grew up near there," Pablo lied. "The blue Pacific."

"Always. And what women!" Gastón shrugged, lowering his head to one side. "My wife Isabelita is from there."

"She lives with you out here?"

"Oh, no." Gastón exhaled, keeping his eyes averted. "She's gone. We lost her giving birth to our first child."

For a long moment, the only sound in the car was that of the wind buffeting through its open windows.

"We lost the little girl, too."

Pablo said nothing, giving Gastón's mourning a moment of its own. He imagined young Gastón, a new police cadet, walking with Isabelita up a Valparaiso beach. She wore a white summer dress and white sandals, a pretty girl who, for Gastón, provided the very blood that surged into his heart, vivifying him with every smile. She too collected shells and, indeed, when—Pablo mused—Gastón offered her a beautiful green mollusk shell as an engagement gift, the sheen of it like that in the dark Chilean rain forests, the gift made her love Gastón like no other man she had ever met anywhere.

"But I'm sure you gentlemen don't want to hear about my problems." Gastón loosened his police uniform tie. "Even though it was just such a beautiful shell that I gave Isabelita the day I asked her to marry me." He handed the shell back to Pablo. "Do you know about those trophons, I think they are? Very rare. They look like a twirl of cigarette smoke, round and round up into the air."

"Of course, I do. From Antarctica. And I've wanted one for years. You have one?"

"No, but my Isabel had the one that I'd given her. She loved it so much, we put it in her coffin." As he fell into silence, Gastón's eyes began to water. "You collect these things, *don* Antonio?"

"I do. I have thousands."

"Catalogued and everything?"

"Completely. I have a system of little drawers. You know, like in the library."

"You have that many seashells?"

"Thousands."

The countryside passed quickly as the two men conversed. To their left, the Andes *cordillera* rose like a precipitous tapestry. Grassy farmlands gave way to rolling hills. Horses grazed in one version of the distance. A farmer tilled a field in another. The air grew warmer. An eagle drifted on an upward draft. Even Alvaro got involved in the conversation, noting to Gastón that few men had as wide a range of knowledge of the birds and bugs in this part of Chile as *don* Antonio had. The Chevrolet sped on.

"But Antonio, look up ahead," Alvaro said an hour later, interrupting the conversation. He applied the brakes.

Gastón turned to look out the windshield. Pablo leaned forward, his sunglasses and beard just over Gastón's left shoulder.

"It's a checkpoint."

"Yes," Gastón said. "Don't worry about it, Alvaro. They'll stop you for just a minute or two."

Alvaro slowed the car and stopped at the behest of the two policemen leaning against the corral fencing that bordered the road. He began opening his satchel, to get to his papers.

"Alvaro." Gastón laid a hand on his arm. "Hang on a minute."

One of the policemen approached the car. He had the demeanor of a beam of wood. He appeared unable to smile. He too had a mustache, although it was far better trimmed than Gastón's, and his boots were excessively well polished, also unlike Gastón's. His self-regard had very few chinks in it. The sweat-stains on his shirt—there were just two, one below each armpit—appeared to be exactly the same size and shape.

"*Buenas, señor,*" the policeman said. "Your documents."

"Atila," Gastón interjected. "These guys are with me."

"Hey, Gastón! How are you?"

"Great. And you? Your kids?"

"Everybody's well." Atila placed his right hand on the car's roof and looked in the window at Alvaro and Pablo. "Who are these guys?"

"A couple of malacologists."

"What's that?"

"Oh, they're guys that collect these things." Gastón took up the seashell from the car seat and handed it over.

Atila inspected it. The mollusk seemed to hold no interest for him. Pablo imagined him sighing, uttering one or two disdainful epithets, and tossing the shell to the ground. Instead, he handed it back to Gastón.

"Where are you from?" Atila asked Pablo.

"Valparaiso."

The policeman frowned.

"You know, where I'm from." Gastón gestured toward Pablo. "I grew up with this fellow's brother. We used to hunt seashells together."

"Seashells! What for?"

Gastón chuckled. "My mother. She loved them."

"I remember," Pablo said.

Gastón nodded toward Pablo.

"Your father, too."

Gastón lowered his head, grinning.

"All right," Atila stepped away from the car. "Keep going." Suddenly, a tight, carved smile appeared on his lips. "Take care of yourself, Gastón."

"Always." Gastón gave a mock salute. "Say hello to Gladys for me."

"I will." The policeman pointed up ahead. "Stay on the main road."

"Yes, sir," Alvaro whispered.

The car hurried away.

"Gladys is his wife, poor woman," Gastón muttered.

For the next while, everyone in the car remained silent. Pablo, eyeing the back of Gastón's head, decided that, well, probably this fellow simply values seashells, and I suppose he really does think that I'm the malacologist Antonio Ruiz Lagoretta. He wished to ask Gastón about it, but the complications of why Pablo wanted to know would make the question too risky. From time to time, Pablo sensed Gastón's glancing sideways at him, as though he too wished to ask a few questions. Alvaro was too nervous to speak at all and kept his eyes on the road.

Twenty minutes later, Gastón pointed to a log fence paralleling the road, at the edge of a meadow. "Up here. From here, I walk."

The car slowed to a halt.

Pablo surveyed the meadow, admiring the velvety green of it. "Who are you here to visit?"

"My girlfriend." Gastón pointed across the meadow to a little adobe building with a garden in front, in the shadow of a half-dozen oak trees. "Alma. A widow, sadly. But happy for me."

"That's good, Gastón."

"Not like my poor Isabel, though."

"But one wishes happiness for widows."

"Yes, at least for this one. But she's not like Isabelita."

Pablo, looking off across the meadow, noticed how softly, in a breeze, the grasses nodded back and forth on it. He reached into his coat pocket. "Take this, will you?" He handed Gastón the mollusk shell. "A gift."

Gastón re-examined it, his investigation of its lines and circles as joyful as the longer one he had made of it earlier. After a moment, he attempted handing it back. "I can't accept it. It's too beautiful."

"It's for your wife, Gastón. Not for you. It's for her heart."

"But, *señor* Neruda."

Alvaro swore, looking out the window into the distance. Pablo's mouth closed shut. He put a hand to his chest. His gullet turned to stone.

"*Don* Pablo." Gastón searched out Pablo's eyes. His own eyes had saddened. He moved to leave the car. "Would you care to sit up front?"

Pablo glanced toward Alvaro, who shook his head.

"No, I'm going to take another nap in the back seat."

"All right." Gastón took his policeman's hat from Pablo and put it on. He stepped out of the car, closed the door, and then put both hands on the windowsill. The seashell remained in one of them. His lips curled downward. He pointed ahead. "Stay on the main road, *muchacho*."

"I will, Sergeant." Alvaro looked into the distance.

"The Andes road is only a few kilometers up. On the left."

"Which road?"

"There aren't any other roadblocks between here and there."

"Glad to hear it."

"And take care of..." He glanced toward Pablo, who noticed for the first time that Gastón's front teeth were lined with gold.

"*'I can write the saddest lines tonight'*, poet," Gastón stood back. "*'On nights like this.'*" He looked up into the sunny afternoon beyond an aging, arthritic oak tree. "*'I had her in my arms.'*"

Barely taking a breath, Alvaro hurried the car back onto the road.

"*Chau, chicos,*" the policeman shouted.

Pablo, turning to look out the back window, saw Gastón examining the shell. He was shaking his head with what appeared to the poet to be a lost lover's regret for what he once had possessed. He looked up at the retreating Chevrolet. Pablo waved. Gastón put the shell in his coat pocket, climbed over the fence and headed out on foot across the meadow, toward the widow Alma.

5

THE COWHERD, THE CAPITALIST, THE LAWYER

Chagrined, Pablo examined the mountain range. He had to look up. Far, far up. The *cordillera* was washed in silver where the snows lay upon it, lit by the full moon that seemed, in its size and glare, to be astride the universe. The mountains gloried beneath this lunar authority. The peaks were diamonded crags.

They had arrived at Lake Maihue that night, at some sort of logging operation, after having picked up a few rifles and some ammunition from a Communist sympathizer in the town of Futrono.

"Who owns this?" Pablo and Alvaro entered the bunkhouse. He laid aside the rifle he was carrying. One of the ranch hands, a sawyer named Ramada Salerno, had shown them in, and Pablo dropped his satchel to the floor, to look around at the cobwebbed ceiling, the clean, simple beds, and the hand-made wooden furniture.

"*El señor* Rodríguez, *señor*." Ramada was a slim, tall man with a dark face delicately beardless, in his twenties. His clothing was workmanlike, the victim of much felling of trees and planing of boards. His voice was soft, to Pablo's mind even deferential in tone, and rather filled with grace. After showing them around, he left the two men alone.

"Who's Rodríguez?" Pablo asked.

48

"José Rodríguez Gutiérrez." Alvaro shoved his satchel into a corner of the room. "Lives in Santiago. Very important businessman."

"An oligarch?"

"A capitalist, *maestro*." Alvaro waited as Pablo's surprise abated. He did not wish to interrupt the pacing back and forth and the stressful sighing with which Pablo was reacting to this news.

"And lately a staunch supporter of President González Videla."

"And you put me here?"

"That's right, *don* Pablo. *Don* Pepe lives far away in the capital. He almost never comes here, and no one would suspect him ever of harboring an on-the-run, criminally indicted Communist."

"Who made that decision?"

"The Communists."

Again, Pablo turned away, this time heading back outside. He took up his rifle, cradled it under one arm, and manhandled the screen door aside. He was scratching his beard as he walked toward the corral and a fire pit in which several logs were burning. He resembled a confused bear that at the moment was pawing at a large wool watch cap that someone had put on his head. He stopped and leaned against the corral fence, his gaze fixed on the ground. Alvaro heard a few profanities.

The mountains remained. As usual, they were covered with snow.

Pablo turned from the view, having removed the cap and now scratching his head. "Who's going to lead us through this hell?" He had several immediate thoughts, not one of them happy. Rather they suggested mayhem and injury, as he saw himself lost in these mountains and trapped beneath the onrush of a major avalanche, swept away down an indifferent, tumbling river, or blown into oblivion by blizzard winds. "Does anyone know the way?"

"*Don* Pablo." Alvaro had followed him from the bunkhouse, and now stood by the fire. He wore a black wool suit and a wool scarf. He was shivering with cold. The moon shone on him as well, giving his scraggly beard the look of a slim-fingered, dark-gray sea anemone. He gestured with his right hand, beyond the bunkhouse.

At first, Pablo had heard only a boisterous crackling of sticks and underbrush. The bunkhouse itself hid whatever was coming, and the sound of the approach, like that of a heavy-breathing creature emerging from a dank forest, was so filled with the insistence upon arrival that for the moment it frightened Pablo. This was an animal of bleak intensities. The creature had no fear. Its advance demanded Pablo's terrified scrutiny and, glancing toward Alvaro, he fingered the safety catch on his rifle, pondering whether to release it.

"Don't worry." Alvaro motioned toward Pablo, a gesture of caution. "There will be a day soon when you'll want a sound like this to precede you."

Pablo turned back toward the bunkhouse. The animal would soon be in sight, and the moonlight, lifting the bunkhouse a bit, allowing it to float before the two men like a spectral shack, only intensified the grotesquery of the sound. Now Pablo heard the creature's breathing, as though it were sucking the air in and blowing it out through tight, phlegm-filled membranes. Its footfalls were like boulders landing in thick mud. Pablo descended into complete fright. He flicked the release, ready to aim the Winchester at the approaching dragon—or was it a Califian griffin, a gilled Neptunian sea-monster, a gargantuan Darwinian antediluvian?—and to take it down with several pulls of the trigger.

A donkey rounded the end of the bunkhouse and came into full view. It was rag eaten, beat up, slow, and ugly, although the garland it wore, a gathering of a half-dozen lengths of knotted rope tied together so that it resembled a rough-hewn tassel, hung from one side of the wooden saddle. The donkey's rider had a similar look. He was a gnarled man of about thirty-five with a heavy stubble of black beard. He was dressed in poor cotton pants and a poorer shirt, dark green or blue, difficult to tell in the light of the moon, with a black wool vest that had only one button holding it secure, the others apparently having dropped off or been lost. His boots were scuffed, as was his hat, a small porkpie that had the look of a *gau-cho*'s, sweat-ringed and dirty. He also wore a white *lengue*, the slim scarf that, tied in a square knot around the neck, serves as a bit of style for South American cowherds, shepherds, and others who escort large groups of animals from one forsaken corral to another over long distances.

"*¡Buenas noches, chicos!*"

The donkey's saddle had no stirrups, so that as it padded its way across the yard before the bunkhouse, the rider's feet hung loose, bobbing out, up and down. His elbows also stuck out to the sides, rickety as they provided balance. Pablo lowered the rifle. In the light of the moon, the donkey appeared disgruntled.

It came to a halt before Pablo and Alvaro, and the rider tipped his hat. "Good evening."

"Good evening, *amigo*." Alvaro patted the donkey's neck. "How goes it?"

"Very well. It's cold, though." The rider leaned forward, crossing his arms across the wooden horn of the saddle. He looked down at Pablo, who realized that he must appear as some sort of strange phantasm to the rider, a bulky, bearded, cantankerous man with a rifle. Perhaps the mule driver was as surprised by Pablo as Pablo had been by him when he had first rounded the end of the bunkhouse. "Who are you?"

Pablo harrumphed. As a world-famous political prisoner who had been kept in dark secrecy for a year, he felt that everyone must know who he was. He gave this up after a moment, realizing that this man may not know who anyone was, beyond a small circle of other cowherds. He doubted that this fellow knew poetry, or anything at all, for that matter.

"Neruda."

"Yes, I've read your, your—"

"My poems?"

"I haven't actually read them, *señor*. They have been read to me." The rider sat up straight in the saddle, looked up at the moon and then the *cordillera*. He raised a hand toward the skies.

"I can write the saddest lines tonight.
To write, for example: 'The night is filled with stars,
And they shiver, blue, the stars far away.'"

He swirled the hand about once with a flourish, then lowered it to his thigh. The donkey remained silent, as did Pablo and Alvaro.

"Who are you?" Pablo asked.

"Juvenal." The rider dismounted. The silver moon illuminated him and the animal with a bright, backlit line of white all around them. Juvenal patted the donkey's rear flank, and the dust that came off the animal also glowed white. "Juvenal Flores."

"They told me about this fellow in Santiago," Alvaro said.

Juvenal slapped his hands together a few times, to remove dust from them.

"They told me he knows these mountains."

Juvenal turned toward the mountain range behind him. Removing his hat, he pointed with it toward the jutting, gray-white *cordillera*. "And you want to go up through that, *don* Pablo?"

"I do, yes."

Juvenal replaced the hat on his head, the movement an almost sigh-like hint of resignation. "Why?"

"Because if I don't get through the mountains, the government will arrest me, put me on trial for sedition, and string me up."

"I see." Juvenal took the donkey's reins in his right hand and stood still a moment, surveying the ground. "Would that be because of this stellar night?"

"Pardon me?"

"They'll string you up because of your poems?"

"No, it's for other things. But Juvenal, listen." Pablo approached the cowherd and extended his hand. Juvenal took it. "Do you think my poems deserve being thrown into prison?"

"Not if they come from your gut, poet." He gripped Pablo's hand even more tightly. "Do they?"

"Do you eat, Juvenal?

"I do."

"What do you eat?"

"Meat, *señor*."

"Excellent. And my poems do for me what meat does for you. They feed me."

"Do you starve if you don't have them?"

"Like the African during the drought."

Juvenal remained silent.

"What's the donkey's name?" Pablo stood back, admiring the animal with comic interest.

"*Miedo-a-nadie*." Juvenal clapped the donkey on its flank. The animal reminded Pablo of an elderly rug. "*Fear-of-no-one*. But I just call him Miedo. Fear."

The donkey's ears twitched.

—

The next day, a very warm one, brought bad news.

Pablo had awakened with a headache, as though a small straight razor had caught between the back of his left eye and the front of his left temporal lobe. It was explained to him over a breakfast of eggs, toast, beans, and coffee that high altitude often causes disorientation.

"No need to worry." Alvaro swept a forkful of beans into his mouth, looking over at Juvenal, who was boiling more water on a wood stove for coffee. "My head is splitting too. But it will go away in a few…"

Pablo put the fingers of one hand to his forehead. "That's all well and good, but you're not trying to write something like *Canto General*." He immediately regretted the remark, thinking that only a self-pitying amateur would say such a foolish thing to the one person trying to help him the most. The protection that he and Delia had been given in Santiago, the escape, and therefore the future of his writing, had all depended upon Alvaro Jara. Pablo wrapped the coffee mug with both of his hands, noting that Alvaro's lips were pursed unevenly, that a sad frown was drawing his face downward, that he was clearly straining to hold in an insult of his own.

"Alvaro, please." Pablo shook his head with charity-seeking aplomb. "Forgive me."

"You have never understood the danger, *maestro*."

Juvenal turned from the wood stove, wiping his hands on a rag.

"I have, it's just that—"

"You have not. You blithely disregard what we're doing for you."

"I—"

"You have never listened to me." With an exhausted look in his eyes, Alvaro stood and placed both hands on the table, a dark glare fixed upon the poet's face. "You've done everything you can to get us all arrested. That foolish Christmas tree and so on. You treat me like dirt and endlessly congratulate yourself for wasting your time writing that..." Alvaro pushed aside his own mug of coffee. Liquid splashed across the tabletop. "What is it called? *Canto Genial?*"

"*Canto...*"

"*Canto Bestial.*"

"*General.*"

"*Canto General* then. *¿Qué carajo es eso?* What the hell is that?"

Sorrow enveloped the poet. "Alvaro, please, I...." Sympathy for Alvaro's misery and anger began to flow through Pablo's veins. His ingratitude to the boy withered his heart. His foolishness. "Forgive me, please."

"I will not!"

"I beg you."

Alvaro walked from the table. Juvenal, growing restive, laid the rag aside and watched the conversation with concerned gloominess. Pablo realized that Alvaro had hid every moment of resentment over the past year in his heart. He had kept his feelings imprisoned. Alvaro had sacrificed his self-esteem for a fool poet, his foolish words, and his foolhardy Christmas parties.

"*Canto Jodido.*" Alvaro fumed, jamming his hands into his pockets. "*Fucked Up Song.*"

Juvenal winced. Confused, as though not understanding the conversation—"Alvaro, please."—yet willing himself to some kind of commiseration for both men, he held out a hand toward the young man. "*Don* Pablo says he's sorry."

Suddenly Pablo, demanding silence, looked out a bunkhouse window at a plume of dust coming up from the road in the distance.

"*Ay, Dios mío,*" Alvaro whispered.

A car drove up the road, a black Ford covered with dust. The plume behind it rose into the air like raggedy brown tail feathers. The road ascended through two rolling hills, meandering a bit, so that the plume then resembled a grand trail of muddied cigarette smoke. Finally, as the car came to a halt on the far side of the corral outside the bunkhouse, the plume collapsed, spreading out unevenly around the car as though a small building had suddenly fallen.

"Who is it?" Pablo asked.

Juvenal scratched the stubble of beard on his chin. "It's *don* Pepe."

"Rodríguez Gutiérrez?"

The three men looked in silence out the window as the dust settled around the Ford.

"What do we do?" Alvaro said.

Pablo took up his cup of coffee. As yet no one had emerged from the car, and he was convinced that, if this were indeed *don* Pepe, he, Pablo, would be in the jail in Futrono within a matter of hours. He sipped from the coffee.

"We didn't know he was coming," Juvenal said. "He comes here once a year at the most. Almost never, *don* Pablo."

The driver's-side door opened and a large man stepped out of it, his straight hair slightly graying, wearing a pair of rimless eyeglasses. He frowned continuously. He was quite tanned, and looked, in Pablo's opinion, continental, Spanish, Andalusian, a breeder of fighting bulls or something. He removed a double-barreled shotgun from the back seat and looked it over, keeping the gun open and unloaded. Resting the gun against the corral fence, he inspected the car. His brown pants and sweat-soaked brown shirt were baggy and poorly fitting. He wore a pair of *gaucho* boots that appeared never to have been shined. They had originally been dark brown, but now had the same color as the dust that covered the car, a kind of mottled, muddy yellow. Something on the windshield of the car grabbed his attention, and he went to the trunk and opened it, to extract a rag, which he used to remove the splotch or abrasion or goo. His mouth, as he worked the rag, tightened with the effort, obdurately angry-looking as the gunk resisted the cloth. The intensity of his lips convinced Pablo that this was a man who prided himself on finishing what he had begun, be it amassing buckets of money or getting rid of a dead bug on a windshield.

Alvaro turned aside with worry. "What do we do, *don* Pablo?".

Pablo replaced the mug on the tabletop. "He knows who Pablo Neruda is?"

"Of course. Who doesn't?"

"He knows that I'm running away?"

"Of that, I'm not so sure."

Pablo sat down, keeping his eye on *don* Pepe through the bunkhouse screen door. "Then let's tell him."

"Tell him!"

"He'll have to go get the police."

"What about the shotgun?"

"It's empty. We take a chance on the idea that he doesn't have any shells. The police are a day or two away and in the meantime, we head into the mountains."

"Do you know how to ride a horse, *don* Pablo?" Juvenal said.

"We'll figure that out later."

"Later!"

"Alvaro, go out there and tell him who I am, and see how he reacts."

Alvaro stood quietly, weighing the possibilities. Finally, scratching the back of his neck, he loosened and re-tightened his belt in a gesture of resolute, frightened purpose. "All right, here goes."

Pablo and Juvenal sat together, watching out the screen door as Alvaro stepped from the bunkhouse porch, circled the corral, and hailed *don* Pepe. They could not hear the conversation, but it was clear as Alvaro introduced himself and then stood talking with Pepe, whose mouth remained closed and without a smile, that Pepe was shocked by what Alvaro was telling him. Alvaro gestured toward the bunkhouse, and Pepe looked at the building, at the screen door, his ire clearly growing as Alvaro continued talking.

Pepe took the shotgun into his hands.

"He's got shells in his pocket, I'll bet," Pablo whispered. His heart seized and he leaned forward, placing his elbows on his knees. Every action at the corral caused his heart to beat ever more quickly. Pepe locked the shotgun into its loaded position, stared at the bunkhouse a moment, having decided, Pablo concluded, to enter the building and capture Pablo himself, here and now. But Pepe did not move; rather remained still for a moment, until he spoke with Alvaro once more, gesturing with the shotgun toward the bunkhouse. There were a few questions from Alvaro and a few answers from Pepe, until Alvaro, again scratching the back of his neck, turned and strode toward the building.

"What does he say?" Pablo said.

The door ricocheted behind Alvaro, its hinges creaking, and then closed tight. His hands were in the pockets of his slacks. His shoulders sloped with what Pablo assumed was chagrin. "First, he swore at me."

"What did he say?"

"First, *'¡Carajo!'* Then, 'You goddamned liar!' Then when I told him the truth once more, he told me he never imagined he would have the opportunity to meet the greatest poet in all of South America."

Pablo closed his eyes, dropping his head forward.

"And he demanded—"

"Demanded?"

"That you grant him permission to come into the bunkhouse so that he can shake your hand."

Pablo swallowed. "But isn't this his bunkhouse?"

Alvaro threw up his hands. "Can I tell him 'yes', *don* Pablo?"

"Yes!"

—

The following morning at about two, Pepe poured the last of the many glasses of red wine that the four men had drunk. They had spent the afternoon, evening, and the few hours since midnight in a state of riot and drunken abandon. They had eaten beef and rough potatoes. They had sat around the fire outside the bunkhouse. They had argued. Politics, literature, women. Now, Alvaro had gone off to bed. Juvenal had fallen asleep in a chair.

"I've learned about you today, Comrade." Pepe leaned forward and tapped Pablo's knee. "You talk tough politics, but really you're one of these romantic Communists, no?"

Pablo sat back in his chair.

"You believe that capitalism is unfair."

"I do, yes."

"Which is true. But you are anything but doctrinaire, anything but a plodding *apparatchik.*"

"Thanks."

"You aren't boring enough to have a system of economic ideas, to lay out five-year plans about anything." Pepe leaned forward and refilled Pablo's glass. "No? You couldn't put together a land redistribution plan for all the tea in China."

Pepe was right. Just the thought of such things caused Pablo to become sullen and ungovernable.

"So, you wouldn't throw people in prison for their ideas, would you?"

Pablo took in a breath.

"You wouldn't murder Trotsky."

"Of course not. I had no gripe with him."

"You wouldn't condemn your entire officer corps to death."

"No."

"Then why did you write about Joseph Stalin—such tripe—that '*other heroes have brought to light a nation./He assisted as well at the conception of his, /at the building of it/and its defense*'?"

Pablo grimaced, taking the cup of wine to his lips. "Because it's true, Pepe."

"He's murdering his nation, Pablo. Something you would never do." Pepe mumbled to himself in search of words. "He assassinates. He pillages. He commits poets to insane asylums and firing squads."

"But what about Franklin Roosevelt?"

"Roosevelt! What's he got to do with it?"

"The New York Stock Exchange. And what do they call it up there? The Blacks? That 'Jim Crow' thing? The thievery of—"

Pepe laughed. "Of course. As you say, capitalism is not fair." He fingered the bottle of wine, resting his elbows on the table. "But it does not murder people by the millions." He sat back. The quivering of light from the gas lantern above them caused a chiaroscuro-like intensity of shadow and skin in his face. His eyeglasses appeared themselves to be on fire.

Pablo glared into his wine.

"And neither would you, Pablo. And that's why I call you a romantic Communist. Your heart quivers with the sight of a poor man in the street, his rags soiled and rotten."

Pablo lowered his head.

"You'd give him all the change in your pocket."

"Yes."

"You'd help him rise up. You would give him coffee."

"Of course."

"A romantic, then. Your kind of communism is all right because it comes from your own individual heart. Not from Lenin and Stalin and their ghastly books, and the terror they visit upon their people." Pepe grinned, Firelight glinted from his teeth. "Books that are boredom itself. Have you ever read anything by Joseph Stalin?"

"Does he write?"

"Does he read?"

"All right." Pablo sighed. "Whatever you say." He took down the rest of the wine in his cup, and then poured himself and Pepe another.

"But in the end what do I care if you're a Communist?" Pepe's voice was now blurring. His diction was growing sloppy. "Jesus, if only I could tell my father about this. You, the greatest poet of this century." He leaned far forward. "This has been one of the most beautiful nights of my life, Pablo." He leaned farther forward. "*'Where are the lilacs?'*" He sipped from the wine, his lips sloppy against the brim of the cup. "*'And the cov-ered metaphysic of poppies?'*" The cup banged against the tabletop, caus-ing a brief tidal wash of wine over its edge and onto Pepe's fingers. He wiped the wine aside with his other hand. "*'And the rain that often beats against/your words, filling them/with holes and birds?'* Eh?" Pepe lurched forward, catching himself on an elbow. He hurried a look at Pablo. "Where is all that, *amigo*?"

He fell forward, his forehead falling to the table. The sound of his collapse was like that of a wet rag slapping against a wooden floor. His head turned aside, uninjured. He slept.

Pablo carefully removed Pepe's eyeglasses, folded them, and placed them on the table. He put a hand on Pepe's forearm, gripping it. He was quite drunk himself, but he knew that, now, it was not the red wine that would cause his tongue to move or his lips to shape the words. It was hardly the wine at all. He stood and placed his coat over Pepe's shoulders, and then turned toward his bed, which was in the next room.

"It's in the great heart that beats in you, Pepe." Pablo moved toward his simple mattress and the sheets and blankets that surrounded it.

—

"So, you have a plan about which way you want to go?" Juvenal asked the next afternoon. It was cold, and he had rekindled the fire next to the corral. All the men had slept, and all were suffering from hangovers.

"No, *amigo*. I thought that was why you're here," Pablo said.

"You know nothing about these mountains?"

"Only that they are the very definition of elegance in granite."

Juvenal sucked on his pipe, in difficulty assessing this observation from Pablo. "Okay. But you don't know anything about the passes? The rivers? The impossible terrain?"

"Nothing."

"Do you suffer from extreme cold?"

"Not if I have a coat."

Juvenal exhaled. "You'll need more than a coat." He leaned forward with a stick and pushed the fire about, which brought up bright flames. "Are you afraid of heights?"

"No."

"You can handle a shotgun or a rifle?"

"Yes."

"Good. You'll need that. We're going out through the Lilpela." He turned from the fire and pointed up at the *cordillera*. "Up there."

Pepe turned his head from the cowherd, and the reflection of the flames shimmered on his glasses. "It's dangerous, Pablo."

"It's all dangerous up there," Juvenal said.

Pablo rubbed his chin. "You can get injured?"

"Look, the way we're going—"

"Pablo." Pepe's voice conveyed a kind of abraded fearfulness. "Many have died trying to go through the Lilpela."

"It's the only way we can get him out," Juvenal muttered.

"But listen, he's not…forgive me, Pablito, but…" Pepe turned to Juvenal. "The señor isn't up to something like that."

"And we're going to go the secret way."

"But there are so many secret trails."

Juvenal nodded. Smoke from his pipe swirled about his forehead. "That's right, and we're going to go through *El Paso de Los Contrabandistas.*"

Here there was a long silence.

"They actually call it 'Smugglers' Pass'?" Pablo asked.

Juvenal kept his eyes on the fire. "It's an old trail, barely known. Cattle rustlers used to use it a century ago. It goes along the west bank of Lake Lácar."

"That's a Mapuche Indian word. The Lake of The Dead."

"*Bravo, poeta,*" Juvenal whispered.

"But 'Smugglers' Pass' sounds like something from a bad Mexican western." Pablo laughed. "You know, Dolores Del Rio. Pedro Armendáriz."

Pepe grimaced. "You won't meet anyone up there at The Lake of The Dead as beautiful as Dolores Del Rio, Pablito."

"Ever." Juvenal stoked the fire once more.

Pablo saw that, even with the calm bravado with which Juvenal was speaking, an underlay of fear had worked its way into his voice, just here and there in the crevices of his speech. "We walk?"

"No, *maestro.* Too far. Too difficult."

"By horse, then."

"Yes. Do know how to ride a horse?"

Pablo lifted his eyebrows, remembering his childhood. "As long as we don't leave the corral."

Juvenal dropped the stick to the ground and gathered his hands behind him. He turned his gaze toward Pablo. His eyes did not move. He was clearly pondering the poet's naivety. *Perhaps*, Pablo thought, *my stupidity*. Now, Juvenal was immobile, not only in his eyes, but everywhere. Disdain flowed from him. He turned toward Pepe. "All right. We teach him how to ride."

"You've only got a couple weeks before winter."

Pablo took up the stick and began stoking the fire "And I can take my typewriter on the horse?"

"Jesus!" Alvaro whispered.

"It's a Royal. A portable. American-made."

Alvaro shook his head.

"My new book too?" Now Pablo pushed the coals around. Small sparks hurried into the air, through the smoke. "I'll want to take that too."

"What's it called, Alvaro?" Pepe asked.

Alvaro had remained almost silent through the conversation. His lips were skewed, as though rough fingers had shaped them into some extreme form of worry, and then left them that way. His thumbs were hooked beneath his belt. "*Canto General*."

"It's your only copy?" Pepe said.

Pablo nodded. "The only one."

Juvenal fell into muttering silence.

"I insist," Pablo said.

———

"It's off for the moment." Pepe took a stool from one end of the porch and sat down next to Pablo

Pablo, reading on the porch of the bunkhouse that afternoon, put the book aside.

"We have to postpone it."

"Why?"

Pepe placed his elbows on his knees and gathered his hands together. "There's a man who works in my sawmill here. An Indian. A Mapuche."

Pablo waited.

"He was shot a couple weeks ago at work, by a foreman, and badly wounded. So, the Indian court has demanded an investigation and wants compensation for the man, which I suppose, I suppose—"

"Is just."

"I suppose. But the trouble is, I learned today that a representative of the court is coming out here tomorrow, and he'll be here for a few days. A lawyer. To talk to people in the sawmill, witnesses and so on, and we can't have you here, or any evidence of your being here."

"I see."

"Which means, Pablo, that you have to leave for a while."

Pablo sighed, distressed by the fact that we would have to pack a suitcase yet once more, trundle himself into some nameless vehicle and drive to some other hovel in which he could hide himself. "So, you're bringing me another Pepe Rodríguez."

"Sadly, yes." Pepe lowered his head.

Pablo crossed his legs and leaned back in the chair. "What if you hire me, Pepe?"

Confusion mottled Pepe's gaze. Pablo stood and, walking to one end of the porch, removed an old handsaw from the wall above a wooden bench, where it was serving as a piece of décor. "I can handle one of these." He waved it before him, as though he were warming up for a fencing match. "Give me a job."

"Too dangerous. Pablito"

"I'll be in disguise. Give me some old clothes, an old pair of boots. I've got my beard. Get me an old hat. It'll be easy!"

Pepe shook his head. He had already become resigned to the idea that everything had to come to a halt. But Pablo, having grown used to such surprises during the previous year, tapped Pepe's shoulder. "I won't intrude." He sat down once more and took up the book. "I promise."

Pepe left the next morning, to go to court. Pablo, outfitted for his new job as a sawyer, modeled his clothes for Juvenal and Alvaro. Alvaro, very worried, yet laughed as Pablo stooped his shoulders as though he had labored for decades in the sawmill and shuffled across the floor, allowing his boots to clomp heavily against the wooden boards, and breathed as though he had spent a long life smoking a hundred cigarettes or so every day.

The following day, just after noon, they spied Pepe's Ford making its way up the road toward the bunkhouse. Yet once more, dust plumed into the air behind the car. By the time it came to a halt, Pablo had positioned himself at a chopping block near the corral, a large pile of bucked logs nearby, and stood mutely, holding an axe in his hand. He did not really know how to handle an axe, but he wanted to look the part. He was at-tempting the stance of a Neanderthal. He also planned to pretend that he was semi-mute, unschooled, and partially deaf. He had practiced it. He was nervous nonetheless, and he knew that Alvaro, who was seated on the cor-ral fence smoking a cigarette, was very apprehensive.

Pepe and another man stepped out of the car, and Pepe gestured here and there toward the buildings and the corral, inviting the man to step into the bunkhouse for coffee. The fellow was plainly dressed in a suit and a white shirt without a tie. He appeared athletic, trim, and even muscular as he pulled a briefcase from the back seat of the car and turned to follow Pepe. His face was worn, though, making him look older than in fact he was. It was beaten and lined. It had been through storms. After a few steps, he spotted Pablo, and stopped motionless. He squinted his eyes at the ap-parition before him.

"Victor!" Pablo startled everyone except for the man whom he was hailing. Dropping the axe to the ground, swirling the hat from his head and raising it into the air, he strode across the yard toward the two men.

"Pablo. You're here?"

"I am."

Pablo hurried past Pepe and embraced the other fellow. Pepe, adjust-ing his glasses and non-plussed, simply watched. Pablo and Victor clapped each other's shoulders. They laughed and turned about in a circle.

"Victor Bianchi. I don't believe it."

"The government…they think you're dead."

"Well, am I?"

"What are you doing here?"

"I'm a fugitive, you know."

"Of course."

"I'm leaving the country."

Victor stood apart a moment. "But the government's been saying for days that they're about to take you, dead or alive."

"Maybe not just yet." Pablo turned to Pepe and the others. "This Victor Bianchi is one of my closest friends."

The others remained stupefied.

"It's true. A superb fellow, cheerful, cordial, open…a great friend of mine." Pablo clapped him on the right shoulder. "His uncle…a fine man, a true diplomat…got me my first diplomatic post." Pablo grinned again. "In Burma, may God help me! Twenty years ago."

Victor looked about at the others. He was especially interested in Alvaro, whom he no doubt recognized from the Christmas Party. He fixed his gaze on him as though he were somehow not to be trusted. Alvaro was a city boy, not like the cowherds. He was wearing muddied street shoes and a pair of slacks.

"Who are these others, Pablo?"

"They're helping the escape."

"And you? Are you ready for such a thing?"

Pablo shrugged. Indeed, he continued worrying that the moment they left the shelter of the sawmill, he would be exposed to the worst that fate could offer him. He awoke at night from dreams of his own violent death. The *cordillera* was waiting, murderous and cunningly happy that Pablo Neruda was coming. The *cordillera* would put an end to all his mindless japing. The *cordillera* would silence him, as no one down in the flatlands had ever been able to do. At night, he shuddered with the expectation of deep, unbearable snow. "I hope so."

"Can you ride a horse?"

Pablo remained silent.

"When was the last time you rode one, Pablo?"

"I believe I was thirteen."

"Does anyone know the route you're going to take?"

Juvenal raised a hand. "I do, *señor*. Quite well." His demeanor, his very presence, seemed to silence Victor for the moment. "But who are you to ask all these questions?"

"A mountain climber," Pablo said. "Almost died on Aconcagua." He lowered his head. "I remember it, Victor." He shook his head. "He was carried down from that mountain as though it had scoured him clean of his own skin. Of his own soul. Wrecked."

"Which it did with those we left up there, Pablo."

"Just so."

"Will you know what to do when everything falls apart?"

With this question, Pablo's heart felt stalled.

"Do you? If these men going with you, if they're injured, or don't know what to do, or are dead?"

There was only silence.

Victor laid his brief case on the porch bench. He exhaled and grumbled a few words that no one else got. "All right. I'm going with you."

6

YOUNG ONE-EYE

El Joven Tuerto had just one eye.

"That's his name," Juvenal said after Pablo remarked on the horse's semi-blindness. "Young One-Eye."

"So, he doesn't see out to the left?"

"Not if he's looking straight ahead, *amigo*." Juvenal patted the horse's neck, and Tuerto shook his head, seeking more attention from the cowherd. "He does occasionally turn his gaze to the left though, to see if there's anything he's missing." He ran his right hand up and down Tuerto's neck. "Horses do that, you'll find."

Pablo, feeling laughed at, studied the animal. It was on Tuerto that he would negotiate the Andes range, and this worried him. "He can take us through The Smugglers' Pass?"

"He can."

"The question, I guess, really is, can he take me through?"

"That depends."

For an hour, Pablo rode in a circle inside the corral. He could not tell whether he or Tuerto were the more impatient. *If this were all there was to riding a horse,* he thought, *we could have left yesterday.*

Juvenal rode behind him on Miedo. "Sit up straight, *don* Pablo. Don't hold the reins as though they're pulling at you. Relax. Be calm. Let your shoulders rest." Two other men sat on the corral fence: Victor Bianchi and the young hand Ramada, who, had he not been so hard-bitten by the ruggedness of his profession already at the age of twenty-five, would have looked like a screen idol from one of Dolores Del Rio's westerns. Wearing a narrow-brimmed black wool hat, a black scarf around his neck, a white shirt the sleeves of which were rolled far up, old Levis and an Argentine *gaucho* belt into which he had sewn a couple of silver coins, he had the most finely delicate profile Pablo had ever seen on a man. Dark-skinned, his eyes with a slightly Asian softness, black like obsidian, and a boy's mustache, barely visible, yet enough so that his masculinity was assured by it, Ramada appeared almost magisterial. His hands were working hands, though, thickened with all the tasks he performed as a logger and a cowhand. As he and Victor smoked and watched, they chuckled, pointing out little stumbles and inaccuracies in Pablo's method of riding a horse. Juvenal had told Pablo that Ramada, too, would be accompanying them through the Lilpela. Pepe and Alvaro stood at the gate watching.

Tuerto did make gestures toward spiritedness but was too confined within the corral's circle to really show it. Only now and then did he break from his slow walk into a mild canter. It was a bit of spice in his step, a little orneriness. Tuerto buoyed Pablo's confidence. *All you have to do is roll with this horse,* Pablo thought. *He turns his head and you flow with him. You turn his head with the reins and he flows with you. Simple as can be.*

Pablo was bored. "When do we go out?" He had turned his head, and now placed a hand on the back of Tuerto's saddle. Behind him, Juvenal held tightly to Miedo's reins as the donkey shuffled quickly along. Where Tuerto strolled around the corral with a certain *savoir-faire*, Miedo seemed always to be attempting to catch up.

"Tomorrow." Juvenal watched Tuerto carefully, studying the horse and analyzing what was happening.

To Pablo's mind, nothing was happening. "Why not now?"

"You're not ready, *maestro*."

They rode in circles for a second hour. By this time lethargy had invaded everyone. Juvenal had dismounted from Miedo and simply followed Tuerto on foot, a riding crop in one hand that he did not need to use at all. Alvaro and Pepe had left the corral, and now sat on the bunkhouse porch drinking beer.

Pablo got down from the horse and patted his head. "I don't know how we'll ever make it through The Smugglers' Pass," he whispered in the horse's ear, "if you walk that slow the whole way, Tuerto." He had noted one thing about the animal, though. Tuerto was half-blind. But his musculature had such formidable strength, in a rustic and harshly made way, that Pablo believed the horse could go anywhere. Tuerto reminded him, in effect, of a young, brusque, and impatient youth. The horse turned his head and looked at things as though he did not particularly trust them, and would insult them if they insulted him. Yes, in the corral he had been quiet. *Outside the corral*, Pablo thought, *it will be a different story.*

So, Pablo gathered himself. He worried about the next day and what would happen to him when Tuerto realized that they would be able to move in a straight line. He would perhaps change his demeanor very quickly… and damn the idiot up above.

—

The following morning, the sun shined like burnished silver through parts of the *cordillera*, casting itself in narrow lines across the forest. Pepe had given Pablo a thick wool jacket that would protect the poet on this morning and, especially, against the wind and snow at the higher altitudes, useful if an unexpected blizzard happened to sweep down upon them.

"You cannot imagine, *maestro*, how cold it can get up there." Pepe grinned. "Even a man of your talent with words, in the face of such weather, would find himself speechless."

Pablo, hurrying the coat over his shoulders, grumbled thanks.

Inside the corral, Pablo mounted Tuerto and immediately noticed that there had been a change of mood in the horse. He was preparing himself for freedom, it seemed. His ears perked up, back and forth. His eyes opened wide, and he surveyed the trail that led from the corral into the forest beyond the bunkhouse. Pablo thought he could actually hear the blood running through the animal's heart, like wind coursing through the great Araucanian woods, reminding Pablo of the actual sound of such a wind when, in dreaming ecstasy, he had listened to it in bed as a child, late at night. Tuerto's hoofs pawed the ground. He took a step forward, a step back, and the hoofs banged into the dirt as though the horse wished to punish it. He lifted his head, trying to pull away from Juvenal.

"No, Tuerto. Calm down."

Tuerto would not listen.

"Juvenal, are you sure about this?" Pablo held tight to the saddle horn.

"I am, *maestro*. You can do it."

Pablo took the reins from the cowherd, who quickly got up onto Miedo. Victor and Ramada waited outside the corral, mounted and ready to ride. Pepe opened the gate and, as Pablo struggled to take control of his horse, Pepe slapped the passing poet on the leg. "Don't worry, Pablito. Be careful."

Tuerto took off.

They hurtled into the forest, Tuerto heading for the first low branches he could find. Pablo ducked several times, until they got out into an open stretch of dirt road, where Tuerto extended himself into a full-headed gallop.

"Hold on, *don* Pablo!" Juvenal's voice was so far off that, with all the noise coming from Tuerto's hoofs, Pablo could barely hear him.

After a few minutes of real speed, Tuerto slowed for a moment. He had spotted a copse of young pines up ahead, on the left, and he began sprinting toward them. As they approached the trees, Tuerto seemed to be measuring his alternatives. Fast? Slow? A gallop? I bring him up against a trunk? I knock him off with a low branch? But before he could come to a decision, Pablo pulled the reins to his right, taking the horse off balance.

"*¡Hijo de puta!*"

Pablo spurred the horse with the heels of his boots, in the opposite direction. Tuerto, confused, suddenly seemed angered himself, as though the blood that had flowed through him like a storm had now shored up against a fearsome dike, and backwashed down the veins, forcing him to stumble and worry.

"This way, damn you!"

The horse turned, grunting, a violent objection as he tried to free himself from the reins. Pablo let them loosen, and Tuerto began running again, away from the trees.

"No!" Pablo shouted, drawing the horse to a halt once more. "No!"

Tuerto stopped. Nervous and impatient, he dropped his head toward the ground. He seemed to look back over his shoulder, as it were, to see what the poet was going to do next.

"¡Salvaje! ¡Cálmate!" Pablo pulled back sharply on the reins. "Savage! Calm down!"

Tuerto, the bit almost bloodying the tissues of his mouth, did not move. He gagged as his heavy breathing coursed in and out.

Miedo approached, followed by the other two horses. All three riders appeared shocked, especially Juvenal, whose hat had fallen off as he had reined in Miedo next to the stricken Tuerto. "What are you doing, riding like that?"

Pablo, enlivened by Tuerto's resistance to him, decided upon magnanimity. "Just wanted to test his nerve, *amigo*."

"That's a fine horse there, *maestro*, and I don't like you mistreating him."

"If he behaves, he gets treated right." Pablo's own heart beat like a snare drum. But he would do everything to keep Juvenal from knowing that.

"You have to have patience with a horse like this."

"No." Pablo brushed off his right pants leg. His butt felt that a large portion of it had been beaten with a club. "I'm supposed to be in charge. The horse should understand what I want."

Juvenal dismounted Miedo and took up his hat from the dirt. "You say the horse should understand you."

"Yes."

"Instead of you it?"

"Right."

Juvenal twirled the hat between his fingers. To Pablo, it resembled a crumpled Milky Way swirling about. The millions of years that it would require to do so, during which thousands of stars would die out and disappear before the next turn was to begin, weighed upon his feelings.

"Worry about your own talents, Juvenal. I'll ride Tuerto. You ride Miedo."

Listening, Tuerto shuddered, as though he were delighted.

—

Ten days later, on March 7, 1949, they were ready. It was fall, an excessively cold, clear morning. Pablo's back hurt from all the riding they had done. His butt ached. His legs felt permanently bowed. The bandages on his fingers darkened here and there with dried pus and blood. But he was ready.

He had asked Alvaro to share a bottle of wine on the bunkhouse porch.

"This is our last moment together."

Crystalline and soft morning sunlight filtered through the trees. Pablo had never seen a morning the likes of this one. The light cut the *cordillera* so cleanly from the clear blue sky behind it that the peaks resembled a universally immense saw-blade's edge. Fresh snow had already fallen up there. The morning welcomed Pablo as though today that blade would open some secret envelope, to reveal long-ancient recollections of the birth of art, the moment that imagination came to some pre-human lout making his way on foot through just such a mountain range. When poetry, music, painting…when they all became suddenly possible for everyone. The moment in which certain animals first felt thoughts coursing through them.

"So, I hope you'll have a glass of wine with me." Pablo had never spent this much time all at once in the Andes, and never in a state of such emotional fragility. Tuerto had intimidated him at first. But now they had become friends, making the task they had of riding together a muscular one notable for its mutual respect. It was a calm day with no wind. The wine filtered through Pablo's heart like an elixir of calm. "And we haven't finished the conversation from that day that *don* Pepe arrived."

Alvaro took in a breath. He had watched Pablo's riding lessons, his cantankerous winning of Tuerto's regard, and then the constant practice, and had seemed during the last day or two to come to admire Pablo's new-found abilities as a horseman.

Pablo's typewriter, a Royal, rested on the table in a leather case with a handle. So did *Canto General*, ordered in separate leaves and wrapped securely in two pieces of British oilcloth tied with lengths of leather.

Pablo laid his hand on the manuscript. "I haven't ever said this to you."

Alvaro's head twitched. Despite Pablo's overture, he appeared to be expecting another of the poet's insensitive barbs, one of his complaints about Alvaro's over-attentive meddlesomeness.

"But I owe you, Alvaro." Pablo moved his hand to the wooden table-top. Its thick fingers caressed the edge of the terra cotta cup from which he had been drinking. He wore Pepe's wool jacket and the pair of blue-jean coveralls that, with the two pairs of woolen underwear, would take him through the Andes. His boots had been badly scuffed by all the riding he had done. "For what you've done to protect me."

"Maestro, I don't think—"

"No, Alvaro. I've been a great trial."

"Maybe. But—"

"Admit it. I have been."

Alvaro shrugged, taking up his wine. "All right, you have been occasionally."

"It's true." Pablo gazed directly into Alvaro's eyes. "What do the Argentines call it? A *boludo*? And the Mexicans, what is it?"

"A *pendejo*." Alvaro smiled, happy to be of linguistic help to the great poet

"Right. All of those. But…" Pablo sat up straight and pointed with an open hand out the bunkhouse door. "Now that this day has come, and we're headed up there" He shrugged, the edges of his mouth turning down. "I want to thank you. And to ask you…"

The sound of approaching conversation came from beyond the corral. Juvenal, on Miedo, hurried along, accompanied by Victor and Ramada, who rode horses. All had satchels and saddlebags filled with rough food and ammunition, ropes, blankets, knives, pistols. Tuerto, saddled and equally burdened, came along behind, at the end of a rope.

"To forgive me."

Alvaro stared at Pablo a long moment. His face was rapt by surprise. Pablo knew that Alvaro had been angry with him for months. Alvaro's silences had stung him badly. Yet he had ignored the boy. He had endangered him.

"I will, *don* Pablo, if you'll do a couple things for me."

"What's that?"

"Be careful." Alvaro grinned, his head held to the side. "I know that will be difficult for you." He gathered his hands on the table, looking back at Pablo, who was reminded of a responsible schoolboy lecturing the ne'er-do-well father that he has just dragged out of a pub. "Do what Juvenal says." The two men stood up as Juvenal and the others stopped at the corral, dismounted, and headed for the bunkhouse. "And don't fall off Tuerto." He shook Pablo's hand. "I have great sympathy for that horse, *maestro*."

They embraced.

"You're a fine man, Alvaro," Pablo whispered. "I'll miss you."

They clapped each other on the shoulders. Alvaro, shaking his head and muttering with comic impatience, took up the typewriter and the manuscript and, putting a hand on Pablo's shoulder, nodded toward the screen door.

—

"All right, Kennecott Copper!" Pablo mounted Tuerto, taking the reins from Pepe's hand. "Ford Motors! United Fruit! See if you can catch me!"

"Pablo." Victor, seated casually on his horse, gestured at Tuerto. "On that animal, in those clothes, you look like a sack of potatoes with a beard."

"I expect the animal feels the same."

"Now, you men." Pepe turned to the others. He took hold of an edge of Tuerto's saddle. Pablo, wishing to get on with it, sat with great impatience. He threw the lower part of his *poncho* around his shoulders and looked up, taking in a breath, into the *cordillera*. "These are my orders," Pepe said. "Do not allow *don* Pablo to fall into the hands of any police. Protect him. Get him to the other side alive."

The others muttered their assent. They were all excited, especially young Ramada, who, like Victor and Pablo, had never been through The Smugglers' Pass. Ramada wanted to get going too, to escape the speeches and head into the *cordillera* no matter what it would bring them.

"If any obstacles keep you from getting him through, drop everything and cut another road through the forest."

"But *señor* Pepe." Juvenal scowled. "That could be many kilometers. The mountains. Unknown territory."

"That's fine, *amigo*. Just do it."

Pepe turned to Pablo and slapped Tuerto on the flank.

"And as for you, poet, I give you my word of honor…" He placed his hands in his pockets, and a sudden glint of mischief entered his eyes. "That I am a capitalist, with all the—"

"Long live usury."

"With all the faults of a capitalist, one of which is that I think Communists are fools." Pepe placed his right hand on Pablo's knee. "I know also that I am a friend to my friends." He lifted his hand and extended it toward Pablo. "And I'm proud that you are my friend."

"As am I." Pablo's voice fell to a considerate whisper. The mountains above so excited him that he could barely speak. He took Pepe's hand. "Goodbye, Pepe, and thank you."

Pepe slapped Tuerto once more on the flank, and the horse bolted. Holding on to the reins with his right hand, Pablo removed his beret with the left and waved it into the air, looking back over his shoulder at Alvaro and Pepe. Pepe placed his hand on Alvaro's shoulder, and the young man raised a fist into the air.

Pablo, his heart racing, spurred Tuerto on toward the high, cold danger of the Andes Mountains.

7

DELIA AND THE AMBASSADOR

Sewing, Delia waited. Picasso had phoned her the previous afternoon, promising flowers. His voice, as always, was demanding, yet sweet in the way of a charming bully. Fernand Leger had also called, asking her to dinner. "I have a special wine," he had said. Jean-Louis Barrault had sent her a note, asking to show her the poster for his new play at the *Comédie-Française*. Then, in a blinding surprise, the Chilean ambassador to France also called, telling her that if her husband Neruda were serious, he would come to the embassy to turn himself in.

"He's alive?" She leaned quickly over the side table and the phone. Her apartment on the Île Saint-Louis had a view of the Seine, which at the moment on this lonely, rainy morning, reminded her of a slab of silver lava.

"Actually, we don't know. We were expecting you to know."

As an Argentine Delia felt she needn't listen to any sort of cross, dictatorial chirping from some Chilean *petit bureaucrat*. So, she told him that she didn't know where Pablo Neruda was, and that if she did know, "I wouldn't tell you…or your idiot president". Waiting as the ambassador blustered in only half-understandable gibberish about how much Delia reminded him of her husband—"difficult, unreasonable and unpatriotic, *señora*"—and that it would be her husband who would suffer from this disrespectful behavior on the part of his wife, she finally replied that she was going to hang up, that she had no more time, that *señor* Picasso was coming up the stairs, as far as she knew with a fresh painting under his arm, and that, as far as she,

Delia Del Carril, was concerned in this year of Our Lord 1949, she would much rather have a conversation with a short, ugly Catalan artist than with an urbane, well-dressed *apparatchik*, "if only because *apparatchik*s, and especially Chilean *apparatchik*s, are all such *boludos*". The word *boludo*, an Argentine specialty, was a very rude one, but in the case of this *boludo*, she didn't care.

She hung up and continued sewing.

8

A DREAM

That first night, near a campfire in a wood, Pablo dreamt of a distant year, far away.

His death.

Sickness flowed from the dream. He had been ill and dying for years. Now he had indeed died, in sorrow for the death of a close friend, a politician who in the dream had died for his politics a few days earlier. A senator, perhaps. Maybe even president. Pablo didn't recognize him yet knew and felt cleanly in his heart that this was a good man who had died defending his country, its honor and all his beliefs from the fierce, sullen fighter planes above, from the revenge of dim-witted generals, from the wrath of the United States and the legions of misled Chilean soldiers who had accosted the capital and killed everyone. Only Pablo himself and a beautiful woman, his companion, his wife, had survived.

Yet he, Pablo, indeed had not survived. Just days after the murder of his friend, he saw that he too had died, in a house in which his lover, the beautiful woman, had nursed him with affection and care through the sadness that had led to his own heart-stricken demise.

He didn't know the location of the house. Perhaps in Santiago, although after a moment he decided that it was probably near the ocean shore.

In the most stellar moment of the dream, his body had been laid out in a casket. The sea's caresses of the shore folded across themselves like rolled, puffed sheets one after the other. The house itself glowed with ancient seashells and ships' wooden figureheads, which Pablo himself had collected, each one uniquely imbued with sunlight coming in the windows.

But the house had been destroyed. Some mindless and disrespectful military force had wrecked it, so that his coffin was the only surviving piece of furniture, and his corpse the only living person in the place. Delirious, faraway conversations came and went. He had only partially understood them. His lover had been asking his advice, now that he was dead, about whether to have him lie in state in the midst of such ruin, or to remove him to a safer place. She had decided to go ahead no matter the condition of the house, to show the destroyers that this was Pablo Neruda, and that he and Death would embrace where he and Death had a mind to.

He lay in silence for hours, alone in the wreckage, until several strangers, people he didn't know, workers, miners, and farmers, rang the bell and entered the house, their wool caps and straw hats hanging from their thick fingers. Their sandals further broke up the glass on the floor and the detritus of the broken stonework left by the soldiers. They passed in silence, asking simply that *don* Pablo not forget them.

Then others came, and the house filled. Poets, novelists he had known; companions from his youth, with whom in the cafes he had argued over Shakespeare and Proust; people he had not seen for decades; friends who had died long ago; the surprise guest…the beautiful niece of the perished president, whoever she might be…Isabel…who in the dream was a journalist who had interviewed Pablo a few months before, whose work as a journalist he had disparaged, and who he had predicted would one day write a beloved novel, a strange tapestry about a house filled with spirits; people who loved the forest and the rivers, who fished, who walked the seashore taking into their fingers whatever little mollusk-remains or shells they could find; collectors of wood and poems, of sonnets and carving knives, of rain and the passage of storms; everyone he had ever known.

They had all helped him in some way, and he knew so in his dream. The problem was, he could not move any of his limbs, to grasp his friends' hands, or to raise a glass to them. His past inundated the house, and he could do nothing but lie in his coffin and think about how grateful he was to that past.

He had ordered in champagne for all.

Finally, his friend the murdered president came to Pablo's side and laid a hand on his chest. Pablo somehow knew him as a kind man, mustached and wearing glasses.

"Goodbye." The president asked for a handkerchief from one of the workers, a railroad man whose hands were soiled with oily grit. The president lifted his glasses from his face and daubed tears from his cheeks. "Thank you, Pablito."

Pablo's funeral would be one spent in the midst of destruction and mayhem. But his friends would protect him, especially as they removed his body from the house, stumbling across the broken glass and cement, over the rags of the knife-slashed draperies and the shattered wood, and carried the body into the sun, to lay it in the dark, salted sand of the Pacific sea.

Pablo awoke in the forest, in the mountains. His dream had moved him to fear. He held his *poncho* close with both hands.

Death.

He enjoyed contemplating it when he wrote about it. But to imagine it in fact, to experience it as he just had…. He felt his heart stop. Opening his eyes, he saw wavering lights in the far distance, in the woods. The other men had fallen asleep, and the campfire had gone to nothing. These lights came from fiery torches, barely visible through the trees, passing in and out of them. The sound of plodding hoofs was so distant from the campsite that they could barely be heard. Only the flames, like tongues of fire afloat and surging, made their way up a faraway path, lighting the path until it slowly disappeared into the dark.

—

The following morning at sunup, Pablo took the knife he had from its sheath. The others gathered around as he approached a large pine tree. The horses waited a few meters away.

"Okay, *muchachos*," he said. "A poem." He laid knife to tree bark. *"Qué bien aquí se respira/ en el paso Lilpela/ donde no llega la mierda /*

del traidor González Videla." ("*How nice it is to breathe here/in the mountain pass of Lilpela/where the shit never shows/of the treasonous González Videla.*") Chuckling, he lowered the knife, nonetheless in a moment of despair. He could die out here. They could all die. There may be no way out.

My Delia. Where are you?

"*Bueno ¿qué sé yo?*" he said. "What do I know? Let's go, boys."

<h1 style="text-align:center">9
THE ROYAL,
DROWNED</h1>

The next morning, Pablo woke to the cascade of waters down the Curringue River. He suspected that this tumbling explosion had been roaring across the boulders and through the enormous, cave-like, precipitous cliff-gates for many thousands of years.

Juvenal shook his shoulder. "Hurry up."

Pablo rolled beneath the blankets that had kept him so warm by the campfire. He had trouble hearing Juvenal.

"We don't have a lot of time."

"But it's only seven o'clock." The walls of the chasm, at the bottom of which they had been camping, were bathed in shadow. "It's so beautiful." Two cliffs, each a hundred meters high, their gray-blue granite partially covered with green moss and other spray-driven greenery, strived toward each other directly above them, as though they were headed for a stony kiss.

"Who cares?" Juvenal pulled the blanket aside. "We have to go."

"Just give me a minute to look at this."

Ramada surveyed the cliffs also. Not much given to the kind of inelegant bravado of which Juvenal was a master, Ramada was a youthful wanderer. Riding up toward the Curringue the previous day, they had talked about music. Pablo liked music more or less. But he knew that he didn't always know what he was listening to. They were pleasant enough, Mozart, Palestrina and all the rest. Debussy. Scarlatti. Stravinsky. Delia liked them, all of them. But music basically did nothing for Pablo, and he realized that this was definitely an oddity in a man for whom the music of language had always been all-important. Pablo understood sound as long as syllables and words were connected to it. He likened the beauties of the Spanish language to olive oil, in the way that the oil was the recondite and supreme condition of the stewpot, the starry key to mayonnaise, so soft and tasty on the lettuce leaves. In Pablo's voice, in his choruses, with powerful softness, olive oil sung. "It is the Spanish language." he had explained to Ramada as they had been riding. "There are syllables in our language that are so useful and perfumed that they must come from the olive."

"Yes, *maestro.*"

"It isn't just wine that sings in the Spanish language, my boy. It's olive oil as well." Pablo turned in his saddle to address the sawyer directly. "It lives in us with its full…"

Ramada's attention had drifted toward a squirrel climbing a tree.

"With its ripe light, among all the goods of the very earth itself." Pablo re-oriented himself toward the path, leaving Ramada to his own thoughts. They rode through the deep forest. The poet felt, sadly, that the boy had lost the thread of his explanation somewhere along the way, as the explanation had gone on, Pablo admitted, for quite a long time…for a kilometer or two through the forest. But if olive oil were indeed the Spanish language, the language was indeed olive oil as well. They both had such golden delicacy. *What could Mozart ever have written—reared in the snows of Austria, for God's sake!—that would bring us to a similar realization? Although,* Pablo thought, *Delia does love Mozart, and Don Giovanni himself was Italian, wasn't he? So….* But Pablo, a master of language with a tin ear for music, had nonetheless never heard such a thing from the cold-bound Mozart, not even in *Don Giovanni.*

He supposed that Ramada hadn't either.

———

Juvenal had saddled Tuerto, and now brought the horse to Pablo. The cowherd's jaws worked tightly as he approached, and Pablo knew that he was about to get some unwelcome news. Juvenal's eyes resembled black marbles that refused to roll in any direction.

"What's wrong, *soldado*?"

"We cross the river this morning." Juvenal gestured toward the Curringue as it raced between the two cliffs, turned abruptly and dropped four meters in a direct falls between a couple of enormous boulders, then continued, scattered, white and foamy down a long narrow draw to a set of rapids.

Pablo grew puzzled. "I haven't seen any bridge, though."

Victor and the others laughed, although Victor, conscious of Pablo's worries, hurried to offer some kind of commiseration. He scolded the other two men with an embarrassed glance, for which Pablo was grateful.

"No bridge," Juvenal said.

"Not anywhere on this river?"

"Nowhere."

Pablo surveyed the cowherd with disbelief.

"Well, perhaps somewhere, *don* Pablo. Up at the summit of the *cordillera* maybe, or down at the ocean. But…" Juvenal cleared his throat, passing a hand across Tuerto's right flank. "Not where we're going."

"So how do we get across?"

"We ride."

Water came down the river's twisted passageway so quickly, so much of it and so noisily, that the men had to shout to be heard. A rigorous, even gorgeous beauty roared from the falling cascade. The blue-green clear flow suddenly turned to white, exploding across huge rocks, swirling so rapidly about them that Pablo imagined that a solid body—his own, for example—being swept past these outcroppings would be visible for so little time that it would hardly be seen at all. The release of air from the buckling, raggedly splintered rapids battered the shrubbery growing up the cliffs. Because it was so filled with water itself, the mist brought shivers to the men trying to protect themselves from it.

"But I can't take Tuerto across that."

"You won't be alone. Ramada and Victor, they'll be with you." The other men nodded, colloquial, nonchalant, and worried. "And Miedo will be helping."

"Where will you be?"

Juvenal pointed to the small gathering of stones and sand on which he stood. "Here on the bank."

Juvenal with Miedo? Not in the river with me?

"Look, it's like this, *don* Pablo. When you take horses across such a river, you always use what we call an anchor-mule." He turned toward Victor. *"¿Correcto, hombre?"*

Victor nodded.

Pablo, his forehead furrowed, glanced at the donkey. "Miedo, you mean."

"Yes, in this case."

"What does he do?"

Juvenal took up a fallen branch and started drawing in the patch of sandbar. "All the horses are tied together downriver from the mule, like in a train." He sketched a design of several circles strung together along a straight line. "And the mule—"

"Miedo,"

"That's right. Miedo is the last animal upriver, and if the horses go down, he's the one who keeps them from being swept away." Juvenal tossed the stick to the ground, a large smile on his lips. "You know, it's amazing what a burro can do sometimes."

"You didn't mention the riders of the horses."

"Oh, them too. As long as they hold on."

Pablo looked beyond Juvenal at a small clearing where the horses had been tied up for the night. Miedo was ready to go and stood quietly in the clearing watching the conversation. He was not a friendly donkey and seemed to view men other than Juvenal as phonies. He had a comic's disdain for false sincerity. He thought that a man like Pablo Neruda, with all his fanciness and words and airs, was a fey bother. Pablo could feel it from Miedo every time he tried to offer the donkey a few kind words or a carrot.

Now Pablo realized that the continuation of his life might well depend upon this animal, and he worried that Miedo cared so little for him that he may simply let *don* Pablo go when the waters got a little too aggressive. The view of the poet's drowning would be a welcome sight, his communist, collectivizing arms beating against the river into the distance, no longer to be worried about.

"Is there no other way?"

Juvenal pushed the twig around in the dirt with the toe of his boot. He held his head so low, his face actually parallel to the ground, that Pablo could barely see any of it. Juvenal's forehead, however, was only slightly shielded by his hair, so that Pablo could see that it was tight with impatience. "No."

Pablo was reminded of Comrade Saturno.

—

Ramada directed his horse to the riverbank. A large pinto that belonged to Pepe Rodríguez, Ángel walked with assured steadiness toward the rushing water. But the moment he first entered the river, his confidence began to falter. He abruptly stopped. Ramada, the braver of the two, urged the horse on.

Pablo admired the young man's change of spirit. While normally Ramada floated from thought to thought, his mind wandering, now he knew the danger he was in. His every attention was on the horse and the river. He whistled, tapped the horse's flank with the reins, and spurred him on. Finally, the horse gave in, and began his traverse of the waters.

Pablo remained on the shore on Tuerto, and Victor sat on his horse behind. The rope that joined the three horses together had been specially tied about the saddle horn of each rider, with ten meters of rope between each horse. Miedo stood at the very rear, the end of the rope secured to his saddle. Pablo saw that the usually bored burro was himself excited now, as though the task before him were going somehow to be fun. His ears were up, his nostrils widened. He had already dug into the shore dirt, as though he had spent several moments preparing the surface, getting his hoofs secured, determined to hold his ground.

Suddenly Ramada's Ángel hurtled into the water. But as the river covered his flanks, he stopped again. The waters swirled. Ángel's head turned back and forth. His eyes were electrified.

"*Ánda, Angelito,*" Ramada yelled. "Keep going." He whipped the horse on both flanks, his own will growing darker as the horse refused to move. Standing still took all of Ángel's courage.

Pablo recalled Juvenal's caution earlier that morning, when he had been describing the idea of the anchor-mule, that the river-bottom was made up of large stones undercut now and then with uneven ledge drop-offs. With almost no flat underpinning to depend upon, the horses attempting to find purchase had to be very careful, all the while being savaged by the unending flow.

Ramada got Ángel walking again.

A voice, as though from a great distance behind him, secreted itself into Pablo's concentration. "You next!" He barely heard it. But he realized that, though far away, the voice spoke to him. He looked over his left shoulder. Victor, seated on his horse directly behind Pablo, shouted at him again, and the river almost overwhelmed the sound of his voice. "Pablo! You! Go on!"

Victor's horse, a black mare named Pajarita, with barely any mane and a very long tail, appeared as frightened as the pinto Ángel had. Ropes and saddlebags hung from her. She stepped to the left, then to the right, unsure of what was to happen. Victor urged her toward the river with the reins. The rope had lost almost all its slack, and in a moment Pablo realized that his inattention would force Ramada to halt once more in the middle of the river.

"Come on, Pablito!" Victor grew angry. "Move!"

Pablo's gullet cinched into a knot. He tightened his hands about Tuerto's reins and swallowed, looking back once at Victor and at Juvenal, who was standing next to Miedo.

"Now!" Both men were shouting, gesticulating. "Go!"

Tuerto moved toward the water and quickly threw himself into it. Pablo held on, his right hand gripping the saddle horn. Tuerto moved with artless insistence through the ragged cold. Victor followed behind, while Juvenal fed rope into the river with his hands.

The way the water ratcheted up about Pablo's legs and waist, the buffeting it gave him, actually calmed him. He sensed that Tuerto knew what to do, and he could also see, as Ramada and Ángel progressed toward the far shore, that Ramada was having an easier time of it now, that the pinto seemed to have found a reasonable path. Ten meters from the far shore, Ángel began walking with more ease, the river roaring so mightily about him, but seemingly unable to dislodge him or to push him off balance.

Then Tuerto stumbled.

Pablo lurched forward. His head fell against the horse's neck. Tuerto, forced to turn so that he was facing diagonally upriver into the flow, fell back, causing Pablo to plummet backwards himself deeper into the water. He grabbed the saddle horn with both hands. The leather gloves he wore were savaged by the water being driven into them, the cold slick of it freezing his fingers. But Tuerto suddenly righted himself and turned back in the direction of Ramada's pinto. Pablo had taken on water himself and was coughing, choking against it. Tuerto found the steady bottom that Ángel had found, and now began to climb up an incline, pulling himself toward the far bank where Ramada and his horse were just coming out of the water. Pablo's breathing eased. He knew that Tuerto had brought him across.

He glanced back and saw Victor go down. The mare Pajarita had been quickly washed over and had fallen. Victor was gone. Then Tuerto went down as well.

The freezing water electrified Pablo. It immersed him. Each follicle, all his muscles, his eyes, his brain and every extremity hardened like arctic stone. Tuerto struggled for footing. He flailed against the water's force, his legs moving so rapidly beneath him that Pablo feared his own body being broken up by the horse's panicked movement. Pablo was drowning. Water entered his entire head. The roughened leather of the gloves allowed him to hold tight to the saddle. The water banged against his eyes and pummeled his face. It froze his lips, taking away one of his saddlebags, and battered his hands, which he tried prying from the saddle horn.

Tuerto surfaced. Pablo looked back at the bank as Miedo, helped by Juvenal, dug in even more. The rope stretched tight in mid-air, strung out to Pajarita's saddle, who, now alone, was just getting her own footing back. The mare wished only for escape. But she could not escape, caught as she was by the rope sideways to the flow, and swept against by the force of the river. Miedo would not move. Juvenal held the very end of the rope and pulled back as hard as Miedo. Both realized that, were they to give in, they too would be swept into the river. Again, Pablo went under. He felt Tuerto's angry panic. He held on.

But in an instant Pablo was swept away.

The water swirled him down, over and over as though he were rolling across a precipitous cliff-face and banging against rocks, struggling for a handhold, a foothold, anything. His nose and mouth were gutted with water.

"I got you, *maestro*!"

Two arms circled Pablo's waist and bound him up, bringing his head finally fully into the cold air. Ramada, bleeding from his forehead, pulled Pablo to the shore, dragging him to a bar where he quickly dropped him on his back, his boots just inches from the roar of the Curringue. Pablo gagged, turning on his side and vomiting water.

"Stay here." Ramada plunged back into the river up to his waist and grabbed at the rope that held Tuerto secure to Ángel. He followed it to Pablo's horse and vaulted up into the saddle, forcing Tuerto toward the shore. As they came up the sand bar, Pablo saw that Pajarita had also been saved by Ramada and Tuerto, that she too was headed ashore. The burro Miedo and Juvenal were now entering the river themselves and, despite their struggles, Juvenal's insistence forced the animal through the flow. Within a few moments they ascended to the shore.

Pablo turned toward Tuerto, to congratulate Ramada for what he had done to save him and his horse. But Tuerto stood alone on the shore. Ramada had disappeared. And so had Victor.

—

Water seeped from Pablo, from everything that touched him. No part of his body had been saved from the cold. Sick, he shivered. The river's ecstatic roar overtook him. Sitting up, bringing his knees up and wrapping them with his arms, he felt like a forest floor slug having been rained upon for months. He wondered how long it would be before moss began to grow on him, to sour his skin and glut the interiors of his eyes.

"Pablo."

The sun had risen above the peaks of the *cordillera* and was lighting the river. The Curringue itself had changed from dark blue-gray chaos to white-blue precision.

A ruined typewriter fell to the sand next to Pablo. It was a small rectangle freed from its case. Many of its keys were broken. Water poured from beneath it. The space bar was bent over upon itself, and the ribbon was gone. Pablo could not immediately make out who it was that had brought the Royal to him. The sun rose above the man's head, blinding Pablo. He raised his left hand and shielded his eyes.

"I don't think it'll work anymore." Victor stood over him.

"You survived, Victor?"

"Always, *maestro*."

Juvenal came up behind Victor. Both men had been beaten down, and were now wearied with discouragement, although Juvenal had come through unscathed. Victor held one arm with the other. The right sleeve of his shirt had been ripped, as had a portion of the skin from the elbow to the wrist. His left leg appeared to have been scoured.

"Where's Ramada?"

The two men grimaced, looking into each other's eyes.

"We don't know," Juvenal said.

10
TANGO
CREPUSCULARIO

Juvenal had made a pot of beans and brought a large plateful of them to Pablo. Juvenal was very distracted, of course, beset by his responsibility for the missing Ramada. He and Victor had been searching the riverbanks for hours. Excusing himself once more, he told Pablo that he wanted to check on the horses. Tuerto grazed in a nearby meadow. The horse walked slowly, his lips caressing the grasses as though whispering to them of the pain he had suffered in the river. Juvenal approached the horse but stood apart from him. Apparently Tuerto did not wish to be bothered just now.

Miedo had been tied to a nearby tree, and Pablo was determined to minister to the poor burro, to comfort him. The least he could do, given what Miedo had done for him. He was a small animal, really…rugged, brave, and made up entirely of weather-beaten heart and rough-hewn courage. He had little intelligence, although his insistent personality, when pitted against Juvenal, drove the cowherd crazy. When it worked in the service of Juvenal though, Miedo's demeanor was indispensable, as had been proven that very morning.

Pablo looked down into the mess of steaming beans, which were so delicious and so sustaining. But…Ramada, he thought. Ramada drowned. Lost. In remorse, he took a forkful of the beans into his mouth.

Pablo loved water, especially the blue glories of the beautiful salt sea. The sand, the shell, the wooden ships' figureheads, of which he owned about a hundred. But Pablo also enjoyed fresh water. He knew nothing as cold and fresh as the simple act of drinking a bit of it from a high mountain stream. Fish celebrated their lives in it, swept down from the mountains in a tumble over rocks and rapids that could be nothing else but fun, Pablo mused, rolling down backwards, forwards, round and round over the rapids, laughing. Such water as that vivified the souls of those fish. *It is surely,* he thought, *a source of love.*

But too much water…

Pablo pulled the blanket that Victor had offered him close around his shoulders. He had almost drowned one other time, in the Pacific Ocean at the town of Puerto Saavedra, where his family had gone for summers. He was seven years old, and a great wave had reared up like a horse on its hind legs and felled him. His father ran down the beach to save him, gathering him up from the waters and, laughing, allowing the boy's sputtering of water and sand, brushing his sodden hair from his eyes. Pablo was struck now by how similar and immediately recognizable to him was the feeling of drowning in fresh water to that of drowning in salt. The taste was different, but the inundation of the membranes inside his mouth and nose was the same, the water attacking his sinuses, and above all the struggle for breath when there was none to be had. Unlike for fish, this was no laughing matter, and even now, thinking about himself flailing head-first down the rapids this morning, Pablo trembled with the memory of the water's force, of its antagonism and smothering anger, allowing him nothing, buffeting him into submission and suffocating helplessness, all in the brightest of clarities.

"Eh. Miedo."

The burro paid no attention. He had himself been wounded and scraped, and it seemed to Pablo that Miedo was ignoring him, that he wished that this clueless poet who had been riding that horse across the river with such clueless abandon, ignoring me, for God's sake, would *¡Carajo!* goddamn well leave me alone and take his sympathetic whispering down to hell with him…*with* the horse.

"Miedo."

The burro glanced toward Pablo. Huffing, he looked away again.

"I owe you my life."

Miedo huffed once more.

The sun was just lowering behind a peak to the west. Down below, in a narrow reach between boulders, the river still cascaded toward the sea. Had Ramada's body slivered between those rocks? Had he suffocated beneath one of them, flailing for the surface? Pablo's soul emptied with the thought of it.

The disappearing light still allowed a little warmth. Once the shadow reached this meadow, though, the startling mountain night cold would begin.

"I know that doesn't mean much to you. But, please, let me tell you a story."

Miedo did not object.

"There was once a poetry book, you see, that saved me the way you just did."

—

Pablo Neruda had just recently become Pablo Neruda. He had changed his name from Ricardo Eliecer Neftalí Reyes Basoalto so that his father José del Carmen Reyes would not know that this new, previously unheralded poet was none other than his own son. Rather than admit to his father that he had decided to become a poet instead of a lawyer, the young man had taken the "Neruda" part of his name from a French violinist. A violinist! he had mused. Pablo knew that he himself had no talent for music. But he liked the name of Wilhelmina Norman-Neruda, a real person who had actually had a cameo part in a Sherlock Holmes story. Neftalí had always loved Sherlock Holmes, so it was, well, ¡Elemental, *querido Watson!* He had tacked on the "Pablo" as an afterthought. All this would allow him to avoid his father's coming across one of his verses in a magazine and thinking to himself that his son Neftalí must be one of those who likes flowers, has a mincing gait, and enjoys books written in French about madeleine cookies.

Such a man was no man at all, Neftalí's father seemed to think. So, several months earlier Pablo Neruda had left Neftalí Reyes behind, had published his slim little volume called *Crepusculario*, had become instantly well-known around Santiago as Pablo Neruda, and now was noted for his odd poetical dress. He wore a large black hat and a long black cape over his suit, silk shirt, and cravat, feeling that this must surely be the way poets were supposed to dress.

In 1923, Pablo was just nineteen, so tall and bony that he thought of himself as The Black Feather, and he looked like a fool walking through the Santiago university district in this get-up. This never occurred to him, usually unaware of the veiled laughter that followed him around. He walked the streets from café to café with a number of books in a leather satchel hanging from his right shoulder, a scholar reciting Shakespeare and Whitman in English, Montaigne and Racine in French, so that few who heard the eloquent declamations coming from this cloaked scarecrow understood anything he said.

But he and other young poets had founded a society. Pablo could not be certain that it was a real "society", the kind of group that has a pretentious name and whose members are all notorious, they assert, for some manifesto or other. Really, Pablo thought that he and the others were just a group of students who went to cafes together, cadged cups of wine where they could, nattered self-importantly about very little, and fumed uncomprehendingly about what constituted a proper poem.

Crepusculario had changed all that for Pablo. The first of the group to have published a book, he caused some consternation among certain of his friends. But the book also had the fortune to be a good book, which caused real jealousy. He had never much been congratulated for his poetry, so that to have certain people be angry with him for what he had done came as a surprise. It was the first instance in his life of his over-zealous celebration causing resentment, a phenomenon that was to hound him all his days thereafter.

After all, he was just now prodding a horse through the Andes as a result of just such a thing.

There were friends, however, that stuck with him no matter what, and they often went out slumming with each other. One night in particular, they decided to go to *El Farol*, a working-class café in a poor neighborhood of Santiago in which small shacks heated by wood fires were nestled in resentful, chaotic warrens around factories and slaughterhouses. None of these students had actually been to *El Farol* before. The rumor was that frequent fights broke out there, even the occasional brawl. But working-class girls went there too, who, the university students dreamed, would actually dance with them.

Pablo arrived late to meet his friends. Riding in a streetcar, its iron and varnished wood surfaces battering each other as it made its way up the cobbled street, he was lulled to sleep by the drone of the car's wheels on the tracks. He leaned against the window. The wooden bench on which he sat discomfited him, but Pablo paid little attention to the problem. He so adored trains of any kind that a rustic lack of accommodation actually appealed to him as part of the adventure. Dozing, he half-dreamt of sitting on his father's lap when he had been a very small boy, waiting for the train on which José del Carmen would be working to leave the Temuco station. In the dream rain fell nastily from the clouds, and the boy rested in the warmth of his father's arms by the small stove in the caboose. Now, riding in the streetcar toward *El Farol*, Pablo sighed, colder than he had been in the caboose, but revived by the recollection of the stove and his father's beard brushing against his right cheek.

El Farol was situated at the intersection of two deserted streets, across from an ill-tended park. As Pablo descended from the streetcar, he could just make out the yellow-brown light from the old streetlamps in the park, which were intended to illuminate its walkways. But he knew that danger awaited anyone who attempted to walk through this park at night. The trees, usually such accommodating structures that provided so much fun for children who wished to climb them, blocked the electric light, so that shadows were cast that were even darker than the open stretches of walk and pathway. A park like this one, at night, held thievery, rapine, and murder.

Pablo turned his back on it, to watch the retreating streetcar. The hanging light bulb inside made the car look, in the distance, like an antique floating lantern rolling away.

The streets in both directions had emptied. A barely visible spotted dog walked up one sidewalk toward Pablo. Down the other street, to his left on the next corner, a couple stood kissing beneath a streetlamp. They appeared rabid for one another, and Pablo worried a moment that their grasping joy could possibly attract someone from the park, someone who could be resentfully distracted by such caresses, and who could do them harm.

The café formed part of a corner building. It had small windows, and its doorway opened upon the raised corner sidewalk. Two stylized streetlamps had been painted on the wall to either side of the door and were now fading with age. The words "*El Farol*" sprawled on the wall over the door. Someone had printed the same words in Victorian gilt script on one of the windows, although the gilt was now flaking badly. The dark wood interior of the café, the old chairs and tables, the beefy, rugged waiter standing at one of the windows, all looked as though they were soon to pass into forgetfulness.

Pablo crossed the street, securing his balance on the cobbles. Tango, the sonorous whine of a bandoneón, came out the door. Tango had only recently come to Santiago, and already was considered a sin by large numbers of citizens, proof that all Argentines were to be condemned. Only *compadrito* rowdies, disrespectful, nervy *cuchillero* guys, minor criminals who carried knives with them everywhere they went, danced it. The Church didn't like tango. Chileans in general didn't like it, and they especially disliked the Argentine *compadrito*, a ruffian dressed in a slouch hat pulled low over one eye, a black coat and black shirt decorated with a loosely knotted white silk neckerchief, black striped pants, shined boots with high heels and, usually, a dagger stuck in his belt behind him. Few of these lived in Santiago. They were bad, intimidating men, and they did the tango as though they could use the dance to kill you, speaking the oddly accented, smart-mouth Spanish that immediately labeled them as low-class Buenos Aires *porteños*.

On this particular evening, a group of these fellows had invaded *El Farol*, and not one of them was dressed like The Black Feather as he passed through the door. Many of them noticed him as he paused a moment looking for his friends, and laughed.

A fistfight had just gotten under way. Pablo passed along one wall, toward a table where a few of his companions sat. At first they didn't notice him, intent as they were on the fight. Two large men, one an Argentine *compadrito*, the other clearly a Santiago laborer, were insulting each other's mother while one of the bar girls, a little blonde, egged them on in the German language.

She was apparently the reason for the fight.

Short, her ankles like thick posts where they entered the high-top, laced-up brown boots she wore, she urged the two men on. Her long skirt, over red and green percale petticoats, extended almost all the way to the boots, although a space between the cloth and the leather allowed a glimpse of stocking. She had embroidered the skirt along the bottom with a strip of white cotton-lace brocade. A thick leather belt circled her waist, decorated with coins. The kind of belt that *gauchos* wore, it was probably a gift from one of the *compadritos*. She wore a short-sleeved, puffy black blouse, low across the bodice, and a necklace made of shells and stones. Brass earrings hung down almost to her shoulders. Her hair was remarkably curly and long and, as she placed her hands on her waist, she tossed the hair back as though taunting the two adversaries before her.

Her laughter rasped, and the further taunts that followed it were riven through with aggression and anguish.

Enormous, with a heavy growth of beard that he had not shaved for several days, the country boy—Andrés, judging from the shouts of encouragement that the other Chileans in the bar gave him—looked like a stupid man, his shoulders sloping enormous, his legs grand and muscled beneath the pair of black cotton pants he wore, which were cinched about his waist with a piece of rope.

He held up his fists and circled the Argentine, who in turn circled him. The Argentine was not enormous, but it was clear that he knew what to do in a situation like this. Where Andrés appeared to slouch, taking a foot forward, a foot back in gargantuan, uncertain steps, the *compadrito* stalked him with feline delicacy, as though the huge man before him were an oaf lacking in all thoughtfulness. The *compadrito* appeared to believe that soon he would pummel this fool.

Pablo found a seat with his friends and removed his hat, laying it on his satchel, which he had placed on the table. Tension flowed everywhere through the café. The noise coming from the patrons at that very moment brought a halt to the music of the little Argentine trio of violin, flute and bandoneón. The *bandoneonista* began packing his instrument in its case so that he could make a quick escape.

"What's going on?"

"The big guy, Pablito." El Pulpón, a dark, squalid journalist, pointed at the Chilean. "He was dancing with the girl. But the girl was complaining about what a bad dancer he is, which is true." Pulpón shook his head sorrowfully. "The guy is a nincompoop. So, the Argentine grabbed her and began dancing with her. Didn't ask permission or anything. And the Argentine can dance."

Pablo reached for the jar of red wine that sat on the table. He filled an empty terra-cotta cup. The girl urged the men on, and they continued circling each other. The Argentine carried himself like a *gaucho* movie star. His long white scarf and the different *gauchesco* accouterments—bits of rope articulately tied into knots, the boots with their drooping tops, the glittering single silver earring in his right ear, the gold around his one still-existing incisor—gave him a piratical beauty. He also had a slim mustache that, because he was smiling as he sized up his opponent, made him appear a kind of elegant butcher who in a split-second would cut Andrés badly, then laugh about it over a cup of wine afterwards. Everyone had already concluded that the Argentine would win this battle.

He took a swing, putting Andrés back on his heels. He threw another punch, which caused Andrés to stagger backwards into the table at which Pablo and the others were sitting.

"Get out of my way." Andrés wiped away the flecks of spittle that had sprayed across his lips. As his back had turned to the *compadrito*, he did not notice that the fellow was preparing to coldcock him the minute he turned around. But like the other blows, this one had little effect. The Chilean rubbed the side of his face where it had landed.

"*¡Anda, Andrés, anda!*" the crowd shouted. "Keep going!"

The *compadrito* took another swing, and this one landed squarely against Andrés's heart, causing him to stagger. To Pablo, the men resembled primitive beasts, dancing obscenely in a primordial forest. The *compadrito* moved in, stealthily taking aim once more.

"You two!"

The *compadrito* glanced to his left. Pablo had stood up and begun shaking the red wine from his satchel. The wine had spilled from its jar when Andrés had stumbled against the table. Now both men surveyed Pablo, who pulled a red-blotched copy of *Crime and Punishment* out of the satchel and rifled through its pages, drops of liquid spraying onto the tabletop.

"Bullies!" he muttered. Looking up, he saw that both men now wished to attack him. "Fat-brained apes!" The *compadrito* dropped his hands. "Fucking scum!" The Chilean glanced toward his opponent, then at Pablo once more, than at his opponent. "This is a farce."

The *compadrito* opened his mouth to reply when Andrés knocked him to the floor. The other patrons shouted out, clapping Andrés's shoulders, and when the *compadrito* rose up, wobbly and estranged, Andrés knocked him out. The uproar deafened Pablo. Even the other *compadritos*, admittedly very outnumbered, appeared to have enjoyed the fight, and they shrugged their shoulders, indicating to the Chileans that there would be no attempt at reprisal. They gathered around their companion and began dragging him by the shoulders toward the door. His boots, still reflecting a shine, bounced along on the rough wooden floor.

Pablo continued fretting about his satchel, and he looked up into Andrés's eyes, who stared at him with a look of sullen rage.

"Get away from me. You're no better than the other guy." Pablo attempted separating a few of the pages of *Crime and Punishment*, which were already being held together by generous leavings of wine. He held the book out before him with one hand and pointed at it with the other. "Look at this, you illiterate fool."

Andrés surveyed Pablo with a look of surprised malevolence. "But I beat him."

"So what?" Pablo examined his satchel once more. "Who's going to pay for this?"

"Pay?" Andres turned and joined the crowd of waiting admirers. "You pay." As their celebration continued, as someone thrust a jar of beer into Andrés's hand, as the *compadritos* cleared the cafe door, their companion just now beginning to come to, Andrés looked back once at Pablo and seemed to whisper to him, "I know you, *puto*. I know you." His eyes resembled black caves in a cliff.

Pulpón put a hand on Pablo's knee when he sat down once more. "I think, *poeta*, that it might be time for you to leave."

"But my Dostoevsky."

"Forget Dostoevsky. You got to get out of here."

"But—"

"You saw what he did to that guy. He'll do the same to you." Pulpón looked Pablo over. "Dressed like a dandy. Looking down your nose at all these idiots." He looked over his shoulder at the crowd, many of whom were now observing the conversation. "'Fat-brained apes!'" Pulpón shook his head. "Jesus, you are a fool."

Pablo turned his back to the cafe. He thought a moment and decided that maybe he had better go. He leaned over, took up his hat, gathered his satchel beneath an arm as he put the Dostoevsky back into it, and tapped Pulpón's shoulder. "Is there a back door?"

Pulpón nodded, taking up his own satchel. "Follow me."

The two men walked to a passageway to the left of the bar, painted black with a single light bulb hanging from a bare wire halfway down the passage. The doorway at the end led to a vacant lot that served as the café's restroom and, as Pablo and Pulpón approached the door, it suddenly opened—crashed open—and revealed Andrés, wiping his hands with a rag. He had bloodied the hand he had used to put the Argentine away, and Pablo saw that the index and middle fingers were badly bruised.

Andrés looked up from his hands. His eyes glittered as he realized who stood in front of him. "I've been waiting for you."

Pulpón took in a breath. Pablo looked around for something with which to defend himself, a stick, a chair.

Andrés tapped Pablo's chest with an index finger. "Let's you and I have a talk." There was barely enough room for one man to be standing at the end of this narrow passage. That there were three, and only one tight avenue of escape, that being a return into the café where Andrés's many friends were festively waiting, caused Pablo's stomach to gather like a stone weighing down on his intestines.

"Compañero." Pulpón rubbed his chin. His eyes radiated. "Do you want me to—"

"Get out!" Andrés shoved Pulpón, who hurried back up the passageway into the café.

Andrés turned to Pablo and pushed him up against the wall. Pablo, in terror and defenseless, shoved him back, which caused Andrés to break into a grin. He was missing a tooth. He reached up and scratched the back of his own neck with his right hand.

"You're Neruda, aren't you?"

Pablo, his own right hand clutching the strap of his satchel, remained still. "I am."

Andrés lowered his head, and then looked back up at Pablo with a sideways glance. He was still smiling. "Here I am, in this little passageway, standing before the one poet whom I truly admire, and he tells me that I'm fucking scum."

"Oh, well, I, I—"

"It's true. I am. And that Argentine? He sells cocaine. We're both scum." Andrés reached into a pants pocket. He pulled out a book, opened it, extracted a folded photograph, and handed it to Pablo. "But you see this?"

A teenage girl in a black skirt, a white apron, a white blouse and a small white heavily starched servant-girl's bonnet stood next to a table in what appeared to be a fine gentleman's parlor or living room.

"She's my Serena, *don* Pablito. Look at her. I'll tell her it was you that I met tonight."

Serena, probably unused to facing a camera, did not smile

"She loves me, *don* Pablito. Look at that picture." Andrés had taken a step to Pablo's side, and the two men examined the photo together. Andrés lay his bruised index finger on Serena's face. "You can see it in her eyes." He looked up at Pablo, who remained frightened.

"She loves me because of you." Andrés smiled once more, pointing to the book, a copy of Pablo's *Crepusculario*. "Because of your poems."

Pablo, offering a smile, shrugged. "I… Andrés, thank you, I—"

"Which we've learned together, which we've memorized, see?"

Pulpón appeared at the end of the passageway. Several of the other poets were with him, and they appeared ready to defend Pablo against the low-class lout.

"*'Deep inside you, a sad boy like me kneels, his eyes on us.'*" Andrés recited the line from memory.

Pablo held up a hand to the others. Confused, they began a retreat, and Pablo assured them with a gesture that everything was all right.

"*'For that life burning in her veins'*, Pablito. That's what you wrote, isn't it?"

Pablo nodded, exhaling, silently in wait for the rest of the line.

Andrés held the bloodied hand out before him and pointed at it. "*'For that life burning in her veins, they would have to* murder *my hands'*".

———

Miedo's ears fluttered.

The sound of breaking twigs and heavy footsteps, those of a small group of men, approached from far away in the darkness. A torch gleamed, and Pablo and the burro stared into the gloom. After a moment, during which Pablo feared that the footsteps were those of Juvenal and Victor, and that they had found Ramada's broken body downstream, the noises suddenly stopped. Pablo could not see anything beyond the circle of light thrown by the fire and the bristling single flame of the torch in the distance. It seemed to him that Miedo had forgiven him for his folly in the river that previous morning. The burro looked toward him a moment and studied him, then turned his attention again into the distance. Footsteps resumed. But instead of two or three people approaching, there was now clearly just one.

The fire wavered.

"*Don* Pablo." A young man entered the circle of light. "I went down the rapids looking for this." Ramada handed Pablo a rectangular package wrapped tightly in oilcloth. "It was in the saddlebag you lost." The package had beaded with water, but it had sustained itself, little dampness having actually entered it. Juvenal and Victor, his arm bandaged, now emerged from the dark, carrying the torch.

"You saved my book?" Pablo examined the package, then took the knife from the plate of beans and began cutting the leather straps that held the package secure. When the oilcloth came away from the hand-written volume, Pablo saw that the edges of some of the pages had shipped water. But they were only slightly stained.

"Yes, *maestro*. It took me a while. It was dark. The water was cold."

Ramada sat down on a log and held his hands out toward the fire. He was shivering, and Pablo quickly lay the book down, took the blanket from his own shoulders and wrapped it around the young man.

"Very cold," Ramada whispered.

11

DELIA AND THE UNIVERSE

The way Delia had fashioned the bodice of the dress didn't work. She knew how much Pablo enjoyed her in a beautiful gown. He had written about her breasts, in poems, journals and letters, and had told her that the finest inspiration for him for a good day's work was to be found in the opportunity to kiss their upper curvature, where it peeked out from beneath a salaciously buttoned blouse.

But this bodice was poorly sewn, and she started dismantling it, to cut a few little slivers of cloth out of it, and to sew it once more.

She had been receiving phone calls from all sorts of friends. The poet Louis Aragon had taken Delia to the ballet a few times, once most memorably to see Igor Stravinsky conduct his own *Firebird*. *Señor* Stravinsky had learned that Delia and Aragon were in the audience and had asked them to come to his dressing room after the performance. He was a tiny man with a round head and very pronounced sharp nose. His eyeglasses reminded Delia of the occasional pieces of industrial glass, worn away at the edges by years of caresses from the seawater coming and going, that she and Pablo would find on the shore at Isla Negra. Pablo collected such pieces of glass as well as, of course, the thousands of seashells that he had been searching for all his life. How could such a man, of such mercurial poeticism, be so interested in mollusks and the oozes that flowed from them? *"Universe in a grain of sand,"* Pablo had once said, citing William Blake as he so often did.

But now she had to re-sew the bodice, having promised herself that, despite her active social life here in Paris, she had come here principally to await her husband Pablo's re-appearance. She would accept invitations to the symphony, dine with this or that writer or musician, take long walks in the *Bois de Boulogne* with Cocteau and the filmmaker Renoir and the actor Barrault.

But she waited in silence, sewing all the while for her lost husband.

12
LOVE, FRUIT AND RAIN

The next morning, as they had coffee by the open fire, Ramada's shoulders slumped. He and Pablo were attempting to dry the wet pages of *Canto General* with the heat cast by the flames, and the book was open before them.

Pablo's Chilean passport, the regular one he had used after his senate passport had been taken away, which he had hidden within the front pages of the book, had suffered more from the river water than had the book itself. Many of the hand-stamped visas within it had blurred, like strokes of watercolor that contain too much liquid. But the two visas he cared for the most, those of Republican Spain and France, remained clear. Pablo's photo was also damaged, although it remained clearly an image of Pablo. He didn't care that he appeared drowned in it. He had never really cared for the image, but actually felt that the photo now did him more justice. It looked like that of a man who, though washed away, had indeed escaped death.

But rain now began falling, and the intensity of it increased almost with each sentence the two men spoke. Ramada sheltered the book on his lap beneath the blanket that both men now held over their heads, so that at least it would remain dry for a while. The fire held its own against the rain for a few moments, but then water began inundating the flames. They were hot and bright at first, then fought back against the wet, then were humbled by it and turned to steam. It took the bulk of the short conversation between Pablo and Ramada for all this to happen.

"You know, trying to dry out these pages…. *Don* Pablo, I've read a little of your book," Ramada said. "And I don't understand it." For the moment, the blanket protected the men from the rain.

"Can you give me an example?" Pablo took charge of the blanket, and Ramada thumbed through the book a moment.

"Well, here. Here it says… *"Mientras tanto,/ por los abismos/azucarados de los puertos,/caían indios sepultados/en el vapor de la mañana…"* ("Meanwhile/into the sugared/abyss of the harbors/fall Indians entombed/in the mists of the morning…")

"And?"

"I don't get it."

Lightning flared in the far distance, among the peaks.

"What don't you understand?"

"There's nothing about love in it."

"Certainly not. That's a poem about what companies like United Fruit do to the Indians."

"What do they do?"

"They kill them."

Thunder rumbled across the *cordillera*. The depth of its anger grew over fifteen seconds to the full fruition of a deafening, insulted roar.

Ramada considered United Fruit for several moments. He scratched his head. "I thought poetry was about love."

Pablo took the book back from Ramada. "I see. You're right, the United Fruit Company is not often mentioned in the same breath with *el amor*."

Ramada nodded toward the still opened page. The rain fell so heavily that streams of it ran down his arms. "I mean, this is okay. But, *don* Pablo, what is love?"

Pablo shrugged. He began wrapping the book and the passport in the oilcloth. The blanket's protection would soon fail, and the men would themselves be beaten down by the tempest. He quickly secured the two pieces of oilcloth around the book and tied it with leather straps. "You don't know?"

"Well, I've never…" Ramada grinned, turning his head away a moment.

"You've made love with a woman, haven't you?"

"Yes, a friend of my sister. But Romina...Romina was one thing, and the other—"

"The other is the other."

"Yes."

Pablo rubbed his chin, the unfamiliar beard feeling like a wire brush against the palm of his right hand. He looked out into the forest. By now, rain came down in a broad cascade. The mountains and forest in the distance were colored blue-gray, with black features. "Love is... It's when you... Look, Ramada, it's when…" He looked up into the storm. "It's when the sun sends down a cluster in your lover's dark dress. When great roots grow hurriedly...uh, from your soul."

"What?" Ramada now had to shout.

"It is when a pale and blue populace born from you feeds itself. It is—"

"What?"

"Erect, it caresses—"

"Erect?"

"Yes, but be careful, *joven*. Because love can be filled with sadness."

Ramada nodded. "Like this storm."

"Yes."

"That was the problem with Romina. She seemed so full of wishes. I couldn't...She was an estuary of wishes."

Pablo's head snapped back. Beside the two men, the Curringue cascaded down a short, steep canyon, as though the water were the same as the rocks that stirred it to such excitement. The water cracked and roared. "What was that? What did you say?"

"A...a... I forget. What did I say?"

Pablo held the wrapped book close. "An estuary. An estuary of... feminine—"

"I can't remember."

"A feminine estuary? I mean, Ramada, such a poetic phrase, so polished, so wise."

"I don't remember." Ramada shook his head. "Me? A poet?"

"Who can tell?"

"You mean…. *Don* Pablo, you don't know what a poet is?"

Pablo shrugged. He could barely hear, and water now seeped freely through the blanket.

"Ramada, sometimes…. You ask me what a poet is? Sometimes you just can't know."

13
RANGO

The rain had abated, and Pablo made coffee for everyone. He spooned the last of the beans he had prepared, a very large portion, onto a plate for Ramada, who was now dressed in an extra pair of trousers that Juvenal had leant to him, his other shirt ("I own just two, *maestro*.") and a pair of fresh wool socks that Pablo had been able to dry out by the fire. All the men now sat by the flames, and it was clear that the food and the drink had relieved Ramada's exhaustion.

"Victor tells us that you were a diplomat, *don* Pablo." Juvenal blew on his coffee.

"I have been, yes."

"What's that?"

The fire popped and crackled, a rattling of surprised reports that ran beneath the men's conversation, a kind of recitative accompaniment, the poet thought, to what they were saying.

"A diplomat is someone who works for the government and deals with other governments."

Juvenal noted this but seemed unimpressed. "That's what war is for, isn't it?"

"But diplomacy gives countries a way to avoid wars."

"Why?"

Ramada sat on a separate log next to Victor. Still eating his beans, he simply listened to the conversation. He had the same sort of unknowing interest in the conversation as Juvenal had. Victor, who knew quite well what a diplomat was, was more actively involved and even amused.

"We should try to avoid war," Pablo said.

"My great-grandfather didn't think so." Juvenal turned toward Ramada. "Yours neither, eh?"

Ramada shook his head, looking into the fire.

"Mine was *valenciano* to the core." Juvenal jabbed Ramada in the shoulder, who now laughed quietly, shaking his bowed head. "His was Araucan. And those two guys would never have understood...what's it called? Diplomacy?"

Both men laughed.

"They would have just tracked each other down until one of them died." Juvenal glanced at Ramada once more. "Right? And that's why I've got such respect for Ramada, *don* Pablo. Because mine did die! Ramada knows what those Indians knew, about how to live out here." Juvenal's eyes glittered in the firelight. "Yeah, the Araucan, they caught my great-grandfather and killed him."

Pablo had a brief recollection of the Spanish Civil War, and the death he had witnessed there as a diplomat. His friend García Lorca. The Lincoln Brigades. Poor Gerda Taro. The refugees on The Winnipeg.

"But I guess that being one of those diplomats is pretty important anyway, no?" Juvenal stirred the fire.

"Now and then."

"Important people talking to other important people?"

"Sometimes."

"And you did this for a long time?"

"Years. Even as a very young man."

"Where was that?"

"Rangoon, for one."

"Where?" Juvenal looked once more toward Ramada. Each seemed startled.

———

Pablo, the new Chilean consul in Rangoon, pulled on the rope that rang the bell. Twenty-three years old, dressed in a white linen suit, white shirt and dark brown cravat, he carried a slim leather case with a letter from the British ambassador in Santiago to the British consul in Rangoon, a man named Basil Fotheringay. Made of black iron, the bell hung from a white-washed wall covered with yellow bougainvillea.

It had rained all night, so that now the entire town of Rangoon seemed to be without air. Pablo felt that, although dressed presentably in a linen suit, he must look like a steamed *dorado*, that great Pacific fish, an hour ago pulled from the ocean, properly gutted and now quite cooked, its eyes open, surprised, to be served with a little Burmese olive oil and some garlic. Maybe a bit of cilantro. A kind of secondary rain still came down from the fronds of the innumerable palm trees. The streets, none of them paved, stunk of animal effluent and mud, and the flowering greenery, which grew everywhere quite beautifully, appeared to be sweating.

He imagined that the plants and trees would surely dry out soon, given the oven of sunlight that, just now at ten in the morning, had turned the entire city into an imitation of Hell's most blistering circle. The youthful Chilean, adjusting the white, damp handkerchief in his coat pocket, felt like a dandified puddle.

The door was much carved, of dark water-stained hardwood, perhaps a hundred years old. The carving presented a view of a forest clearing, a large monkey in the middle of it, and a covey of Burmese maidens bathing in a stream beneath some palm trees. A serene monkey, it appeared, happy in his viewing of the semi-nude young women. But only parts of this scene could be seen. Weather had so deteriorated the carving that the door was a slivered dream, many surfaces of it having rotted away. Pablo recalled the early nineteenth century maps of the Congo that he had seen in university, where the great river appeared, but the nature of what there was on either bank had not yet been completely explored, and so had to be left partially blank. In the case of this door, patches of bare wood, without illustration and discolored—little hearts of darkness, Pablo mused—bordered on the designed remains of the ornate stand of perfumed trees, the distant gathering of maidens washing themselves, a few water birds here and there, and some bunches of bananas.

An orangutan opened the door.

Pablo did not know what to say. The orangutan retreated into the courtyard, passing an elderly Chinese woman who, with the help of two wooden canes, approached the visitor. At first, she appeared to be walking on point, the way the Russian ballerinas did who now and then danced on the Santiago stage. But the ballerinas were twenty-year-olds, while this woman was about seventy. Pablo had never seen a woman with bound feet. Her clothing appeared ancient, made of silk, and faded, so that the bright Rangoon sunlight did little to enhance its elegant design. For Pablo, she resembled an illustration of a Chinese noblewoman from an eighteenth-century travel book. As she tottered across the courtyard, the red and green silk of her long gown shimmered in the light. The Chinese collar, like a priest's except that it was colored a washed-out yet torrid red, made up a circle of precision against which her complicated amber earrings swung forward and back. Her hair, which Pablo knew had once been black like obsidian, now silvered with gray, but so coiffed as to be itself of such sensuous precision, the bun held together with a carved amber barrette, that it appeared to have been lacquered.

She was surely the mistress of the English consul Fotheringay, to whom Pablo was presenting his diplomatic credentials. He imagined one of those wasted British colonialists, something else from Joseph Conrad, stuck here in backwater Rangoon for the last forty years, sporting a grubby gray stubble, beset by opium, his shirt smelling of old sweat, the braces that held up his mold-spotted trousers themselves stained, the wooden buttons in slivers around the edges...whose concubine this woman, whom he had bought from a rich Chinese merchant well before the turn of the century, had once been. In those times she had been a glorious, delicate flower.

She greeted Pablo. She spoke no English and, of course, no Spanish. But she gestured to him that he escort her into the large wooden house with a broad porch all around. Its palm-thatch roof had an architected design of thick slopes beneath the dank sway of the palm trees.

They had to walk very slowly. Her feet made it almost impossible for her. The canes and the toes of her shoes sounded in an uneven four-tap rhythm across the tile courtyard. Pablo walked at a glacial pace. They struggled up a short stairway to the porch, where she showed him to a mahogany table on which was a platter of sliced mango along with a setting for two of English tea.

Suddenly Fotheringay appeared. "Right. Neruda, is it?" Like Pablo, this English consul was actually in his mid-twenties, very correct, dressed as precisely as Pablo himself, with a small brown mustache, brown shoes, rimless spectacles and a sharply curved pith helmet. A rather pretty Burmese boy dressed in white and barefoot followed him up the porch.

Pablo hurried to speak. "Quite."

"One of the servants let you in?"

"The orangutan, yes."

Fotheringay grimaced, gritting his teeth. "Yes. Rango, we call him."

"He always—"

"Always answers the courtyard bell. Quite talented, if you ask me."

"I should say." Pablo presented Fotheringay with a leather folder, containing his introduction papers. "Perhaps I could have a conversation with him some time."

"There you are." Fotheringay's mouth tightened. "You're the poet, aren't you?" His forehead furrowed as he hurried a hand toward his gut.

"I am, yes."

"Don't know much about poetry myself."

Pablo remained silent.

"Donne and those."

Pablo's eyebrows rose. He adored Donne's work. "Yes. *'Send not to know for whom the bell—' '*"

"Doesn't matter much out here, does it?"

Pablo shrugged, immediately appalled by this nervous Limey priss.

"The truth is, I'd be happy to speak with you, old boy. But I'm damned sick."

"With what?"

"The stomach" Fotheringay had blanched, pain etching his forehead. "I struggled from a latrine to come here to introduce myself. But a conversation... I'm afraid it would be much interrupted, you see." He looked over his shoulder into the house. "Would you mind if we met another day?"

"Not at all, *señor* Basil. We'll both be here for a while. We needn't...."

Fotheringay ran from the porch, followed by the boy who, before he rounded the corner of the porch, placed a slim-fingered hand against the edge of the wall, glanced back at Pablo and smiled. His eyes, like black jade, fluttered with light.

Left alone, Pablo did not know what to do. Should he leave the documents for Fotheringay's later perusal? Should he see whether Fotheringay needed a doctor? Should he....

Rango came around the corner of the house carrying a ceramic pot with a ladle in it. He placed the pot on the table before Pablo, and then retreated up the porch on all fours, disappearing. Pablo looked into it and saw that the pot contained beer. He sat back and waited, until Rango reappeared with two clay cups, which he placed on the table before jumping up onto one of the other chairs, the better to survey the Chilean consul. Pablo imagined that Rango wanted to talk, but Rango didn't say anything. He appeared impatient, his eyes flickering toward the pot of beer, and then to the cups. Pablo poured out two cupsful, one of which Rango pulled toward himself, bringing it quickly to his mouth. Much of the beer fell down his front. Pablo poured him some more, and took up his own cup. The two drank together.

"I've read your work," Rango said.

"Which?"

"All of *Crepusculario*." Rango sipped from his beer. "Whatever that word may mean. Perfectly marvelous, though. A whole new way of writing verse, old boy. Revolutionary, I should say, especially the way it departs so from the European traditions."

"Less structure, you mean."

"Perfect freedom. No one's written like that."

"Whitman, maybe. And Gerard Manley Hopkins."

"Well, yes." Rango nodded. "There is Hopkins."

They drank some more. Actually, that's all they did together. Pablo had imagined the conversation, as it could have taken place with the British consul. But Basil Fotheringay was ill-disposed, most certainly, the Chilean consul thought, for as long as I am to know the *puto mariconito*.

So, a conversation with Rango, another cup of beer for each of them, wit, pleasure, and laughter.

14
ALONE IN A BOAT

In the forest the following day, they came upon a wooden coffin, placed atop an assembly of stones. A sturdy box, roughly made, it had been beaten against by the Andean weather, they soon were to learn, of thirty-one years. More stones lay in a pyramid at one end, and a wooden crucifix was secured by the stones. The box itself was inscribed on its lid with carved-out letters: "Dominguín 1898 – 1918". Also, an old Paraguayan coin with a hole in the center had been nailed to the top of the box.

"We'll see more than one of these." Juvenal leaned forward on his saddle and surveyed the rude construction, the roughly lettered inscription, and the absence of any ceremony of any kind. "I just hope it's not one of us inside the next one."

Pablo took a low branch from one of the trees by the trail and cut a sprig of needles from it. He leaned down and laid it on the box. "Out of respect, I guess, for whoever this Dominguín was." He fingered the coin, and then surveyed the nail, which had been pounded only partially into the wood.

"What's the date on the coin, Pablo?" Victor said.

Pablo leaned closer from his saddle. "It says...here, just a minute...it says 1851."

"Almost a hundred years, then."

"Yes, but what's interesting is that the nail is new." Pablo examined the nail more closely. "No rust. Somebody put this coin here just a few days ago, it looks like. A few weeks."

—

There was a lake.

Very high up on the trail, it filled a sort of concave shelf at the bottom of rock-face cliffs three hundred meters high, the tops of which were deeply serrated for a kilometer in each direction. Several rock moraines scattered down the steep slopes at the bottom of the cliffs, the detritus of glaciers that had meandered by, a million years ago.

The lake was two hundred meters across, with a small, tree-covered island along the far shore and surrounded by woods so thick with larch trees that the forest floor was made up entirely of deep, black-gray humus. The larches' needles had shed themselves and fallen to the ground every fall, along with thousands of pinecones. Larches were a favorite of Pablo's, so broad a tree when fully grown that Pablo and the entire crew with him now could pass through a tunnel carved in the base of one of these, horses and all. Maytens held to the edge of the lake as well, smaller evergreens that Pablo called *leña dura*, "hard wood", also a favorite of his.

As they approached the lake, the horses sunk into the humus to a level a half-meter above their hooves.

"What's it called?" Pablo pointed to the water.

"*El Lago de Preguntas*." Juvenal leaned forward on his saddle, surveying the cliffs across the way. "The Lake of Questions."

Pablo chuckled. "Perfect."

Juvenal explained that this lake was so isolated from the main trail passing up the Lilpela, which was now very far below them, that almost no one knew about it. "You have to be brought here. You may have noticed that, on this part of the trail, we followed no trail at all."

There had been a small dispute the day before about the route they were following. Every fifty meters or so, Juvenal and Ramada had cut a blaze on the side of a tree, marking their path. Victor had objected. "The police, the army, they'll follow us right up here because of those."

Juvenal, waiting for Victor and Pajarita to come up even with him and Miedo, held the machete he had been using in his right hand. "*Señor* Victor, it was you, wasn't it, who cautioned *maestro* Pablo about what could happen to him if we were to perish."

"Yes."

"Then would you have him freeze to death out here because he can't find his way back?"

"That's not—"

"Would you have him lost forever, wandering in these woods, raving with hunger, riveted with madness?"

"No."

"Good. Then I think it's a small risk to take, to make sure he finds his way, no?"

Victor had had to acquiesce.

They pitched camp, and while Juvenal and Ramada prepared a fire and started cooking the food and making coffee, Pablo went out to explore. Many broad plains of granite bordered this edge of the lake, and from the declivities and shallows in the granite, some form of greenery had been able to grow. Maytens struggled from many of these places, their roots having found purchase, although not enough to keep the trees from being deformed, in tortured shapes, quite small. Pablo recalled Basil Fotheringay's servant woman in Rangoon. These trees suffered as she had, and to Pablo had a similar beauty to that of the Chinese woman. They were elderly, they flourished, they were hobbled, yet elegantly alive.

When he got to the very edge of the lake, he saw that, across the way, a falls came down from the cliff far above. Tremendous water plummeted from a fissure in the lower precipice, from some channel cut through the rock. It made a faraway roar, so frightening in its distant, constant rumble that Pablo imagined it came from the very center of the range through which they were wandering.

He wished to circle the lake to take a look at the falls, and he set out across an enormous granite slab. There was no trail, and he had to walk through trees and underbrush that had probably not been trod upon by any person for centuries. The forest grew so wildly here that, without someone like Juvenal to show the way, no one would find this lake. They had reached an end of the world, Pablo mused. Perhaps no one had ever been here before.

He came across a boat. A small rowboat, very old and upside down, ashore at the foot of a rickety landing made of sticks. Two oars lay on the ground below the boat, and the entire craft and the oars were covered with green-black slippery moss.

Pablo turned the boat over and examined it a moment. He wanted to tell the others about it. But even more, he wanted to shove it into the lake and see if he could row it somewhere. He cast off, and immediately imagined that he was Poseidon splashing across the seas in his watery chariot, pulled by, of course, One-Eye Hippocampus, the sleek, golden, semi-blind sea horse of the deep. He put aside for a moment the rowboat's actual decrepitude. Rather, he thought, this chariot was festooned with gold and diamonds whose glittering was only enhanced by the frothy seawater running just below its gunnels.

Then as he began rowing, Pablo recalled the Norse boat. *What was it? Naglfar, that's right.* A flood had come to the world. The stars had disappeared. The earth had flailed in such a quake that the mountains themselves had fallen to the ground. Trees were blown down. All prisoners and animals had escaped because what had bound them had been loosed. Naglfar itself had shed its own moorings and sailed into the oceanic darkness. Naglfar, a ship made of the fingernails of the dead, so fearsome in Nordic childhood dreams that the Scandinavians always keep their nails clipped so as not to have them ripped from their fingers upon their deaths.

Or how about the canoe of Máui-Tikitiki-a-Taranga? Pablo mused. *What a name!* conjuring up dark men in loincloths going to battle in militant canoes, beautiful Maori women bare-breasted and generous with themselves. He leaned back, pulling the oar handles toward his chest, and the rowboat slipped across the black waters. Máui's mythical canoe that, placed upon the great Pacific Ocean, became the southern island of New Zealand, the plot of land on which Máui placed his foot in order to pull fish from the sea. The baby Máui, thrown by his goddess mother into the sea, yet protected from the cold of the waves by her splendid hair. The baby, crying, descending, seeking light from far above, all the while wrapped in seaweed, later to be discovered by the Deep Spirits.

Or The Argo, Jason's ship with a prow made of the sacred wood of the Dodona forest. Its most important piece was a magic wooden beam that carried the future in its finely hewn grain. A boat like that, Pablo mused as he rowed with even more enthusiasm, carrying its muscled crew toward the discovery of the fleece of the golden ram, a boat that in its voyage sailed every sea. The boat that now sails the skies, the constellation Argo Navis.

Moses among the Nile reeds.

Huckleberry down the Mississippi.

Marlowe up the Congo.

Washington across the Potomac.

Bolivar down the Magdalena.

Pablo wished that this little rowboat be all of those, with himself as the captain-poet, Walt Whitman Neruda afloat in the Andes. He looked beyond the port gunnel and saw, simply, the black deep. So, Pablo leaned to the side and searched its mysteries.

Water seeped into the boat, slow enough at first that Pablo felt no need to try to get rid of it. He glanced up at the darkening afternoon, floating toward the falls where they emptied into the lake. He so loved boats and ships. Above all he admired a craft's fragility. Like a small wood fragment floating over an enormous void, any boat or ship could easily disappear, taking all hands with it. The surprise was that so few boats did perish, despite their nervy existence. He knew as well of course that no body of water was a void, and he imagined himself disintegrating as he sunk into the depths, with pieces of the destroyed craft sinking with him, his face brushed with broken seaweed, his own body wrapped in it. The creatures and fish searched for him as he slowly fell to pieces, and then they ate those pieces. The fishes' leavings—Pablo Neruda—would be spewed into the waters and lost at sea, eaten again, spread into clouds of nothing, eaten once more, dispersed, and finally lost.

For him, such oblivion was a goal. Surrenders to emptiness and total forgiveness led to ecstasy. What was it that Queen Gertrude had said in her sad, duplicitous mourning for Ophelia, the queen's description of the girl as she fell into the rushing cold stream while singing old songs?

"Her clothes spread wide;
And, mermaid-like, awhile they bore her up...
But long it could not be
Till that her garments, heavy with their drink,
Pull'd the poor wretch from her melodious lay
To muddy death."

Her drowning had saved poor Ophelia, Pablo thought, from a long life of mad rage and the immolation of her soul. Had she not allowed herself to fall (and surely, she had allowed herself, willfully) she would probably still be imprisoned in that nunnery, muttering dismayed non-sequiturs for the rest of her life.

During these reveries it had gotten quite dark. Pablo had succeeded in reaching one end of the island. But as he headed for the falls, he realized that the boat now was shipping quite a bit of water. His boots were soaked in it. He turned the boat about and began rowing quickly for the wharf that he had left behind. When he rounded the end of the island, he searched for Juvenal's campfire. But there was no sign of one. He could see nothing.

He rowed into emptiness.

He looked back toward the island, and it too was almost gone. He floated heavily in the still water. The boat declined into it. Pablo continued rowing but realized that he was making no progress. The gunnels sunk below the level of the water, and the boat eased into the blackness.

Pablo was overcome.

He held to the boat, calling with wild hopelessness for help. But with the roar of the falls behind him, no one could possibly hear him. The island's enormous larches looked like spread-armed ghosts in an amphitheater, watching in glacially slow, slow-breathing silence as Pablo commenced to drown. He clutched the now over-turned rowboat. The moss, like a thick scum of raw oil, clung to it. His hands slapped against the curved planks of the keel. He could barely hold on, and cold water surged over his shoulders. It too felt like oil, and it seemed to Pablo that it was pulling him down. He would fall through it, immersed, until he disappeared.

Pablo glimpsed light in the forest from men on horseback. A half-dozen torches revealed that they were struggling to get several dozen head of cattle to progress through the woods. The cattle protested. The men whistled at them, whipping them, prodding them with sticks. The scene glowed in dim yellows and browns. The *gauchos*, their horses, and the cattle all appeared to Pablo, but barely, to be floating between the trees. In his panic Pablo called to them for help. They continued on, paying no attention and disappearing into the woods. One man, though, looked back into the gloom. His eyes burned with light.

Pablo called to him. "Save me! Help me!" He went under and drowned.

—

He awoke on a bank of the lake, on a sand bar through which the falls bled into the black waters. In the black-gray dawn, the trees above him appeared to be adorned with giant gray webs. He realized after a moment that these were just the outer, lowering branches, the older growth, of the great larches that bordered this side of the lake. He rolled over, stiff with cold, and saw nothing of the boat or its oars. His clothing was wet, but he realized that this had come from the night air, not from the lake. A patina of crusted, frozen dew had congealed everywhere all over him. It made noise when he moved.

Sitting up, he placed his hands on the rocky sand to either side of him. His right hand fell across a gathering of sticks tied together. A pitch-filled cotton rag had been wrapped around one end. He reached into his jacket pocket for a packet of dry wooden matches and lit the rag with one of them. It burst into flame. A fire had been prepared a few meters up the bar but left unlit. He thrust the bundle of sticks into it, and it too hurried into flame.

"Pablo!" Victor's distant voice barely registered above the roar of the waters cascading into the lake. Worry lined his face as he approached, and he carried a flaming torch of his own. "How did you get here?" Pajarita waited in the distance. Victor arrived at the fire, where Pablo was warming his hands. Pablo's distraction, the intensity of his looking into the flames, and the cold, all made it difficult for him to respond.

"We've been looking for you all night."

"A boat…"

Victor gripped Pablo's shoulder. "You didn't come back."

"No, I…"

He embraced Pablo. "How could you just walk off like that?"

"I found a boat."

Victor took a canteen from Pajarita's saddle. Pablo sipped from it, whiskey that, descending through him, warmed his gut.

"What do you mean, a boat, Pablo?"

"By the lake. Near where we camped. There was a little wharf."

"A wharf."

"A rowboat." Pablo sighed, suddenly feeling run through with a wire that carried water-borne electricity. "Those *gauchos*." He turned toward the lake, placing his hand over his mouth. "Phantoms." The lake was as he had first seen it the afternoon before. Nothing had changed. "I saw them in the forest. They must have been cattle thieves."

"Juvenal says there hasn't been a rustler up here for fifty years."

Pablo turned back to Victor. The mix of gratitude and relief that now swirled through Victor's eyes was itself a relief to Pablo. *I drowned,* he thought, *and now I am saved.*

"How can you say that for sure, Victor?"

"No boat, *maestro*. No wharf."

"But Victor, there's this fire."

Victor glanced at the flames. He tossed his own torch into them. "So what? You made the fire."

"No, no. They did."

15
THE MUSE

He devoured a plateful of beans and a handful of beef jerky.
Victor had brought him back to camp, and after he had told what he had seen—"It was all there, in front of me."—Juvenal had replied, "How can nothing be something?"

Pablo didn't understand the question.

"It was just a dream, *poeta*." Juvenal laughed. "All poets have dreams, yes?"

"But what about the *gauchos*?"

"Rustlers stopped coming up here way before you were even born." Juvenal held out a hand. "Nothing personal, *don* Pablo. You saw what you saw. But you didn't see them. Too many of them died up here."

Thinking about the rowboat and surveying his companions, Pablo worried about his responsibility for these fellows' lives. What if one of them did die trying to get him out of Chile? What if they all died? What if he, Pablo, left alone and responsible for the deaths of the others, did drown alone? In the unsteady light from the fire, the salted meat in his hand reminded him of old betrayals: ones he had instigated and others that had befallen him. His first loves, Teresa Vásquez and Albertina Rosa Azócar, written about with such heart in *Crepusculario* and *Twenty Poems of Love and One Desperate Song*, but abandoned in the end. His first wife María Antonioneta Hagenaar, the Dutch woman with whom he had lived when he had been the Chilean consul in Java, and from whom he had ultimately run away. His father Carmen del Reyes's never-resolved disappointment in his son Neftali and the boy's useless versifying. Francisco Franco's ruining of Spain. There were so many such things. Was Pablo to add the names of these guys here in the Andes mountains to the list of betrayals that he himself had perpetrated in his life?

His heart sunk. The beans had turned cold. He knew that such a response as this, inspired by a tin plate and its trivial coincidence of grease and light, could be explained simply by the extreme danger they were facing in these mountains. He worried that in the end his fame and that of the others could in fact come to an end here in the sodden, brutal Lilpela at the behest of Gabriel González Videla, a tinhorn politician, rather than being sustained by the glorious applause of Paris or Madrid at the behest of, say, Pablo Picasso or, of course, Delia.

—

The others had gathered around the fire, and Juvenal had brought a bottle of Chilean red from his saddlebag. "A special gift, *muchachos*." He had uncorked it with a knife.

"So, gentlemen." Pablo sat back, took up his own now-filled tin cup and held it out. "To Federico García Lorca."

"Who?" Juvenal's cup paused before his lips.

Pablo replaced the cup on the ground at his side. "A poet I once knew."

"Chilean?"

"A Spaniard."

"*¡Epa! Menos mal.*" Juvenal smiled. "Hey! Even better."

"He knew how a fire like this one is like a good poem."

Juvenal glanced toward the flames. "You often say things like that, *poeta*."

"Because it's true."

"But what good does a poem do?"

Having seldom been asked this question—never, in fact—Pablo did not have a ready answer.

"Words? A lot of shaped burps, if you ask me." Juvenal tossed another piece of wood on the fire. "Can a poem get you a job?" He looked up at

Pablo. "Can you put it between a couple slices of bread with maybe a little cheese?"

The other men waited, their faces wavering in the firelight like roughly hewn masks.

"Can a poem save your life?" Juvenal appeared to know what the answer would be. The silence that followed his question suggested that there was none.

"It can." Pablo leaned forward and sipped from his wine.

"Come now, *poeta*."

"It can do even more."

"You can prove that?"

Pablo, his own face shimmering light to dark in the firelight, shrugged. The flames illuminated his bent shoulders. "There was a donkey I once knew, Juvenal. Like Miedo. Only this one was called *La Musa*."

—

A Spanish jenny named after the muse, small and feminine, trotted up the canyon every day to the print shop at the great Montserrat monastery, in the mountains outside Barcelona, ridden by the printer Manuel Altolaguirre. Musa did not belong to Manuel. Rather, her owner had enlisted in the Republican forces on July 18, 1936, to defend the honor of the duly elected Republic of Spain against the invading army of Francisco Franco, and been blotted out within a few weeks, dead in an *arroyo*. So now Manuel and Musa ascended from Manuel's cabin to the monastery print shop using a little-known trail up through the rocks and gullies, by which they could escape detection by Franco's spies or soldiers. Those kinds of people lay in wait for intellectuals, writers and the like, artists, Montserrat being a refuge. General Franco fumed at such criminals. The jenny knew the secret way by heart, so that Manuel could also recite as he rode.

"*Anda, Musita*," Manuel would say, and he would begin declaiming. Sor Juana de La Cruz. Rubén Darío. Manuel's Chilean friend, already so lionized, Pablo Neruda, who had been editor of Manuel's review *El caballo verde* a few years ago when he had been living in Spain. And the Spaniards, of course. Fernando de Herrera "El Divino", Bartolomé Leonardo de Argensola (whose *The Conquest of The Molucca Islands* Manuel particularly cherished), Miguel de Cervantes, his left hand almost taken away by flame and cannon-shot during The Battle of Lepanto in 1571, so badly wounded that, he said later, his right hand had had to bear all the weight of composing *Don Quixote*.

And of course the best of them all, Manuel's friend Federico García Lorca.

"Ay, Musa,*"* Manuel said one January morning, patting the burro on the neck. Cold mist obscured the path ahead, but not Manuel's memory of Federico's verses. "*'The guitar mourns.../Mourns the arrow that has no target/and the afternoon without a morning,/ the first bird dead/upon the branch.'"* Federico, a handsome lyric genius who loved boys, had been murdered by the fascists in 1936.

Musa moved on up the trail as Manuel's voice quieted to silence. Fascists didn't understand such things. They had shot Federico, but for what reason? His poems? His plays. That he was queer? Who knew?

He rode on. Manuel was an athletic-seeming man, handsome in a rough sort of way, thirty-four years old, whose unkempt hair fell down over his forehead. He rode Musa easily, not wishing to tire the little jenny, who was so lovable an animal and so conversant. His hands were blackened by the printing ink with which he worked every day at the print shop. It was the oldest such shop in the world, its first work having been published in 1499. Now, in 1939, the books Manuel was making faced mortal danger. The fascists wanted them, to burn them, the bastards.

Musa came to an urgent halt behind a wide pine. Manuel, as always, marveled at how the jenny had so much a sense of self-protection. She could feel the path ahead and knew when something threatening was on it. Manuel and Musa craned their necks to peer around the edge of the tree trunk. In the distance, nothing showed but other pines and the enormous yellow outcroppings of rock, smooth and rounded, through which they had been climbing the trail.

A man stepped out from behind a tree. He was a ghost, or at least so he appeared. Out of focus, gray-white and cloudy in the gloom of the pre-dawn light, he seemed to come and go. The fellow carried a rifle, with a bedroll tied to his right shoulder by leather strings. A Republican army overcoat, soiled and ripped, covered him. His black pants and gray shirt were equally mud-stained, and he wore a black beret. This was a beefy man with thick, soft hands. The beret stuck like a small cloud to his head, ever shifting in the distance.

The jenny stepped back. She took in a breath, seized with doubt. She wished to turn and run.

"No, Musa. Wait, wait."

Manuel knew the man well and viewed him with astonishment. "Pablito. What are you doing here?"

Musa still held back, as though wishing to insist to Manuel that something odd emanated from this fellow, something below the surface and not fully readable. But Manuel already knew that, and that's why he had always liked Pablo Neruda. Pablo could look at a flower and feel its blood. He saw the universe in the brightening eye of a tiger, in a blade of grass, in a train engine or a printing press. He saw the universe in all things.

"Have you finished printing my book, Manuelito?" For such a large man, Pablo had a high voice. The smile that accompanied this question appeared immediate and uncomplicated, so like the poet himself, so celebratory.

"Almost."

"We'd better finish it tonight, then. Because…" Pablo looked back over his shoulder, toward the broad plain below. Barcelona lay in the distance. "They're coming."

"Franco?"

"His army, yes. They'll be here shortly."

Pablo began to disappear, and Manuel had to think hard about him, to conjure him back. The poet wavered, then began to re-materialize. He smiled. "They know you have *Spain In The Heart* up there in the shop."

Manuel had almost finished printing Pablo's new poems, *España en el corazón.*

"What a book! Eh?"

"But we told everybody that we had no paper, Pablo. That the press was shut down."

"They don't believe you."

"They think we have paper?"

"They know you have it, Manuel. That Franquista flag you had in the basement. And the shirt, the one you took off the Moor prisoner. Those old Republican uniforms. That's why I'm here. Everyone knows you made a new batch of paper from them. They know the book is coming."

Manuel grimaced. He patted Musa's neck. The jenny shivered with fear.

"We have one more folio to print." Manuel scratched his chin. "We could have it done by, oh, I don't know, midnight I guess."

"All right. Let's go." Pablo abruptly disappeared up the trail, leaving both Musa and Manuel startled and alone.

—

"What does it say?" Pablo's large head hung over the platen press, which he was wiping with a dirty rag. The rag had a ghost's gray ghastliness. His sweat-stained gray shirt was also splotched with black printer's ink, the sleeves rolled up, his forearms and hands similarly stained.

Manuel scored the printed press-sheet with an index finger, examining it carefully in the fading sunlight from the window. "Ah, here it is." They had just lit candles. They were almost finished with the printing. He took the sheet up into his hands and began reading out loud:

"And one morning all was aflame,
and one morning bonfires
leapt from the earth
devouring humans,
and since that day fire,
gun powder since that day,
since then, blood."

During Manuel's recitation, Pablo had placed his hands on his waist and looked out the window. "It's good. Very good."

"If you say so."

The poet turned. "You don't like it?"

Manuel joined Pablo at the window and looked out, down the trail toward the plain below. It seemed to him that he could see tanks and troops gathering at the foot of the mountain. Hell readied itself to ascend. "It's good as far as it goes, Pablo. But, but—"

"You think it needs something else."

"Well, this last part here." Manuel searched the sheet once more. "Where you say of yourself, '*Why doesn't his poetry/tell us of the dream, of leaves/and the grand volcanoes of the land of his birth?*' Pablo, you leave it off there. It's as though you don't have an answer. You don't know how to finish it."

"Hmph, they should all come here to Spain and see the blood in the streets."

The remark, a cliché, stunned Manuel. But like all clichés, the idea of blood in the streets, especially here in Spain, carried something of the truth. He laid the press sheet down on a table. "Say that, Pablo."

Pablo wiped his hands with the rag, shrugging his shoulders. "No, it's not such a good line."

"But it's a plain one. It tells the truth. It ties the knot."

Pablo looked back over his shoulder at the press. Doubtful, he tightened his lips. He wiped his hands once more. "I guess it would only take a few minutes to set the type for it."

"That's right."

"Before the ink dries on the press."

"Yes."

"So that we don't have to clean and re-ink the press."

"That's true."

They went about setting the type. Manuel took out a boot, Pablo searched the different cases, upper and lower, for the proper sequence of letters, and they set up the last stanza of the poem to contain the phrase *"Come and see the blood in the streets!"* In fact, they liked the phrase so much that they repeated it twice again, one after another.

"And what's the poem called?" Manuel was inking the press with fresh black. "I forget."

"*'Explico algunas cosas'.*"

"That's right. *'I explain a few things'*"

"Not bad, eh?"

"Not at all, poet. The fascists will hang you high for it, though."

"They have to catch me first." The candle on the table flickered, causing Pablo to partially disappear.

They printed far into the night, suspending each press-sheet from clotheslines that were strung from one wall of the shop to the other. In the candlelight, the press-sheets looked like evenly made small shrouds, the letters runic markings telling some sort of future.

"And now that they've dried, we fold them and bind the books." Pablo fingered one of the sheets.

"No, there's no time. Do you hear that noise?'

It was a rumble of far-away machines, monsters charring the countryside. "Tanks?"

"Tanks, trucks, horses." Manuel began walking along one of the clotheslines, removing with delicate care the press-sheets that hung from it. "An army, Pablito."

A half hour later they had packed the folded sheets into two large leather satchels and now hung them across Musa's back, securing them with leather straps. She protested.

"Don't worry, *mi* Musa," Pablo said. "You're carrying words."

Manuel, standing on the other side of the jenny, laughed. He pulled tight the last of the straps.

"And they can be heavy, *querida*, I know." Pablo patted Musa's neck. "Once we're out of here and it's safe, Musa, take a moment. Read some of them." He took Musa's rein into his right hand. "They're about your beloved Spain, *borriquita*." He gestured toward Manuel and they set out.

They descended and descended until finally they lost the way. Enormous boulders hid the trail, and even Manuel could not tell where they actually were going. The trees above hid the moon, and the trail had simply, utterly disappeared. Below, they heard the clanking of tank treads and the throatiness of heaving diesel motors as they made their way up the dirt road toward the monastery. It was the sound of the world's end, Satan and his rotting legions advancing upon the parapets of heaven. They could even see the rising, in the distance toward the starry night, of the tremendous exhaust put out by so many engines. They could not see much else. Were they not captured by the Franquistas, Pablo worried, they would be taken into the terrible gloom of night, causing the three of them to fall down some cliff, the press sheets floating after them like large meandering petals.

"I'm afraid, Pablo. Franco's army, they kill people like you and me."

"And Musa."

Furrowing his brow, Manuel grimaced. "No, burros mean more to them than poets do." He sighed. "Ask Federico."

Both men grieved a moment, in silence for their assassinated colleague.

"Federico," Pablo muttered, cold and fear causing his voice to waver. He leaned close to Musa and whispered in her right ear. "'*Do you recall,/buried there in the earth,/do you recall my house and its balconies where/the June light drowned the flowers in your mouth?*'" The words of Pablo's verse, that he had written for Federico García Lorca, broke his heart as, despite his present terror, he fell once more into mourning. "'My brother.'"

Musa's ears suddenly went straight up, rigid in the night air. She peered into the darkness, toward some trees ahead. Her tail went limp. The very silveriness of her coat seemed to turn to lumpish gray. But Pablo could see nothing ahead. No trail. Shadow upon shadow. All Pablo knew was that somewhere ahead an abrupt drop-off surely awaited them, through the yellow boulders down which the disappeared trail made its way. The trail had been well-tended for centuries, by many, for just such an escape as this: by disgraced monks caught in bed with other disgraced monks; royal prisoners who had bribed the guards; whores who had had to use the trail's dark passage in order to keep secret their assignations with the bishops and papal emissaries visiting the monastery.

But Pablo, Manuel, and Musa were now quite lost.

A burst of white light flew up from a gorge far below them. Enormous and stellar, it began settling down from the sky upon the men and the jenny.

It was an apparition, of arms, a chest and a massive head bearing down. It had two fiery black eyes and black hair unkempt and great among the stars.

Pablo's heart barely moved. Manuel appeared paralyzed with fright, his hand clutching the side of one of the satchels. Only Musa was entertained by this explosive, terrible brightening. She seemed delighted by it. As the apparition gestured toward them, motioning them toward the suddenly visible trail, the jenny moved away from Pablo and Manuel, as if convinced of the two men's cowardice. She ran to the ghost's embrace.

The phantasm gestured. "This way, fools."

Right away Pablo recognized the voice. "Federico!"

The vision began once more to blaze, the light from it almost too glaring to be borne. The forest lit up with a roaring wind. Lightning blurted from the heavens. Shielding his face behind his right hand, Pablo set out once more, in pursuit of the frolicking Musa as she raced after the light. Federico flew ahead, showing Musa the silver path, the clear, marvelous avenue to escape. Braying, laughing, she led Pablo and Manuel down it.

—

"So, in the light cast by those silver trees, hurrying down the trail, unsure of where the Franco troops were, where the stones were, the obstructive roots of trees, Manuel and I followed the apparition. Federico's floating hands pointed the way. His eyes were black jewels, *chicos,* lit with confidence and joy. And do you know why?"

The attention of Juvenal and the others had occasionally wavered, but Pablo had continued with the tale because he was himself so interested in how it would come out. Until this moment, because he had been making most of it up, he hadn't known what the end would be.

"Because *don* Federico had come back to this earth to avenge his death at the hands of General Franco, and he did so by saving my book." Pablo glanced at his now empty tin cup. Juvenal hurriedly refreshed it with wine. Victor and Ramada's as well. "When he called out to us, Juvenal, Musa's soul flew to him." Pablo placed his left hand in a jacket pocket. By now the air had become quite cold. "Usually books save lives, you see. But in this case Musa and the dead poet saved my book." He grinned. "And thus, my soul and my life." He lifted the tin cup to his lips, and then turned toward Ramada. "So, you see what that means to me?"

Grateful for the recollection, Ramada extended his hand to the poet, who shook it and then held it a moment.

"And I hope you believe every word I said, *amigos*." A sigh brought an even softer glow to the firelight, which had gathered as Pablo had been telling the story. He let go of Ramada's hand. "Even though the part about me and the part about Federico…" He sipped from the wine. "…was something I just concocted. I wasn't there. And neither was he." Pablo exhaled. He missed his poet friend. "But the rest of it is absolutely true." He sipped once more from the wine, and then examined the half-empty cup between his fingers. "Manuel Altolaguirre. Montserrat. The book. The tanks. All of it. Absolutely." He finished off the wine and, thrusting a stick into the diminishing fire, he re-stoked the flames.

Juvenal looked to the others, smiling. He was obviously pleased by having been brought into the great poet's company and introducing the others finally to Pablo's much vaunted, and now proven, ability to compose a fanciful late-night entertainment.

16
DELIA AND THE RUSSIAN

These flames were like most others. They emerged from the pieces of wood with the usual fury. But as Delia sat back in the chair, having replaced the slim iron shovel in its stand next to the fireplace, she knew that the fire appeared pedestrian only because she had seen other flames on a particular occasion that had seized her heart.

Just now, she waited for Igor Stravinsky on a rainy evening, with whom she would have dinner at Maxim's. Just the two of them. She wore a long black skirt that Coco Chanel had given her, along with one of Coco's long-sleeved white silk blouses with a sailor's collar, and the necklace of emeralds that Pablo had given her on the evening he had won the election for senator.

Stravinsky was twenty minutes late.

Those other flames had emerged from a stone fire pit that Pablo had built outside their house in Isla Negra. Not far away, the sea buffeted the shore, its muffled reveries like soft, constant sighing. The moon seemed to call the flames to itself. As Pablo moved the pieces of wood about, the sparks were galactic fireflies, alive for much too short a time before their light expired, climbing so hurriedly into the darkness. Delia watched them go, and Pablo laughed, holding the stick at his side. *"Eres su fuego femenino de rosa, mi hormiguita." ("You're the feminine fire of the rose, my little ant.")*

Delia loved the nickname, used as often by Pablo as her actual name.

All their friends now referred to her as Hormiguita. But the intonation of Pablo's voice when he said it contained such playful love that Delia's heart itself felt that it was being caressed.

"Ay, Pablito," she said, her eyes wavering with the disappearing light." A rose—"

"*Sí, un solo pétalo que la luna y el mar combaten.*" ("*Yes, a single petal in combat with the moon and sea.*") Pablo's eyes remained fixed on the fire in the pit. The light wavered across his face, so that his eyes and mouth were at once alight, yellow and white, and thrown into dark, slivered shadow. When he studied flames like this, his heart grew engaged with words, and they flowed from him like air being shaped into clouds.

"I'll always love you," Delia whispered.

The phone rung, and Delia stood and walked to the table near one of the windows looking out on the river. She pushed the dressed mannequin aside, closed the small velvet sewing kit with which she had been working, and took up the phone. The concierge, a thin man with bright teeth whose name was Jean-Louis, announced that M. Stravinsky was in the lobby waiting, and that he wanted Mme. Neruda to hurry since their reservation was for nine o'clock. She could hear Stravinsky speaking to Jean-Louis, his Russian accent a little brassy in an oligarchic sort of way, insistent on what the doorman should say to the Madame.

"So inconsiderate," she sniffed.

17
THE WEIRD SISTERS

It rained again in the night. Not the slow inception of a storm that you can watch and feel over several hours. This torrent began right now. Having predicted such an occurrence earlier in the afternoon, Juvenal and the others had set up a low shelter of pine branches, which had had only partial success keeping the water out when it had finally come in a jolt from the sky. A lot of the gear in the shelter was quite wet by the time first light came. Pablo's two blankets were mostly dry, saved from the worst of the wet by a large sheet of oilcloth that Pepe Rodríguez had given him. The other men awakened soaked. To Pablo's citified surprise, they did not seem to care.

Juvenal struggled to put on his boots. "In our lives we've been washed over by more rain than you've ever even seen, *don* Pablo."

"It rains in Santiago."

"I expect so. But you have buildings there, no?"

"We do."

"That you can run into for protection."

Pablo nodded.

"That's not the case out here." Juvenal went out into the storm.

Right away, water streamed from every centimeter of the brim of his *sombrero* like a swirling beaded curtain. Victor and Ramada, similarly awash, walked around in the tempest as though there were no tempest. While breaking camp, Victor had even succeeded in making a fire beneath a smaller version of the pine-bough shelter. It was an astonishment to Pablo. Just now, Victor was boiling a pot of coffee. "It can be a problem, Pablo.

Dry snow is easier to defend against than rain. Rain will kill you faster than snow, hypothermia and all that."

Steam rose from beneath the lid of a second covered pot, and caressed Pablo's interested nose.

"Corn mush." Victor grinned from beneath the heavy coat that hung from the top of his head. Hunkered down over the fire, his boots in two inches of mud, he removed the lid and stirred the mush with a stick. "Delicious on a bad morning."

Juvenal knelt down on one knee before Pablo. His hands cradled a cup of coffee. "So, *don* Pablo, today, today…"

The two men braced themselves against a gust of cold wind.

Pablo shivered. "What have we got?"

"It's a particularly difficult section of trail, heavily wooded and rocky." Juvenal looked up, shielding his eyes from the downpour. "It's some of the highest elevation we'll see." He kept his gaze on the great canyon ahead. "It will be painful."

"Not much traveled?"

"Not for many years."

Victor handed each man a bowl of mush with a spoon. Pablo scented the corn, a vegetable he had always loved.

Juvenal slurped a spoonful into his mouth. "Now we begin the real Smugglers' Pass. A century ago, *gauchos* would bring stolen cattle up here and use this trail to avoid the authorities." Taking in a breath, he savored the heat. "See, they knew that they could have come up the regular trail, which is a much easier one. But they had cattle with them. Thirty, fifty, a hundred head."

He took another spoonful and accepted more coffee from Victor. Pablo sipped from his tin cup also, trying to avoid burning his lips.

"So, they had to take this other trail, the higher one, hidden, so that they could get the cattle through. But the trouble, the trouble was—"

"That the cattle made the hidden trail really difficult," Pablo said.

"Exactly." Juvenal blew across the surface of his coffee as he waited for it to cool. "You'll see. This is going to be difficult just for us. And if you had a bunch of cattle with you, all of them struggling for footing, complaining the way steers do, stupid animals refusing to go, bawling, hating you, you'd be unhappy too." He looked into the distance. "That much complaining from a bunch of dumb beasts can get you killed."

They set out into the torrent.

In such a forest, rain gathers in the trees, slipping down the thicker branches to the slimmer ones, gathering weight in ever-growing globules of liquid that then drop like cold, wet lead. So, the rain itself, in this case strident and ruinous, was accompanied by a ragged falls plummeting from the trees. Pablo had never been this cold. His wool jacket had been soaked immediately. Everything had been. The extra poncho contained more water now than wool, and when Pablo wrapped it tightly around his throat to keep further water out, icy liquid drained onto his shirt collar nonetheless, flowing across his chest and back. The wind blew in a deep roar.

They rode for hours. The horses grumbled, refused to move, tried to throw their riders off. The trail, a cacophony of rigid angles, giant roots, slippery rocks and boulders, offered no forgiveness.

The light began to fail at about three in the afternoon, and Juvenal called a halt. His *sombrero*'s brim had lost whatever shape it had had, so that it looked like a clump of black mud straddling his skull. His *poncho* resembled a teepee long abandoned and fallen down. His clothing clung to him, and Miedo stood stock still, the only movement being in the foggy breath that he expelled every few seconds.

Juvenal raised a hand to his face and wiped water from it. "We've got another couple hours to go." He tightened his lips. "Many hours."

"What do we do?" Pablo said.

"It may snow tonight. So, we have to get to the lava tunnel." Juvenal pointed up the trail, which at the moment disappeared beneath a fresh squall coming down from the canyons. "But there's a cave, I remember, up ahead, close by."

"The lava tunnel, did you say?"

"We've got to get out of this rain."

Victor, whose mare Pajarita shivered with cold, leaned forward on the horn of her saddle and clapped Pablo's shoulder. "We can't stay out here,

Pablo, for…" He pointed into the *cordillera*. Fresh assaults of rain surged down through the passes. "For obvious reasons."

"A cave?" Pablo held a palm to his right cheek, to protect it from the wind.

—

They stopped at a shallow opening at the bottom of a cliff face and set up camp inside. The men slept cocooned within their watery clothing, the storm outside blustering at them angrily. Juvenal had built a fire just inside the cave entrance, and Pablo was awakened from time to time by his re-stoking it and adding wood to it.

It snowed all night.

"Can you handle an axe, Pablo?"

Pablo took the axe from Victor into both hands. He held it up, parallel to the ground, and admired it. In the morning shadow from the *cordillera*, its blade scarred and scraped, its handle rough-stained, the axe appeared to him the most utilitarian thing he had ever seen. He recalled Vulcan. A factory for the human hand, this axe could destroy and build. Were it to be clothed, it would wear soiled cotton pants, no shirt, a rag around its head and a hod for carrying distressingly heavy loads on its back. Its teeth would be soiled. Several would be missing.

"Now and then I guess I have." Pablo handed the axe back. "I'll cut up a few pieces of wood for Delia, you know, on a cold night."

Victor grinned. "In other words, you don't know."

"That's right."

The storm had abated a little. Because of the temperature, the snow was very delicately dry. The cave itself was at the bottom of a gargantuan granite precipice that went up at an angle away from the men two hundred meters. Far above and beyond it, invisible in the thick roiling clouds, but well imagined by Pablo, the summits of great adjoining peaks were bur-dened with snow. The forest grew almost to the cave entrance, and fresh snow had patterned itself in lace-like curtains on every tree.

"You're going to need to know about using an axe, Pablo." Victor pointed into the forest. "Because we have a few extra concerns today."

"That we're going to freeze to death in these wet clothes?"

"Precisely. The other is that eventually we're going to need wood for our fire later tonight. Knowing how to use an axe means that you'll be able to work up a sweat cutting the wood, and then you can relax in the heat when we're burning it."

"You learned this on Aconcagua?"

Victor shook his head. His eyes tightened. "No. We were way above the tree line in that storm. An axe does you no good when there's no forest."

"I suppose not."

"And those people would have died no matter what."

Saddened by the downturn in Victor's voice, Pablo stuck his hands into his jacket pockets. Victor stared at him, his eyes almost unmoving.

"How come you didn't die, Victor?"

"Plain luck."

"God's intervention."

"Not a chance." Victor swallowed. He was suddenly angry. "He was nowhere present up there, believe me. Even the people beseeching Him that day, their tears frozen on their skin, poor bastards, they all died."

Victor had hewn a portion of a very thick branch into a small chopping block. He took up the axe and gestured toward some of the other branches. "Help me with that one, will you?"

Pablo took one up and, holding it at a right angle to the ground, secured it from above while Victor trimmed it.

"OK, now lay it down sideways on the block, and hold on tight at the far end there."

Victor began chopping and, within a few minutes, had bucked the length of wood into three short logs. "Now we quarter them." He picked up a log and set it upright on the block. Handing the axe to Pablo, he stood back and gestured toward the rude construction.

"*Bueno, poeta.* Cut it in half."

Pablo remembered his father cutting wood. He recalled how his grandfather had done it. He placed one foot a half meter in front of the other, at an angle to the other, and raised the axe over his head in both hands.

"No." Victor moved forward as Pablo lowered the axe before him. "The one rule in chopping wood is that you don't put one foot before the other."

"Why?"

"Because…look." Victor took the axe from Pablo. He assumed the same stance as Pablo had had and, in slow motion, pretended to strike the log. "If you miss?" He feigned losing control of the axe-head and made it look as though the blade were to run directly into his forward knee. "You see?"

"Of course."

"That's no good." Victor took a stance once more before the log. "So, here's the one rule. You face the log with your feet planted to either side, equidistant from the block, about three-quarters of a meter apart, eh?" Again, he rehearsed the falling lunge of the axe toward the log. "If you miss? The axe goes between your legs, between your feet, and into the ground, no?"

"I see."

"OK. So go ahead and try."

An hour later, Pablo had demonstrated immediate prowess as a woodsman. His back hurt. His nerves had been frazzled by the abrupt clash of axe and log. But otherwise, no problem.

"So, we leave this chopped wood for the next group of rustlers who wander through here." Victor nudged one of the pieces of wood with the toe of his boot. Three dozen pieces lay in a humble pile at his feet.

"Might be a hundred years." Pablo smiled, surveying the axe.

"Even better. The wood will be well cured in that case." Victor pulled his jacket close, to protect against the snow. "It'll burn brighter."

—

They left the cave behind, riding into a forest papered with snow.

"We want to get to the lava tunnel by this afternoon." Juvenal patted

Pablo's shoulder as they passed through a large copse of larch trees. "It's interesting, the tunnel. It's huge. Formed by lava flow when these mountains were formed. Who knows how old it is."

"From the inception of the range?"

"Certainly from when these were volcanoes. Hundreds of millions of years."

They rode on. As the damp humus ground cover grew semi-frozen and unstable, the footing for the horses became grueling. They climbed higher and higher, and all of the animals, even Miedo, had difficulty making their way. In some of the granite plains, shallow pools of water had frozen through, and if they were covered with humus or snow, neither the riders nor the horses could see what was below. So, the riding had to be very skillful. Juvenal told Pablo to ride in the middle of the single file of horses, while he and Miedo brought up the rear.

The snow kept on.

During a stop after a few more hours, Juvenal dismounted from Miedo and approached Pablo, who was at the moment lighting one of the half-dozen cigars he had brought on the journey.

"You're doing fine, *maestro*."

"Thanks." Smoke swirled around Pablo's head. "You guys want a little of this?" He extended the cigar toward Juvenal.

Smoke billowed up around Juvenal's face. He held the cigar in the gloved fingers of his right hand a moment, savoring it, and then handed it to Victor. Pablo realized that Juvenal was enjoying himself, something that had not much happened during this trek, except for the occasions back at the sawmill on which Pablo couldn't get Tuerto to go or to stop, depending on the situation. On those occasions, Juvenal had laughed. But even so, Pablo would not have been able to say whether the cowherd was truly enjoying himself or simply chortling at the expense of the poet dandy.

"It's good, the cigar." Victor passed it on to Ramada.

"Cuban," Pablo said. "We deserve a little pleasure, with weather like this."

"*Don* Pablo." Juvenal looked to the side, holding a fist before his mouth. It was a shield that did little to hide the smile that appeared. "You've been riding well. Came as a surprise to me, I'll admit it, but, well...." He turned away.

Two hours later they made their way up a shallow streambed. Water purled down the rocky ravine up which they struggled. Snow blew up and down the ravine to either side. Pablo imagined that, were anything to go wrong on this day, it would surely be here. *And it will be a horse falling,* he thought, *going down, breaking a leg. Such a disaster far from anywhere safe.*

A single cracking explosion came from a tree above the ravine, like broken thunder. The top twenty meters of the tree fell directly into the stream. Tuerto had sensed the wood coming down and scrambled up a bank of the ravine. The tree had fallen up the streambed, at a slight angle to it, so that it had come down all the way to the waterline. Pablo and Tuerto were separated from Juvenal and Ramada, who had ridden ahead. Once he had been able to calm Tuerto down, Pablo looked about him for Victor. He heard nothing of Victor's voice. No sound of any sort, except for the stream and, suddenly, a neighing from the mare Pajarita. She had turned back downstream and now stood fifty meters away, to one side of the water. She waited before a circle of snow-driven larches. She was alone.

"Victor!"

The tree trunk, lying on its side, was four meters thick. The forest remained completely silent, except for the panicked voices of Juvenal and Ramada far ahead, coming closer. The snow seemed to hold itself up on the trees and the humus. Of Victor there remained nothing. Pablo dismounted and began walking the length of the trunk. With so many branches, he had to scramble through them, beneath them, fighting through the snow that covered them, searching for his companion. Needles pushed themselves into his face, jabbing into his hands through the cloth of his gloves. His heart stumbling, Pablo lurched up the portion of the stream bank that had not been covered by the fallen trunk. The stream swirled over his boots. He slipped on the stones, occasionally falling to his hands and knees.

He found Victor unconscious, lying to the side of the stream. His left leg was caught among some stones, hemmed between them and held there by an edge of the tree trunk. He was out of the water. But he could not be freed.

—

"I'll chop from up above." Juvenal then pointed at the trunk at a spot about a half-meter above Victor's imprisoned ankle. "Ramada, you cut from down here, into the side. We chop so that eventually we meet…" He made an X with his finger on the side of the trunk. "Here. Then we'll have an easier time of it getting you out, *don* Victor."

"How long?" Victor's speech had faltered as he had grown colder.

Juvenal looked at the upper edge of the fallen trunk, then back and forth a few meters of its length. "Three hours."

Victor lay back, his eyes fixed on the snow-laden tree canopy above. His skin had paled to a mottled gray.

Within an hour, two large notches had been cut in the trunk, from above and from the side. Pablo's job had been to try to keep Victor warm, which he had done by following Victor's own example of building a canopy, struggling to make a fire, boiling pots of coffee and cooking beans for everyone. At one point he lit another cigar and shared it with Victor, followed by a second one. Victor himself fell into unconsciousness a few times, wearied by the pain in his ankle and his struggle to remain calm.

They did not know whether the ankle was broken. Pablo kept Victor talking, to hold his attention and to take it away from the entrapment. Victor worried aloud that he was going to die out here.

"No. No future in that." Pablo nursed Victor, wiping water from his face and keeping him covered with his own semi-dry blankets. Pablo talked about everything, and demanded answers from Victor, about the rain and snow on Aconcagua, about Victor's climbing, about the beaches in Viña Del Mar and Valparaiso, the sun during summer, fishing streams in Bariloche, Victor's enjoyment of beef and vegetables cooked on the *parilla*, about poetry, books, and legends.

Victor struggled to speak. "Yes, I remember, somebody…. An Indian who was a friend of my grandfather, he told me a story, Pablo, about a certain kind of woman who, even as she gets in your way, can save your life."

"Why?"

"She warns you about what's going to happen. The Indians here have many such women."

"Like Cassandra."

"The Greek?"

"Who could tell the future. But the worst part about the future, Victor, at least what she knew of it, was that it was all bad."

"Yes. Destruction."

"The ruination of the kingdom. The downfall of the just ruler, all that."

Ramada ceased chopping. His shoulders and forearms quivered. "This is an old story, *don* Pablo?"

"Very old." Pablo stood and handed him a cup of coffee. Victor, surveying from his back the deep wound that Ramada had inflicted upon the tree, admired it with a sickly exclamation. Up above, Juvenal was working as well, and the sound of his axe striking the wood set up a kind of irregular thwacking rhythm that syncopated the steady lilt of snow that was once more descending.

"I know those kinds of stories." Ramada put the coffee down on a nearby rock and took up the axe once more. He gazed at it for several seconds, his eyes riveted to its banged-up blade and chipped handle. Pablo, who had sat down on a small boulder, sensed that Ramada's pause was like one of his, in the middle of writing a big poem, when he didn't know where he was going with it or how he could possibly complete it. Ramada was surveying the details. He was trying to determine whether the tools were right, the words, whether they would work, given the numberless choices that were open to them.

Just now though the goal was simple: to get Victor 's leg freed before he froze to death. So, Pablo realized the frivolousness of his rumination. Nonetheless, he thought, although Ramada's poem had just a few essential lines, each was of supreme importance. This made the options fewer and far more important than would regularly be the case.

"There are all sorts of old spirits that you need to know about in a forest like this," Ramada said. "Trails that will jump up to trip you. The widow-makers from the trees." He frowned. "They're not just fallen branches, *don* Pablo, those widow-makers. They're the revenge of disappointed wives." Ramada shrugged, turning away again.

"How do you know these things? A young guy like you."

"Mothers. Grandmothers. My *abuelita* once told me, for example, that there are dark night animals up here. The ghosts of the Araucan."

"I've met a few." Pablo fed the small fire with some sticks.

"Araucans."

"Sure. And ghosts."

The Araucans were the tribe that had given its name to the region of Chile in which Pablo had been born. Of all the Indians, they had defied the *conquistadores* for centuries after the invasion in the sixteenth century. Pablo's father had admired them. You feared the Araucans even when they were dead.

"And in a forest like this, they'll find you." Victor turned his head to the side. "Did your grandmother tell you that, Ramada?"

"She did."

"Well, luckily," Pablo said, "we have only this tree to worry about."

"True, but it's formidable, *don* Pablo. It's..." Ramada stood before the fallen larch, surveying the work he had already done. Above, Juvenal continued working. Ramada raised the axe above his head. "A tree like this, the spirits in it, they can surprise you." He let the axe fall. It ricocheted from the wood. The head banged into his leg. *"¡Ay mierda!"*

Pablo hurried to help Ramada. Blood oozed from the glancing wound the axe had inflicted on him.

—

"It's up to you now, *don* Pablo." Juvenal handed Pablo the axe. Ramada's knee had swollen and bruised terribly. The dressing on it, one of Pablo's shirts, was stained dark with blood.

After two hours of chopping, Pablo had to struggle to keep going. His back had grown angry with pain. His hands, though protected by his gloves, had blistered nonetheless. He had remembered everything that Victor had told him about how to chop wood and, although the axe did from time to time ricochet in some unforeseen direction, Pablo was able to keep it from turning against him.

Victor and Ramada had asked him to keep talking, even as he chopped. They had grown so cold that they needed some sort of distraction, something besides the coffee and beans to keep them going. Pablo thought about Scheherazade, and told the story of her telling stories, how each night for a thousand and one nights she saved her own life by never finishing the story. He considered the Brothers Grimm, and told them *Snow White* and *Sleeping Beauty*, in which Pablo exaggerated the sensuality of the two heroines to a point that would have offended readers a century before. Large breasts revealed, seductive smiles offered, unusual caresses enjoyed. Ramada liked the tales. Finally, Pablo began telling Victor and Ramada about Persephone and her threats to lay waste to Hades' underworld universe. Her erotic love of pomegranates, which bled across her fingers as she sucked on them. He described her return to the world. And how, with that return, the seasons came, as did destruction, aging, ruin, and rebirth.

Pablo also knew about certain North American tribes, so he was able to talk about the Apaches' renowned horsemanship, the beauties of Algonquin face painting, and the feathered war bonnets of the Sioux.

As Juvenal's axe from above came closer and closer to his own, Pablo described some of the things he had learned from the tribal groups in Sumatra, where he had once been the Chilean consul. The Garuda bird, the instantaneous conflagration of fire and gases that enveloped the whole universe when the bird was born, the Garuda's battle against the gods for possession of the Elixir of Immortality, and his ultimate task as the winged carrier of the god Vishnu through all the worlds of good and evil.

Pablo explained the myth of The Frozen Children, who had been sacrificed to the Inca gods on the upper snow-ridden reaches of Llullaillaco, a mountain seven thousand meters high in Argentina. He knew of it because Llullaillaco was a sacred place for the Atacama Incas, who had lived there for thousands of years, many of whose descendants had voted for Pablo for senator. "They say that the children live, even though they were put to death, and that they stroll through the universe dressed as princes."

He described The Weird Sisters, predicting the mayhem and blood of MacBeth's ambition. *"Like a hell-broth boil and bubble,"* they had said. The bearded women. *"Aroint thee, witch!"* MacBeth had responded. Get thee gone!

Shakespeare, that marvelous man, Pablo thought. *If only I could write as well as he.*

He chopped and talked until finally, exhausted, he came to the place at which Juvenal, equally done in, had arrived, in a kind of giant cradle at the center of two large, open wounds in the larch's trunk. The wounds had come together as one cut slash, at a ninety-degree angle, with perhaps six inches of wood still left to go until the two men could expose Victor's imprisoned leg.

"So now the third cut." Juvenal scratched his head. "The last one."

"I brought that saw, you know," Pablo said. "The little handsaw I was posing with when Victor arrived at the sawmill. I have it with me, as a memento." He sighed, dropping the axe to the ground. "Wouldn't that be safer?"

"Get it."

—

Within an hour, they had freed Victor.

His ankle was quite badly bruised. But with help he could walk. Pablo surveyed the tree trunk. A giant slice had been cut out of it, the ultimate result of three separate cuttings, three gouges where once the tree's eyes may have been, Pablo mused. Eyes chopped from its face, blinding the tree forever. The Weird Sisters, the three of them, had snickered at the vain efforts of these foolish men to free their compatriot. All three had dictated the future, and all had been defeated. Cassandra's foretold disaster, of Victor's slow freezing to death before the very men trying to save him, had not taken place.

Victor sat with a final cup of coffee by the side of the tree, nursing his ankle and thanking the three other men, all of whom appeared slothful and exhausted on the stream bank. "You all look far worse off than me."

"We are." Amused but exhausted, Pablo turned over on his side, wishing to sleep.

—

The light was failing, and they arrived at a clearing.

As they set up camp, Pablo noticed—as though for the first time—how ragged his companions looked. Fatigue had overcome them all, and they moved about slowly, as though the fading afternoon light had weight that, as it sighed away toward darkness, pressed down on them more and more. Ramada and Victor, ever the workhorses, had both been battered, so that when they moved, the pain they were in seemed anchored within them, like devouring worms in their entrails. Their faces and hands were equally soiled. In Ramada's case his face had previously appeared twenty years or so younger than his hands. Now his face was creased with dirt, abrasions, and fatigue, just as his hands were. Victor lurched about with a stick he had found in the woods, his battered ankle unable to hold his weight. Juvenal, usually so imperturbable and given to willful disdain or, at best, humorous muttering in his speech, now was mired in silence. Even a dismissive tone of voice was not possible. He was too tired to talk.

Pablo had secured Miedo and the horses, taking special care that the animals be protected from the wind within a circle of larch trees. The horses too were slouching with fatigue. As Pablo emerged from the grove, Juvenal, his shoulders sloped, his entire body listing to the left, awaited him by the fire. His dark eyes glowered at the ground. His lips were tightly pressed with what appeared to be defeat and anger.

"*Don* Pablo. We'll rest here."

Pablo nodded.

"Everyone needs it."

Pablo lowered his head. "Yes."

"But I must tell you... I've thought of you that you didn't understand the danger."

"Yes?"

"That you thought we were all just your servants. Your footmen."

"Ay, Juvenal."

Juvenal held up his hand, demanding silence from the poet. He would allow no back talk. It was clear to Pablo that Juvenal was about the berate him for.... What would it be this time? His ingratitude? His disdain for these men and their well-being?

"But I see that you're a strong, brave man."

"Not an ingrate?"

"No. A man who can learn to ride a horse like you, who can handle an axe like that? No."

Within an hour, there would be no light at all. Pablo was shaken with surprise.

"We all appreciate what you've done over the last few days, *don* Pablo, and especially what you did today."

"Juvenal, I—"

Juvenal held up a hand in a gesture that once indeed would have indicated disdain. But now Pablo realized that the hand was offering him welcome.

18
WHITE

The next afternoon snow tumbled down across the *cordillera* in an immediate blizzard. It was the worst snow that either Juvenal or Victor had ever seen.

As Tuerto plodded across an enormous open meadow from which not a single tree grew, snow burrowed into Pablo's eyes, so that the other riders before him broke up into blurred shards of gray and black. No amount of brushing the snow aside and no attempt to shield his eyes from it saved him. He was battered by the snow...everyone else as well, until finally, leaning abruptly into the wind, spurring Tuerto, Pablo brought up the rear of the small column. There lay before him only a colorless sheen.

He floated into invisibility. Snow…so much of it, like a whitening universe all-surrounding, yet invisible in the wind-roiled glare…. It made the rest of the universe an elusive foolishness, disappeared, not worth worrying about. Snow…white…. What had Melville said? *The muffled rolling of a milky sea….* The fright of endless sightlessness. *The wretched infidel gazes himself blind at the monumental white….*

So it was that Pablo himself went blind, his sight turning to nothing at all. *The invisible sphere formed in fright,* as Melville had said.

The one indication of a forest anywhere came with the noise it made all around them as the blizzard winds snarled through the trees at the edges of the meadow. The roar they made resembled that of an Alpine avalanche. But even that, Pablo surmised as he tightened the collar of his wool jacket around his neck, even an avalanche like that would be mild by comparison to this. Pablo could see few trees. In fact, none. He tightened his collar against the unleashed cacophony of the wind attempting to blow the forest down. The Andes *cordillera*, as though plagued by disappointment and betrayal, lashed out at everything. Were the sun and another star to collide, this is what it would sound like, this the noise that must have accompanied the beginning of the universe.

Had there been any noise at all….

The skin of Pablo's face, where it was not covered with a wool scarf and the cotton kerchief that he had tied about his head to shield his nose and mouth, burned like ice. His hands were encased by his gloves, and he felt only pain within the hands. Not surface pain; rather the numb eccentricity of deep cold coming from the very bones of his fingers.

Tuerto walked more slowly with every moment, as though his musculature were hardening, the tendons growing shorter, and his determination becoming skeletal. The horse's reins froze to Pablo's gloves.

He looked ahead once more for the others. For a moment, the flanks and rear of Ramada's Ángel were visible, as was the appearing and disappearing head and back of Ramada himself who, like an escaping dream, yet appeared to return, each time less forcefully.

Pablo drowsed in the storm. Everything moved slowly. He slouched forward, barely fingering the reins. The now-rigid gloves would not allow him to take the reins in hand. He gave Tuerto his lead, knowing that the horse would stay with the others of his own accord. After several minutes, feeling a kind of general warmth particularly in his hands and feet, Pablo lowered his head, and his eyes closed easily…slowly…into sleep.

He fought against it. Pepe Rodríguez had warned him about the cold up in the mountain passes, that it could betray you into a sense of fellowship and kindly drowsiness that then would kill you. The warmth did fool Pablo, although he did not realize it at the moment. He looked up, and the others had disappeared. He didn't care. He knew that Tuerto would save him, and that no matter what, Tuerto's name was, as Don Quixote had phrased it when thinking of his own Rocinante, *"aristocrático y sonoro,"* noble and sonorous, "a name just right," Pablo murmured to himself, "for a stallion like my Young One-Eye, no, Cervantes?"

Pablo awakened once more. Alone, Tuerto had ceased walking. The wind battened itself about the two of them, as did the heavy snow. It didn't matter. Pablo lowered his head and slept, the warmth in his jacket now running up his belly toward his chest and neck. The cold comforted him. He dreamt.

Delia.

She kissed him once more, inclining toward him, her hair sweeping across his chest. She held tight to his right hand, the fingers of her left clutching it as her excitement flourished. She was about to come, sitting on Pablo the way she enjoyed doing, and allowing his thrusts to rivet her with intensity and shock, everywhere in her. Her hand caressing her clitoris. When she kissed him, Pablo worried that he would not be able to withstand her demanding wish that he keep going, that he not stop. Her lips caressed his. She wetted his with her tongue, and then kissed him again just as the warmth of her orgasms took over everything, and a heated cry came from her.

To his surprise, in the dream, she bled. She rose up from him, ascended into the white, slowly disappearing in every way except for the blood that flowed down her thighs. She had not in fact so bled for a number of years. But now she appeared as a rising mermaid through a white, swirling sea, her blood dropping to the snow and staining it, rose-colored currents flowing over the colorless briny drifts.

Moments later Delia, as always scattered and unable to speak after such lovemaking, lay on the sheet, sunlight coming through the white organdy curtains of their bedroom in Isla Negra. The sea flowed, the Pacific Ocean blue and at this moment hardly calm. Indeed, the shore break tumbled like great muslin sheets folding over upon themselves with a delighted roar, the ocean so deep in the distance that its blue more resembled the stellar blue of the universe on a full moon night. Delia's breathing palpitated. Her quick inhalations caused her skin to quiver. She laid a hand across her right breast, and murmured as her fingers covered it. "Ay, Pablo." A strand of her long almond-colored hair lay across her eyes.

Pablo's heart floated, the back of his right hand against his forehead. He could barely dream, as the memory of Delia's skin against his own caressed his skin like the ooze of fine oils entering each other. He listened for the sea.

"Pablo."

He turned his head toward her. She had disappeared, and everything surrounding him now was blind white.

"Pablo!"

He dreamt that he had been laid out in his grave. Made up of blue ice and white snow, the ice like sagging diamonds, the rectangular hole surrounded his body. There was no coffin. Rather he lay in the wool coat and coveralls with which he had been making his escape through the Andes. The gravediggers scrambled about in the hole with him, digging further and expanding it. He wondered how he had died. *Alas, poor Pablo.* It amused him, death. *I knew him well.* Just like that, gone! With none of the brouhaha and fear that he had always been certain would accompany his demise. *A fellow of infinite jest...* No struggle. No blatant war against the deterioration of his flesh and the mortification of his heart.

"At least we got him out of the storm." One of the gravediggers continued digging. Pablo wished to continue sleeping, but these men wouldn't let him.

"Wake up!" one of them shouted, leaning over him. The man slapped Pablo and shook him by the shoulders. "Pay attention."

Pablo noticed that the fellow hunched against the wind, which blew along the surface of the ground above the grave.

"Falls off his goddamned horse in the middle of a storm...."

"Delia?" Pablo murmured.

"No, I'm not Delia."

"Who are you?"

For a moment there was no answer.

"You have that saw?" Victor shouted at him, shaking Pablo by the shoulders.

"The saw? Yes, I, I—"

"All right. We dig the cave."

Juvenal shouted. "You need a shovel to dig a cave!" A battering wind passed over him. "A saw's not going to do us any good."

"You've got a shovel?" Victor asked.

"Yeah."

"Then get it, too."

Climbing out of the grave, Juvenal disappeared into the white.

"And don't argue with me like this, *hijo de puta*," Victor shouted after him. "Bring one of the torches." Victor surveyed a drift of snow that rose up before him, beyond Pablo's head where he lay in the grave. "Ramada, take care of the animals."

Ramada disappeared into the storm, and after a moment Juvenal returned.

Victor knelt down at the base of the drift, his right knee just inches from Pablo's left temple. "Give me that torch." Juvenal handed it over, and Victor plunged the handle-end of it horizontally into the drift, then took it out and plunged it back in, many times. "Okay, there aren't any rocks or logs or anything. We can dig here." He turned to Juvenal and pointed at the base of the drift. "You dig. Use the saw and the shovel."

"All right. But what do I saw?"

"A hole in the side of the drift, idiot."

Juvenal began sawing into the snow. "How far?"

"Inside, the hole should be three meters square."

As Juvenal labored, Pablo watched Victor, whose anguish—his head wrapped in a wool scarf the ends of which were jammed beneath the collar of his wool coat—seemed to convey that this hole in the side of a snowdrift wasn't going to do any good. It was hopeless foolishness. He remembered speaking with Victor in the hospital in Santiago, after he had survived the disaster on Aconcagua. A night storm had come in on their camp six thousand meters up. They had planned on a bid for the summit, starting at two the next morning. But now, all the tents had been destroyed, and Victor, panicked and near death, had been able to find only one other person alive, an Indian guide and porter whose name he could not remember. "A strong climber," he had told Pablo, "a man you wouldn't think would ever die." In his hospital bed, Victor had turned his face away from Pablo, releasing his hand from the poet's as he glared at the featureless white ceiling of the room. "A man whom even Death, we all thought, would be afraid to take."

"What happened to him, Victor?"

Victor's face, blackened in several places by frostbite, had seemed unable to move. The whites of his eyes were riddled with red veins. They looked to have been attacked by shock electricity. His lips barely moved as he gathered his resolve to answer. "He gave up."

"Did he say anything?"

"Yes, he asked me to tell his children how..." Victor had swallowed, for a moment unable to speak. "What a fool he had been."

Juvenal sawed the snow as though it were an enemy to be obliterated.

"I didn't know how, then, to make a cave like this." Victor grabbed the saw from Juvenal and cut further into the cavern that expanded into the drift from the head of the grave.

Is he digging everyone else's grave, too? Pablo, certain he had died, guessed that they were burying him. *If Victor is digging the graves of everyone else, who will bury Victor?*

With each cutting, another block of snow came out of the drift, and soon the surface around the edge of the grave was piled high with the blocks, lessening the wind even more. Within an hour, Victor and Juvenal had sawed and dug a cave into the drift large enough for all the men to enter. There were two shelves on either side of the cave, between which was a passageway that was a meter deeper than the shelves.

"Why the shelves?" Juvenal asked.

"Heat rises," Victor said. "The cold goes down. We'll be sleeping on the shelves, and it will be warmer up there."

He had also fashioned a curved ceiling, which he smoothed with the back of the shovel. "The body heat could melt some of this snow up here. So, if the ceiling is wet, and it's smooth, the water flows down the walls, rather than falling on us." Victor took up the torch once more and punched a hole in the ceiling that opened to the outside. "The body puts out carbon monoxide, too, see? If we close the entrance to the cave with some of those blocks of snow, we don't want to suffocate, and that's why this vent is here." He turned to Ramada. "What about the horses?"

"They're all right. We're not far from the forest, and I secured them in the trees. Like *don* Pablo did the other day. They'll huddle up. Protection from the wind."

Pablo had sunk again into sleep, which as before he mistook for death. But this time, he tried imagining how it would be for him to describe such a thing. Here he was, the greatest lyric poet of the twentieth century—"in any language," Picasso had said—slowly turning into a block of frozen meat. What would some poor novelist eventually writing about this event be able to say? *How do you imagine the thoughts of the greatest lyric poet of the century if you're a plodding hack writing for money?* Well, the Englishman Samuel Johnson had said that only a blockhead would write for anything else but money. Cervantes writing the second Quixote novel because he had run out of cash. Shakespeare, a player desperate for sales to his own plays, writing to entice the audience into The Globe. Charles Dickens not wanting to disappoint his readers, who were paying good money for the magazine they were buying. He had had a practice of writing the exact number of words it would take to get to the very end of the column he was expected to fill. Pablo himself, writing endlessly and publishing unceasingly because his salary as a diplomat was the equivalent of a few forsaken *centavos* by comparison to his sales as a poet.

So, a plodding hack may not have a problem at all, Pablo mused, *writing about the slow death, in an ice-lined grave far from God, of the other hack Pablo Neruda.*

But what would I say about it, he wondered, *if I had such an opportunity?*

Pablo mused. *Delia. Love, so like Delia. Blue, the starry night now turned black, the stars faraway intimations of the presence of love. Diamonds, like ice, except that ice, in blindness like this, becomes silver and galactic, its stars drowned in endless light.*

19
COW HEAD

A cold sky shone down upon them the next morning, the sun like a jeweled coin. The most that Pablo could muster was to console Tuerto, who had spent the night out in the storm. The horse was in better shape than he was though, so that Pablo actually wished that Tuerto would pat his neck and flanks, instead of he Tuerto's.

But tradition prevailed, and the man offered solace to the horse.

The clearing in the middle of which they had spent the night opened into a high valley meadow. With no tree cover, the meadow revealed itself as a broad snow-bound bowl surrounded by forest that shined in the bright daylight like white marble. The meadow, velveted with drifts that were shaped by the undulant ground beneath them, appeared fully undulant itself. To Pablo's mind, the drifts too would benefit from a caress. The glacial mountains on both sides of the meadow reared up like stallions in ragged, glittering lines into the distance.

As Juvenal and Ramada were digging out a fire pit from the snow, they came upon a skull, buried in white. It was very old. The bull had been enormous, and each of the two horns had a majestic S-shaped curve, the left one of which ended in a precise point. The other had been broken at some time in the past, so that the delicacy of a finely honed horn had long deteriorated. Now it was simply ragged broken bone. Pablo liked that because, in his imagination, it made the bull into a lumbering working-class laborer that had had to struggle for everything he had attained. A Communist steer. A bull huge and low to the ground, muscled and slow, barely capable of thought, but a grand animal.

"I believe I know the man who put this here," Pablo said. He watched as Ramada placed the skull on top of the snow a short distance from the fire pit. Pablo had awakened badly weakened by his exposure to the storm the previous night. But the fact that he was indeed not dead had settled his anxieties considerably. Kindling a fire, Juvenal pushed the sticks about, seeking the right combination of dryness and space to draw the heated air up through the wood.

"In fact, I knew him well."

Juvenal grunted. "You seem to be recovering, *don* Pablo."

Pablo looked to the others. The startlingly well-etched lines of the *cordillera* mountains formed precisely lush vectors, straight and clear after the blindness of the snow the afternoon and night before. Here in this vast open space, with this fire and the beans and potatoes that they were about to cook and eat, the sky pulsed with such light that the blue canopy above seemed to absorb the very height of the peaks all around. Indeed, to Pablo the mountains appeared literally to have fled the earth and joined the sky, like terraced gargantuan stalagmites.

"His name was Álvar Nuñez Cabeza de Vaca."

Victor leaned back against the fallen log that supported him and laced his hands behind his head. "I've always wondered, Pablo, how a man's family name could be 'Cow Head'. We all used to laugh at it when we were students. Imagine! What kind of Spaniard would have the name Cabeza de Vaca?"

Pablo imagined that Álvar himself had asked the same question.

—

"It's because, my son..." Álvar's mother Teresa held the boy's head against her cheek, to sooth his sadness. Boys at the local church of Cristo El Rey, where they were training as acolytes, had teased Álvar that afternoon about his name. "Cow Head! Cow Head!" They had laughed at him, chasing after him, and the boy had run home crying.

"There was a very brave man many years ago, to whom you are directly related." Teresa was so kind, Álvar's mother, a refuge for him in any difficulty, with whom the boy, who was eight, could share all unhappiness. On this afternoon, she dressed simply in a long gray skirt and a plain blouse with puffed long sleeves, and old wooden shoes. She had been supervising the washing of linens by Rowena, her servant girl. But she had not allowed the workaday necessity for plain dress to diminish the beauty of the amber necklace she wore, a gift from her husband, the *hidalgo* Francisco Núñez de Vera, or the intensity of the dark blue wool turban with which she had circled her head. The only trouble with the turban for Álvar was that it hid his mother's generous black hair, something he had dreamed about even as a very small boy. Teresa had all of Álvar's love because, although she did not herself read, she loved how important it was to him that he please the priests and his own tutor, a Christian blackamoor named Gabo Menesis, when they tasked him with reading verses from The Bible. "Three hundred years ago, that man fought against the bloody Moor at a place called Las Navas de Tolosa."

"He was a soldier, *mami*?"

"No. A shepherd. But he was Christian, and the Moors, who had lived in our country for many centuries, were of a different faith."

"They weren't Catholics?"

"No, heaven forbid!" Teresa laughed. "And the Catholic armies were trying to push them out of our country. So, Grandfather Martín..." Teresa took Álvar's left hand in her own and played with his fingers as she spoke. "Martín Alhaja was his name. The Moors had hidden an army in the mountains, and Martín knew where they were. He told the Christians that he would place the head of a cow on the road before them that led into the mountains, and that they should not follow that road because the Moors would be waiting further along it, to ambush them." She smiled, taking up Álvar's other hand. "The Christians took advantage of that information and were able to circle behind the Moors and attack them. So, the Christians won the battle."

"And what happened to Martín?"

"The king made him a nobleman." Teresa placed a hand on Álvar's head.

"A count? A duke?"

"Something like that, yes. And because of the way in which he had helped the Christians, he decided to change his name to Cabeza de Vaca."

"Cow Head."

"That's right. He was your great-great-great..." Teresa smiled, fingering her necklace. "I don't know how many 'greats' he was. But he was the grandfather of my grandfather's grandfather's grandfather. And so, my Alvarito..." Teresa released Álvar and helped him to sit up straight. She looked into his eyes and tousled his hair. "That's why your name is Cabeza de Vaca, and you can tell the other boys in church that the original Cabeza de Vaca made himself a great hero in the Crusade against the Moors."

—

The sun had passed mid-sky, and no shadow appeared anywhere in the meadow. The canopy of the sky remained calm over a windless, motionless sea made from snow.

"Thirty years later..." Pablo stirred the fire. "In 1527, Álvar was shipwrecked on the coast of North America." Smoke blew up into his eyes, and he turned away, waving his hand before his face. "He had been the treasurer of an expedition of four ships to the New World, with four hundred men, which had been led by a Spaniard named Narváez."

"I had an uncle with the same name," Ramada said. "Celedonio Narváez. He was a carpenter."

"It's a good enough name, Ramada, although this fellow unfortunately was a fool."

"As was *tio* Celedonio."

Pablo sensed from the young man's tone of voice that Ramada may indeed have loved his uncle despite whatever the older man had done to gain his reputation. "Narváez had been given ownership of the southern third of North America by—"

"More than just a meadow, eh?" Juvenal said.

"Yes. By the king, even though they didn't know much about the southern third of North America. And in Florida, where they had first landed, the Indians had attacked and killed half of the men on the expedition. Narvaez made a number of rafts out of trees, and the survivors sailed to the west, away from Florida. But a great storm attacked them from the sea, and those who were not killed by the storm were captured by Indians. After a while only Álvar and three others were still alive."

"But not Narvaez?" Ramada grinned, intuiting the answer.

"Sadly, no. He floated out to sea."

Ramada shook his head.

"Face down. So maybe he *was* like your Uncle Celedonio."

"What happened to the four survivors?" Juvenal asked.

Pablo nodded. "They walked to the west coast of Mexico."

"That's far?" Juvenal spooned beans onto his tin plate.

"Thousands of kilometers, *amigo*. A lot of jungle, and then mostly desert."

"How long did it take them?"

Pablo leaned forward and caressed the broken horn of the bull's skull. What had once been white bone was now yellowed and pitted with the effects of many decades of mountain weather. If anything, the ruin of it gave the skull a kind of manly brio. This had been a tough animal that had died reluctantly.

"Eight years."

He took a cigar from his jacket pocket and chewed off one end of it. Now the meadow glimmered with late morning light, and there was no movement in any of the trees all around. Lighting the cigar, Pablo took in a few puffs, removed it from his mouth and examined it. Smoke gathered before him.

"And in those eight years, they were taken captive many times by Indian tribes along the way. Enslaved and imprisoned. But Cabeza de Vaca was some sort of genius. For one, he taught the Indians how to till. One man in front with straps around his shoulders...." Pablo gestured toward the others. "Imagine a man named Cow Head pretending he was a bull for people who couldn't even imagine what a bull was. How do you explain a bull to someone who's never seen one?"

Pablo pointed to the skull.

"This might even be…" He laughed. "Cabeza de Vaca himself, for all we know." He patted the skull on its pate. "So, one man in front, another behind, the straps attached to a stout stick. He taught them how to seed, how to grow. He learned the Indians' languages, many of them, and became a kind of *brujo* to them. A sorcerer. And a *curandero*, too. A medicine man."

"He could doctor to them?"

"Even more. He contended in the book he wrote about it that he brought people back to life."

Juvenal shuddered. "They say there were people like that up here in these mountains too. In the very old times." He looked around him, into the distance of the sun-livened snow. "And I believe it." He turned back toward Pablo. "I suppose a man like you, though, *don* Pablo, a man of books and words, an educated man...you wouldn't believe such a thing."

"I most certainly do believe it, Juvenal. For me it's as true as—"

Ramada held up a hand and pointed into the distance, at a small trail that emerged from the trees on the far side of the meadow. A single horseman appeared. He spurred his animal several meters into the meadow, then halted and remained still for a moment as he studied Juvenal's fire and the men enjoying it. The horse was quite ragged, with a wooden saddle and wooden stirrups. The rider, a *gaucho*, wore a long red and black poncho similar to Juvenal's. A rolled-up wool blanket circled his neck. His broadbrimmed hat was made of black felt or some such, the brim turned up in back, angled down in front. He had a great black beard, and the *bombacha* pantaloons he wore were ripped on one leg. They were probably the only pair he had, it being clear that they were quite old.

After a moment he turned and gestured back up the trail. A herd of about twenty steers came out into the open, along with two other *gauchos*, followed by a two-wheel flatbed work wagon pulled by a team of very slow beaten-down oxen. The wood-spoke wheels were enormous, coopered around the outside edge with tooled iron, constructed, Pablo knew, so that the wagon could make it over fallen trunks and across deep snowfields. He had seen such wagons in the port of Buenos Aires, which had been used to transport cargo from sailing ships through the shallows of the harbor before it had been dredged and deepened for deep-hull craft. Now those wagons were displayed as charming artifacts from a romantic past.

This wagon, however, proceeded with ragged creaks and groans. It was half fallen apart.

The other *gauchos* kept a distance from the fire, not wishing to speak to Pablo and his friends. Juvenal held the plate below his chin, the spoon in his right hand. His lined face had a general downturn. It was not of anger. Nor was it a frown. Rather his eyes widened into an expression of astonishment.

"Who are they?" Pablo asked.

"Don't know."

"And you say that rustlers don't come up here anymore?"

Juvenal laid the plate on the snow and leaned forward, his elbows on his knees. He pushed his *sombrero* to the back of his head. The *gauchos* did not speak, and indeed appeared unwilling to risk any sort of contact. The cattle were barely able to walk. Dying—"Maybe dead," Pablo mumbled to himself—they complained and moaned as they advanced. All three men appeared to have come through the same terrible storm as Pablo and the others, something they had barely survived. Their clothes hung in rags. They were so gaunt that their very bones pressed out against the skin on their faces.

"That's what I've always been told." Juvenal took up the plate and fingered the spoon. "In my lifetime I haven't seen such people up here."

Finally, the first of the *gauchos* spurred his horse forward, angling through the drifts across the meadow. Juvenal stood. Pablo did as well. The *gaucho*'s horse moved very slowly, his head hung down. The man scratched his beard with his left hand as he approached. He appeared to have difficulty sitting up straight in the saddle.

"*Caballeros.*"

No one spoke. The *gaucho* and his animal seemed insubstantial to Pablo, like mere suggestions of a man and a horse.

"Forgive me, *amigos*. You know the way, don't you?"

"Yes," Juvenal said.

Pablo, standing next to him, felt Juvenal's fright.

"We're going to San Martín de Los Andes."

"That's good." As the *gaucho* pulled once more at his beard with the dirt-scummy fingers of his right hand, it became clear that he had only half his teeth. He turned in the saddle and pointed back to the west, back into the *cordillera*. "We weren't sure you knew where you were. It's so bad back there. So easy to lose the way."

"You saw us?" Pablo asked.

"Yes. That is, *señor*…" He pointed at Pablo. "We saw you." He leaned forward in the saddle. "Back there by the lake. And we saw you were in difficulty."

"What kind of difficulty?"

"The soul." The *gaucho* rubbed his chin. "I mean, we're in difficulty like that, so we know what it is."

"What troubles do you have?"

"Dreams." The *gaucho* grimaced. His face appeared to lose its musculature. "And, of course, so much snow." He gestured toward the sky. "We wander from snow to snow, year in, year out."

"I see."

"You do see. That's why we wanted to help you." The *gaucho* nodded toward the skull. Light shivered across his hands as they took up the reins of his horse. "I watched that steer being born, you know. *Una bestia de fina estampa, digamos.* A beast of a fine stamp, we say." He sighed, leaning on the wooden horn of his saddle. "But now he's been dead a very long time."

Movement came from the other *gauchos*, who were impatient to go.

"So go with God, *amigos*. San Martín de Los Andes, it's far from here."

"Thank you, *hermano,* we know." Pablo pointed to the fire. "May we offer you some food?"

"No…no. We—"

"What's your name?"

"Dominguín, maestro. And yours?"

"Pablo Neruda."

Dominguín scratched his beard once more, shaking his head. "I don't believe I've heard of you."

"No, I expect not."

"Well, *chicos*, good luck." Dominguín turned his mount away. The horse moved with sighing slowness through the drifts. Suddenly Dominguín brought the horse to a stop and looked back toward Pablo and the others. "You know the lava tunnel?"

"Yes," Juvenal said. "It's up ahead, isn't it?"

"Yes, and after a storm like the one we just had, you'd never make it out of here without the tunnel."

"I agree."

The other *gauchos* spurred their horses, and once Dominguín had rejoined them, they moved slowly toward the forest. In the gleaming sunlight and the snow, each movement of each animal became clarified and so enhanced by the glare that Pablo and the others could miss nothing. The cattle—*debased animals*, Pablo thought, *moth-eaten*—moved as well, as did the oxen and the wagon. Dominguín touched the brim of his hat with the fingers of his left hand and took up the long reins with which he had been guiding his horse, snapping them against the horse's flank. The others began shouting at the cattle and, frightened by the *gauchos* and their mounts, by their shadow-like voices and whistling, the cattle moved arthritically toward the trees at the far side of the meadow, into the black shadows of which they disappeared.

20

DELIA AND THE PHOTOGRAPHER

Robert seemed glamorously distracted, as indeed, Delia knew, he had been since Gerda had died so long ago. Delia herself had been distracted before that event because Pablo had been briefly in love with Gerda Taro, smitten by her extraordinary and immediate rise to world fame, and by her beauty. "*La pequeña rubia*" was her nickname, and Pablo had once said to Gerda, in Delia's presence, that he was only sorry that it had not been he who had given her the nickname. The Little Blonde.

"Robert, how wonderful to see you." Delia kissed her guest's cheek as he entered the apartment and embraced her.

"I've missed you too, Delia." Just with these five words, Delia recalled how she had cherished his Hungarian accent, so lovely in his speaking of Spanish that she had on occasion asked him to read for her…something from García Lorca or de Argensola or Cervantes, just so she could listen to his tremulous, strange accent.

"Have you got any news about Pablo?" Robert laid his Leica on a side table as Delia took his coat. "Here's something I brought for you." He handed her a slim, flat box.

Robert Capa had briefly been a close friend of Pablo and Delia, a dozen years before. By then he had already become famous, and his politics for the Spanish Civil War had been, before they had all met, so much in concert with theirs that a friendship seemed a natural probability. With Gerda Taro, Robert had come to Valencia for an enormous convention of writers in support of the Second Spanish Republic, in July 1937. The war had entered a chaotic phase, and Pablo had been given money by the Republican government to organize the convention. Robert and Gerda had asked for press passes, and Pablo had hurried to arrange them within minutes after he had met them and been taken by Gerda's sweet loveliness. He enjoyed the irony that, judging from her photographs, she seemed to be afraid of nothing.

One picture by Robert himself had especially convinced Pablo of this. It had been taken in an urban setting, with what appeared to be a multi-story apartment building in the background. In the foreground, their backs shored up against a high mound of dirt, two crouching people were under fire. One—a Republican soldier, his rifle in his left hand as he looked over his right shoulder, seeking an opportunity to fire back at the sniper or the gun emplacement whose fire had forced the two to take cover—was terrified. The other figure was Gerda Taro who, dressed in a wrinkled shirt with rolled-up long sleeves, a pair of pants and dirty shoes, was also looking over her shoulder, in the same direction as the soldier. She had a Rolleiflex in her hands and was waiting for the moment to take her next picture.

"Look at her, Delia," Pablo had said. "The soldier's more afraid than she is."

When they had finally met, Pablo's first congratulation went to Gerda and her calm during that moment. Later he recalled who else had been there, and he had taken Robert's hand, thanking him for the photograph.

Now, Delia took the box from Robert into her hand.

"Those are the pictures I took of you that day." Robert sat down on a chair by the apartment window. "You remember? In Valencia."

"Oh, Robert."

Robert was as grim, swashbuckling, and handsome as he had been in 1937, although now he was thirty-six years old and had in the meantime covered World War II and a few of the post-colonial wars. He had aged, looking weathered now, as though the wars had scoured him. She had read that he was thinking about going to Vietnam, a country about which Delia knew very little. He had just arrived in Paris from Israel, where he had photographed the founding of that country and its 1948 war.

"I wanted you to have these because, Delia, I…." Robert gazed at her in silence. He smelled of whiskey.

"Would you like a glass of wine?"

"Please."

When she brought him the wine, Robert told Delia that he loved the dress she was making, still on its mannequin in a corner of the living room. "Gerda never did that sort of thing. She never had time. She wasn't very fashionable."

"But I've seen the picture of the two of you in Paris." Delia sat down across the coffee table from Robert. She fingered the box he had given her. Fred Stein's photograph had showed Robert and Gerda at a Parisian café, outdoors, enjoying some sort of intimate moment in the conversation. They were in their mid-twenties, dressed quite fashionably, especially Gerda, who was wearing a little French beret and a precisely fitted wool suit. They were both smiling, a couple in love, sophisticated, sensual….

"Yes, but a needle and thread?" Robert smiled. "Never."

That day in 1937, Delia had been suffering from jealousy of Gerda and her toying with Pablo. Pablo was some years older than Gerda, but Delia was twenty years older than Pablo. The young woman's freshness and youth fascinated Pablo. He wanted her.

But Robert too had been jealous because Gerda had been distracted by the great Neruda, who was the bard of South America and the famed apologist for the Second Spanish Republic. So, while Pablo and Gerda had gone out for a walk around Valencia, Robert had escorted Delia to the apartment in which she and Pablo were staying and had asked her if he could take some pictures.

Delia was ravenous to open the box, to see what he had done. But as she looked up at Robert, to get his permission, she saw that for the moment he barely noticed her presence.

His face slumped in some thoughtful sadness. "I miss her, you know. It's never been the same, really, since…" Robert scratched the back of his neck, shaking his head. "Since she died."

Delia posed for many pictures that day, and Robert's manner, his lovely accent, and his eyes all seemed to her bewitching. The camera had a sensuous gaze all its own, as though relieving her of her skirt and blouse, caressing the white silk of her slip, removing it to expose her shoulder, her thigh, and her wishes for Robert. They spent an hour together, and Delia's wishes were…well, in a way…realized. Robert asked her to stand, to recline on the little day couch in the apartment, or to lean against the doorjamb that led to the narrow balcony with its view of Valencia rooftops. The sound itself of the shutter opening and closing excited Delia, as though each photo were a suggestion from Robert that they kiss or that he caress Delia's neck, or she his.

But no.

He left finally, to meet Gerda in a café. Robert was to travel a few days later to Paris, and Gerda was to go to the town of Brunete, to cover a battle there that could be very decisive for the Republican forces. The word was that they were in house-to-house combat with Franco's troops.

"Yes, I should never have let her go there." Robert fell into further sorrow, as though he were quite alone. "How could that driver not have seen the tank? How is it he didn't swerve, Delia? How could she die so quickly?" Robert looked up into Delia's eyes. Light from the windows shadowed his face. "I would have photographed her had I been there." He put the glass of wine aside. "Imagine photographing your lover's ruined body." He grimaced. "The way she just…disappeared beneath that terrible machine. Gone. My love. Always my love."

Delia poured a bit more wine for Robert as she recalled her own tattered anguish during the funeral service in Paris, attended by thousands, at which she had had to minister to Pablo as he too had wept for Gerda Taro.

21
LOS DUENDES

The three men with Pablo relaxed, exhausted about the edges of the fire pit. Fed and rested, they were nonetheless spent, especially Juvenal, who, after the conversation with Dominguín, had lain down by the fire beneath his coat and a blanket.

"I'll be able to stand up eventually."

Pablo had helped bed him down.

"But not until tomorrow, damn you, poet." A grizzled smile came up from the snow. "Don't wake me until then."

The men dozed. They were crumpled and exhausted like piles of rags. To Pablo they all appeared as newly materializing specters, closely gathered in the late afternoon cold sun. The light caressed them with diminishing warmth. Pablo assumed that he looked as beaten as all the others, and that made him feel that, together, they had become *duendes de las montañas*, ghosts of the mountains, although he well knew that a *duende* is far more than just a ghost. The word, so old in Spanish, defines an elf, a magical being. *What do they call them in English?* he thought. *That strange word, so difficult to pronounce. A hobgoblin. And the other English word, what is it? A bogeyman? A trickster. All those things.*

And also the striving spirit that enables life itself. Tongues in trees. Books in the running brooks.

So, this small gathering of men and horses had come together for a profane congress of some sort, to bewitch this snow-crusted clearing and all that surrounded it. Juvenal's rough features peering out from beneath the blanket appeared chipped and badly gouged. Ramada snoozed, a figure of

Indian masculine serenity but for his wounded knee and the anguish it had caused him. The badly lamed Victor's head lay sideways on his gathered hands, he the rugged searcher, wounded woodsman, and counselor to the naive poet Neruda. Victor, who could explain the forest to the poet and, more important, explain the poet to the forest, for which—Pablo grinned— the forest had punished Victor...although it had allowed Victor to save Pablo and all the others with The Cave of Snows. The horses and poor, grumpy Miedo, they too were *duendes*, witless animals that could do such fantastic things nonetheless.

Could The Weird Sisters have predicted this, back there in the woods? It had been just one tree, battled with in three different places. But as he had been chopping at it, trying to cut a way through, Pablo had also told Victor and Ramada about the Graeae, the three sea-demons, all gray from birth, who were the waves of the gray-capped sea who constantly murmured imprecations and cautions. Between them, they had one eye, but with that eye they saw the truth, the future, and the meaning of the past. They handed it back and forth, and, chopping, Pablo had recounted how as a boy he had imagined that the eye must be slathered with blood and hanging tendrils, ripped from one forehead and shoved into place in the next.

"You know, we're lucky, *don* Pablo." Juvenal, not yet asleep, intervened in the poet's thoughts. Light from the sun rippled across him.

"Yes, we're free, Juvenal. We survived the snow." Pablo was certain now that he and the others had rendered The Weird Sisters blind, and that the great *cordillera* and all its misery were a failure.

"But—"

"We evaded the darkness at the center of the forest. We survived the black night. We were blinded by snow, Juvenal. Nearly drowned."

"Yes, well, that too." Juvenal had come close to sleep. "And we can still see. Far into the distance."

Pablo looked off toward the mountains. These particular peaks upheld the sky and surrounded the four men. Others further east awaited them. Still others surrounded those that waited, and all were beset with snow. All could kill you. *And in this light*, Pablo thought as he turned himself to the last bit of meat on his tin plate, as the lowering sun nudged against the edge of a peak far to the west, causing the snow on other mountains to burn yellow and, farther away, soft-hued pink and somber blue, *in such light we can now see clearly, and assure each other that we are alive.*

22

EL HISPANO

But soon, still subdued by the unperturbed mountain range before him and the troubles it would bring to him and the others, Pablo allowed himself a particularly dark moment of worry. After what they had seen, what more could there be? Oddly and luckily the single remaining chunk of beef on his plate reminded him of *El Hispano*, the laughter of Ezequiel Ruibal, as well as of *The Winnipeg*, so smelling of fish.

Yes…Ezequial's glee, the kind that remains in the hearts of the saddened, those deprived of their family, those far from home. Laughter, nonetheless.

—

"Welcome to Buenos Aires!"

Pablo and Delia were visiting Argentina for a few days before sailing for France. He had been asked by the new president of Chile, Pedro Aguirre Cerda, to become a special consul for Spanish emigration, to help Republican army soldiers imprisoned in France to emigrate to Chile. The waiter Ezequiel had brought menus to Pablo and Delia a moment earlier, and now placed a glass each of malbec before them on the table. He stepped back and took out his pad and pencil. It was January, 1939.

"What would you like, *señores*?"

He was a celebratory man, glancing for a moment from his notepad out the window onto *calle* Salta. With a mustache and a jowly smile and large hands, he had a kind of priestly authority, although really he more resembled a Spanish laborer, someone who would look quite right carrying a bag of sand on his shoulder. As in Madrid, the *de rigueur* clothing for Buenos Aires waiters was a long-sleeved white shirt, a black bow tie, black slacks and, occasionally, a long apron either white or black. Ezequiel's was black with pin-striped gold thread, a jaunty adornment. He was about thirty years old.

Pablo and Delia had just made it through the front door of the *Restaurante El Hispano* before a summer tempest had broken open, the beginning of a massive storm of rain and hail. Outside, the street flowed silvery with the ricochet of great water in many directions, and there was little foot traffic. A woman under a slender umbrella tried to run from the storm. A taxi driver hurried from a doorway to his parked cab. Otherwise, the empty street showed little in the dark. Its buildings were from the late nineteenth century, two- and three-story apartment complexes whose *persiana* wood shutters were shut tight against the storm.

The street had a romantic feeling, lit as it was out their tableside window by just a single streetlamp. Pablo thought of the many tangos whose lyrics extol the loneliness of a single light on a dark street. The way this rain took advantage of the light made the rain appear like wayward sparkling glass as it fell to the street. Shattered lightning. The parked cars were animals hunkering down below the fevered cataract. Once the taxi had driven away, there was no foot traffic of any kind and no moving automobiles. The storm took over, fiercely so, a rage of water and wind.

The *Restaurante El Hispano* was one of many in an old *gallego* neighborhood in Buenos Aires, "*gallego*" being the descriptive term for all people of Spanish Iberian heritage in that city. Not altogether a flattering word, it is often used to express an opinion about someone's slowness of perception, someone's stupidity. Luckily there were such words for every ethnic group in Buenos Aires. In this city you could call someone a name and have it be simply a humorous part of the discourse. As such it made Buenos Aires Spanish a complete pleasure for Pablo, as he hated over-respectful and therefore phony politesse. In any case this neighborhood, off the *Avenida de Mayo* near the corner with *Avenida 9 de Julio*, was central to those who had emigrated from Spain.

The interior of *El Hispano* held many simple wood tables that were stained dark brown, with similar chairs. A number of wrapped cured hams hung over the bar, and yellow-white curtains covered the windows. The lyricism of Spanish song flowed through the place, the feel of *The Three-Cornered Hat*, of Enrique Granados (that poor fellow, Pablo thought, going down on a ship sunk by the Germans during the World War, his jaunty music cut short), the Moorish garden, the colonial town plaza, *los flamencos*, Miura bulls, and *la guitarra*. Maps of Spain decorated the walls, along with old photos of Spanish street scenes. The restaurant's blood beat with the lush warmth of a Spanish village.

Water in the street rose almost to the sidewalk. Lightning flashed often and not so far in the distance, so that the accompanying thunder was immediate and extremely noisy. As a result of the storm Pablo and Delia were the only patrons in the restaurant, and the warmth of the place, enhanced by its very Hispanic romanticism, made them feel safe from the savagery of the wind and the rain.

"How beautiful the storm is." Delia used the word "*tormenta*", perfect for the tortured immediacy and sheer largeness of the lightning strikes. She had glanced out the window just as a jolting brilliance broke from the sky. The green cotton dress she wore, which Pablo had bought for her in Mexico a year or so earlier, was ankle-length, embroidered across the bodice with a dozen tightly woven blood-red cotton roses. When she crossed her legs, the dress seemed moved by light filaments that were part of the cloth itself. She wore a silver necklace, a Mapuche Indian design of a ceremonial bird in flight. In conservative Buenos Aires such dress was a decorous oddity on a beautiful woman, and Delia enjoyed the comments it caused. "I wish that all stormy unhappiness could be as exciting as this."

Water gushed down the windowpane as though the flat surface were a set of rapids.

"Yes, *señora*," Ezequiel said. "It reminds me of the war."

"Which one?"

"Ours."

Delia and Pablo waited a moment for more explanation. There had been many, many wars in Argentina: colonial ones, conflicts with the Indians, civil wars. But Ezequiel spoke with an unusual accent for a Buenos Aires *porteño*. He was a Spaniard. So, Pablo had a sense of what he would say next.

"Yours?"

"Yes, *señor,* the one in the restaurant. Here."

Startled, not understanding, Pablo imagined an assault upon *El Hispano*, its front corner door of heavy ironwood maybe a hundred years old, decorated with iron fixtures, its glass panels expertly beveled. A large barricade, maybe, with an Argentine flag flying from it, sandbags and turrets, Ezequiel at the ready with a rifle and a helmet, taking his stand. But against whom?

A flash of lightning lit the street.

"Where are you from, *amigo*?"

Ezequiel tapped his notepad with the end of the pencil. "Madrid."

"And your family's still there?"

"I hope so." He removed the point of his pencil from the surface of the paper. Two other waiters stood at the bar talking. "I haven't been able to get any news for months, things are so bad there."

"We know. I was my country Chile's cultural attaché in Madrid for a few years."

"Recently? During this war?"

"Yes."

Ezequiel nodded.

"And that's where we're going now."

"To do what, *señor*?"

"You know about the concentration camps in France?"

"Of course, where they're keeping Republican troops."

"That's right. And my government has given me the job of bringing a couple thousand of them to Chile."

Ezequiel grimaced, suddenly so saddened that he cast a sidelong glance at the floor. "Would you keep an eye out for someone named Gustavo Ruibal? Or Pedro and María Luisa Ruibal?"

"Who are they?"

"My brother and my parents."

Pablo centered his gaze on the pencil, noting how steady it was in Ezequiel's hand. He glanced up at the waiter and saw that he was studying the bright illuminated circle that came from the small lamp that rested on their table. Pablo recalled, as though they too were a splash of warm light, the words from the great Carlos Gardel's first recorded tango:

"Y la lampara del cuarto
también tu ausencia ha sentido
porque su luz no ha querido
mi noche triste alumbrar."

(*"And the lamp in the room*
also has felt your absence
because its light has not wished
to illuminate my sad night.")

"I don't know if they're alive."

Pablo and Delia remained silent a moment, respecting Ezequiel's worry.

"But what war did you fight here?" Pablo asked.

Ezequiel pointed to the high wall above the restaurant bar. "You see those flags?"

There were about six of them, on angled standards that came out from the wall itself. They were made up of three horizontal stripes, of red, yellow, and a kind of purple.

"As you know, those are the flags of the Second Spanish Republic, may God protect them." Ezequiel folded his arms as he looked up at the wall. "Communists. Anarchists. Socialists." He shook his head slowly. "Good people, every one of them." Sighing, he turned and laid the pencil once more on the notepad, ready to take the order.

"They're different from the Franco flags," Pablo said.

Ezequiel looked up. "Right. Francisco Franco is a simpleton. So, his are just red and yellow." He gestured around the restaurant. "And this place, this is our land here. This is a Republican restaurant."

"There are Franco restaurants in this neighborhood?" Pablo gestured out into the street.

"There are. And there have been battles between us. Luckily there's a Communist cafe down the block that fought on our side." Ezequiel smiled. "A cheese store, too. No anarchist places, though. It's tough to have to argue it out every time over how to make a good flan."

A gust of wind peppered the window with rain.

"The cooks in all the restaurants on this block are Republicans. The waiters, Republicans, every one of them. The customers, too. A Franco customer would get thrown out." Ezequiel began laughing. It was a sudden turn to full-throated enjoyment that brightened the entire restaurant. "And there have been fights in the streets, when our waiters have gone after theirs."

Ezequiel used the pencil as a kind of kris, in a brief cartoon knife fight with an invisible enemy.

"Or theirs after us. A year ago, we fought a battle here, when a bunch of bastards from a place called *El Tiburón* came in through that door and attempted taking down our flags." Ezequiel frowned. "Imagine! A seafood place." He frowned even more deeply. "They invaded the kitchen with soup ladles and rolling pins. *Maldito* fascist soup ladles."

"Who won?" Delia asked.

"Who won!" Ezequiel's frown was quickly replaced by a broad, gold-lined smile. He placed the hand holding the pencil against his heart. Lightning dazzled the street outside. "*Che*, with all due respect to you, *señora*, what do you think? Our guys won."

"Bravo."

"But enough of that, *amigos*. It's kind of you to ask."

"It matters to us." Pablo took Delia's hand and kissed the backs of her fingers.

"I can see. But for the moment I care about the state of your hunger, especially on a night like this." Ezequiel gestured toward the sidewalk. The storm had increased. "And we can't have our Chilean Republican friends go hungry, especially someone as distinguished as you."

"No, Ezequiel. We're simple travelers looking for a meal."

"But you are Pablo Neruda."

Pablo shrugged. It had happened again, as it seemed to be happening more and more.

"I've read your poems about Federico García Lorca, a great hero. We can't have a man like you come to Argentina without feeding him." Ezequiel smiled toward Delia. "And…" He glanced toward Pablo. "…*Con permiso, señor*, his beautiful wife."

"Thank you." Delia squeezed Pablo's hand.

"Poor Federico." Pablo surveyed the rain a moment, which made him feel that he and Delia, Ezequiel and the restaurant itself, all of Buenos Aires and even all of Spain could soon be washed into the Atlantic.

"You were close friends, I know," Ezequiel said.

Observed in silence by Delia, both men fell into momentary mourning. Each other's suddenly discovered feelings intermingled in a moment of longing for just one more conversation—in Ezequiel's case through the poems composed by a cherished compatriot; in Pablo's a muscular exchanging of poetic ideas, how to progress a thought, how to extend a metaphor, and how someone like Emily Dickinson might have done it—with their mutual old friend, Federico.

"What may I serve you, *maestro*?"

"The *paella, hermano*. We'll share. *Una ensalada mixta y una botella de vino tinto*. And please, bring a third glass for yourself."

"*Muy bién*." Ezequiel wrote it down with a flourish.

23
DELIA'S SLEEVES

"No, the sleeves aren't right." Cocteau peered at them through his glasses, picking at one of them with his fingers.

Delia examined one of the leg o' muttons that she had sewn. She had thought they were beautiful, striped a kind of egg-white blue and emerald-green. They bloomed from either side of the dress's bodice, two large puffs of silk that then gathered themselves into wrist-length narrow tubes that sensuously followed the narrowing line of the dress's waist. Perfect, she thought, for the long green gown that she was making for Pablo's arrival.

She had sewn several versions of the sleeves, toiles for each. Her favorite kind of sleeve was a ruched one, but it took forever to do and, if you made a single mistake, the bunched cloth had to be un-ruched and then re-ruched. Delia liked short, pleated sleeves too, with a bit of scalloped embroidery. But that hadn't seemed right for this dress. Too flighty. Her mother had taught her about blind hemming, and Delia was expert at it. For a lover to actually see the stitching was an unacceptable compromise, so she had done the extra work to make sure that her hemming was totally blind. Even so, the sleeves had bored her. Delia thought about interfacing, also, but it was too much work if you were forever taking apart the sleeves you didn't like. Besides, it was difficult to figure out the seam allowance.

To make a long story short, Delia was frustrated.

Cocteau had arrived a half hour earlier, and Delia had shown him the dress on its mannequin. The leg o' muttons were basted to the dress, a temporary solution for the great Cocteau to approve.

When he saw it, he laughed. "Oh, honey. You want a man to take in a breath as though it were his very first when he sees you, *non*? But those bags hanging from your shoulders? It won't happen."

Everyone knew that Cocteau was in love with Picasso. So, would he know what a man wants to see in a woman? Cocteau was himself dressed in a dark gray wool suit and vest, a white shirt and one of the new Hermes silk neckties, introduced by the company a month or so before. They were already just the thing for the well-dressed Parisian. His hair was gummed, so that it fit his skull like lacquer. He moved very slimly, his fingers like silk feathers.

"But put it on anyway, *ma belle*." He brought a cigarette to his lips. The smoke rose across his face like a filament of airy fleece.

They had had dinner the week before, at a small place Cocteau knew on the Île Saint-Louis, the *Saint-Regis*. He liked it because the food was good and the waiters young. They had been talking about *Beauty and the Beast*, Cocteau's movie that had premiered in Paris a few years earlier.

"Oh, Jean, the dress Belle wears when she's letting the beast drink water from her hands—"

"You liked it?" Cocteau spooned his soup.

"Beautiful, the way it reveals her shoulders."

Cocteau placed the spoon on its plate and daubed his lips with the napkin. "I'd love to make a dress like that for you, Delia."

"Oh, my Pablo would love it."

Cocteau's face fell. He liked Neruda well enough, but Neruda was a kind of beast himself. One of these wild South Americans. Tall, baggy, and so much disorganized poetry. How had such a slovenly-minded artist become so famous? But Cocteau kept that opinion to himself. Neruda was perhaps dead, and Delia clearly loved him in a way that, Cocteau knew, he himself did not understand.

He waited now for Delia, who had stepped behind a screen to put on the dress. He grumped impatiently and silently, exhaling as he glanced toward the screen. He brought the cigarette to his lips and inhaled as though the cigarette were so beneath contempt as to be unfashionable. But suddenly Cocteau glimpsed small rivulets of Delia's bare skin in the spaces between the three cloth sections of the screen. The movement excited him, the possibility to examine her skin and to touch it. When she stepped back out into the room, having also put on a pair of quite beautiful lime-green pumps, she was nonetheless embarrassed by her dress.

Delia didn't know what to say.

"No, the whole thing is wrong." Cocteau reached for one of the sleeves and pulled it off, breaking the basted stitching with one tight-lipped motion. He examined it a moment, impatient with its design, and then let it slip to the floor. "This one, too." The second sleeve came off, and Cocteau stepped back to observe what he had done. He appeared shocked. "Those arms, Delia. With arms like those, you don't need the sleeves." He gestured toward the mirror on the armoire behind her. "Where did you get such skin?" When she turned to look at herself, she too was stunned by the beauty of what she saw, how, without sleeves of any kind, the dress fell down her slim body like water flow. Her shoulders and arms gleamed, also like water.

She noticed how Cocteau, his cigarette in his right hand at his side, surveyed Delia's back. His eyes passed through a second or two of envy. He then glanced toward the mirror, caught by Delia in the indiscretion.

"Well, honey, that's a dress that *any* man would…would like to…."

24
THE WINNIPEG

The rain that had begun as they had entered *El Hispano* continued with them across the gray Atlantic to Bordeaux. A taxi left Pablo and Delia off at a wharf in Pauillac, the port of Bordeaux, and rain was falling with such force that they had to run up the wooden wharf toward a dilapidated wooden shack on the pilings, in which several men were sheltering themselves. At the far end of the wharf, a quite rusty ship sat heavily in the water. It was an old ship from the World War, Pablo guessed, and smelled of fish. Rust seemed to hold up its very stacks. Its name, *Winnipeg*, struggled to be seen amidst the mold and rust on its stern. Pablo liked the ship. For him, such a vessel showed what work was like. It celebrated difficult tasks. It seldom spoke. It summoned itself to move, although it would never be able to run or fly. Nonetheless, Pablo knew, it always arrived.

—

Numbers of people waited in the line, vying for the last dozen berths on the *Winnipeg*, which the following morning was to take two thousand Spaniards to Chile. The selection of the passengers had filled some of the most guilt-ridden days of Pablo's life. Those he had turned down were as qualified to escape from France as those he had accepted, and there were thousands more. The ghastly, deadening odors and fear-ridden conversation that came from the refugees filled the warehouse. Delia passed coffee and bread to the people waiting. A woman accompanying her pushed a wheelbarrow along that was loaded with old shirts, coats, pants, and shoes, which they distributed to those who were in the worst condition. The line was almost formless, the peoples' faces and desires filled with wounds and scrapes, mud, grime, and the certain pain in the eyes that comes from having been routed bloodily from their homes.

Two men appeared before Pablo.

"What's your name?"

"Leonel Goyeneche."

"Basque?"

"Yes, *señor,* from Álava."

Pablo smiled. "*Babazorros ¿eh?*" Bean-eaters.

Leonel was a very thin man whose face was grizzled with a matted gray beard. "So, you know about us. You've been there?"

Pablo took his hand. "I have."

Leonel wore a long black coat, badly ripped on the right sleeve and threadbare everywhere else. It had no buttons. The collar stood up around Leonel's neck, and Pablo could see that his neck had also been bloodied, a flesh wound of some sort only barely hidden by the long piece of cotton wrapped about his neck. He carried a stained cardboard suitcase in one hand and a wooden cane in the other.

"How old are you?" Pablo said.

"Sixty-one."

"Any papers?"

"Just this." Leonel pulled a deed from a pocket of his coat, a document muddied and slightly torn, and folded in fours. It showed that in 1927 he and his wife María Fernanda had bought a house.

Pablo wrote down the information. "Nothing else?"

"No, *señor*. I lost all my papers during the war."

"How so?"

"That house. It no longer exists. All my papers went up with it."

Pablo added this information, finally turning toward the second man "And you?"

The fellow shrugged. "I'm his brother, *señor* Pablo. Donaldo Goyeneche." He handed Pablo his Spanish Republic identification papers.

"What happened to you?" Pablo pointed at Leonel's neck wound.

"I fell out of a tree."

Pablo wrote this down as well. "Forgive me, but were you were hiding up there?"

"I was."

"Had you deserted?"

"No, *señor* Pablo. I was covering my son."

"What was he doing?"

Leonel took in a long breath, and then leaned forward on his cane. "He was attempting to take out a machine gun nest. He had a grenade."

Pablo looked up. "Did he succeed?"

"No, *señor*."

"What happened to him?"

Leonel's back slowly buckled. He began weeping, and Pablo placed the pen on the ledger book, to wait. Leonel could not speak for several minutes.

Pablo lowered his head. "I'm sorry, Leonel. But after your son…after he…what happened?"

"Leonel killed them all." Donaldo was a very small man with meaty, filthy hands. His clothes were tattered, including the scum-stained beret that held loosely to his black hair. He carried a rolled-up blanket on his back, tied there with rope. He appeared to have eaten almost nothing for quite some time. Despite his filthy wool jacket, he shivered as he spoke.

Leonel continued weeping.

"It took him all night, *señor* Pablo." Donaldo turned toward Leonel. "Didn't it?"

Leonel nodded, placing the palm of his right hand against his forehead.

"Leonel wounded himself coming down from the tree." Donaldo's voice was slurred by his extreme fatigue. "He could barely walk, so he crawled. He waited. There was mud. Rats. Thorns. Then over a couple of hours, he crawled to the perimeter of the machine gun emplacement. Maybe they fell asleep. Maybe they were just careless. It was four in the morning. But Leonel threw a couple of grenades…and killed them."

Pablo continued waiting.

"Every one of them. For his son."

The line behind the two men was impatient. But they seemed to understand from Leonel's lowered head, his bent back, and his weeping, that the conversation was a particularly difficult one, and they did not complain.

"What's your specialty, Leonel? I mean, your line of work."

Leonel wiped his nose and eyes on the sleeve of his coat. He was glad to be diverted. "I work in cork."

"Cork?"

"Yes, *señor*, both of us. Our family. Our father was a cork man. My son was. From the moment it is removed from the cork oak tree to the time it's been cut, cured, shaped, and handed to the vintner for bottling." He nodded, still unable to look into Pablo's eyes.

"That's a pity. There are no cork trees in Chile."

Now Leonel looked up. He was suddenly charged with combativeness. "No cork trees!"

"As far as I know."

"Listen, you." Leonel leaned over the table, put an index finger on Pablo's chest, and tapped it three times. "You put me on that boat and leave the rest to me. I'll make sure that cork trees suddenly appear in your country."

Startled, Pablo quickly signed the chit that allowed Leonel onto the Winnipeg. He began filling out another. "Is your wife here?"

"She was killed, *señor* Pablo."

Wincing, Pablo continued writing, and then passed both chits to Leonel.

"And my brother?"

Pablo pointed at the two pieces of paper. "The second one. You'll see. He goes too."

25
THE TUNNEL

He saw the entrance. Far above the tree line, approachable only by a switchback trail cut into the cliff face that appeared so narrow that just one horse at a time would be able to ascend it, the cave resembled a dark orchid, twenty meters high, twenty wide, the surroundings of which were curved petals made from the flooding of long-ago fiery liquids.

Right away, the horses had trouble. A stream ran down the lava tunnel's length, and the porcelain-like stone surface was so smooth that the animals could not keep their footing. For the first four kilometers, Juvenal said, the tunnel would be a steep incline, and he guessed that they would go up about seven hundred meters in altitude. "There will be a lot of snow outside. So, I'm glad we'll be in here." Horseshoes sounded against rock, causing sparks when they walked up the parts of the tunnel floor that were not underwater. Although this surface did not have the treacherous instability of the Curringue River crossing, it was icy-slippery, and the passage was made even more difficult by there being no light at all in the tunnel. After the first hundred meters, the light from the entrance had faded to nothing, leaving Pablo and the others immersed in a blackness, as Pablo observed to himself, like that of dreams riveted with worry.

As Juvenal attempted lighting a torch, Tuerto fell and Pablo went sprawling. He was blind, but he heard Tuerto's angry crying out as he went down and scrambled on his hands and knees to get away from the fever of the horse's efforts to right himself. Neither could see the other. Pablo followed Tuerto's struggles by the sound of them, frightened that the horse would trample him without even seeing him. The way his hooves battered the rock, the way Tuerto's large musculature banged against it, probably injuring the musculature, caused Pablo to scurry even farther away.

Juvenal's torch hurried into flame, and suddenly Tuerto appeared standing alone before the four men. The horse's legs were bloodied. He appeared for the moment almost hobbled. But the light revealed that, huffing and snorting, he disdained all that.

Quite suddenly herds of animals gathered everywhere above them. Great lizards slithering about one another. Heavy-headed lumbering bison. Horned deer as they leapt across meadows. Green-gold Andean trout swirling about each other in circles. Human hands and depictions of human battles with spears and sticks. These were painted on a rounded ceiling from which slim silver stalactites hung like individual threads of a spider web. They glowed like water, and water dripped from the very ends of them. The paintings had been organized around the stalactites, so that a kind of musical notation of cold stone and artful pigments gracefully turned and hurried its way across the immense ceiling.

Juvenal gave each of the men a torch. When they were all lit, the tunnel expanded, and they saw that it was the size of a grand railroad station, only far-more decorously appointed than even the *Estación Central* in Santiago that, Pablo well knew, had been designed by Gustave Eiffel himself in 1897. The lava tunnel's size took Pablo's breath, especially as he recalled with what rhapsodic language his father had once described to him the *Estación Central*. Pablo—still called Neftali in those times—had been ten years old. José del Carmen had told the boy about how the steam enveloped so many train engines all at once that they looked like struggling iron angels in the clouds. The great wheels spinning into movement and trying for traction on the rails imitated celestial systems twirling about themselves. His father had re-created the sound of all this. He had explained the echoing of the engines, the talk and the train whistles, and the laughter and footsteps of the hurrying crowds rising to the station's ceiling. Neftali, his hands gathered against his right cheek as he sat at the kitchen table listening, and seeing the wonder in his father's face, had determined on that day, at that moment, that he would not allow himself to die until he himself had seen the *Estación Central,* something he first did when he was sixteen.

Pablo recalled visiting the Eiffel Tower the first time as well, in 1927. Pausing in his voyage to Rangoon, he had joined the Peruvian poet César Vallejo for coffee and pastry in a café at the edge of the military parade grounds next to the tower. Pablo's hypnotized awe while viewing the tower was only slightly distracted by Vallejo's telling him that he, Pablo, had become the greatest poet in the Spanish language since Rubén Darío, even though, "sitting there sipping your coffee, Pablito, looking like a kid...." Vallejo frowned. "How old are you?"

"Twenty-three."

Vallejo, a chunky, thin man in a beautiful pin-striped Parisian suit, with black hair and a squashed nose, himself already a notable figure in South American writing, leaned forward on a cane, his mouth hanging open. "That much?"

"Look at those." Ramada pointed to the ceiling. Victor and especially Juvenal craned their necks staring at the display of so many hundreds of figures.

"I remember this," Juvenal said. "My father brought me here when I was a little boy. I had forgotten that it actually existed, though. I always thought it was something I'd dreamed." He held his torch high. The animals above moved with each changing of the light.

Birds as well. Pablo made out renderings of the black giant coot, of flamingos and female lesser rheas, the andean flicker with its lightning-struck feathers, the penguin-hued andean goose, the amazing cock-of-the-rock, whose jet-black body seemed to do battle with its own head, colored orange as though it were of pure flame, different kinds of miners and sierra finches, diuca-finches as well, the andean highland blue-crowned motmot (with a name like that, always one of Pablo's favorite birds) and from several different angles andean condors. He knew these were the largest birds in the world and had seen them only through binoculars from a distance of hundreds of meters. Indeed, the lava tunnel ceiling gave Pablo the most close-up view of a condor he had ever had.

They progressed farther up the tunnel, the light from the torches lessening. The path ahead became dim, then murky. Water dripped down on the men and horses from the ceiling, and Juvenal lit another torch.

"I made a mistake back there, *don* Pablo."

"How?"

"I shouldn't have let everyone light his own torch. It caused us...." He looked down at Miedo's saddle, where the bundle of remaining torches was secured by a rope. "I think we've got enough to get through here." He turned back up the tunnel. "We have a long way to go, though." The new torch lit the way, if not the entire tunnel itself. Shadows, like dark trolls, danced about before them. "We've got to be more sparing with these things." He rode in silence a moment. "Although I wouldn't have missed that chamber for anything, no, *don* Pablo?"

"Not for anything."

An arduous hour later, the tunnel leveled and, deep in darkness, they came to a lagoon. Its waters were darker than those of The Lake of Questions. It was not as large as the lake, and the water was as still as glass.

"This is new." Nervousness filled Juvenal's voice. "It wasn't here the last time I was."

It filled the space. They could find no discernible way around it, no path for the horses. The curved walls rose, encircling them, and at the highest point disappeared. But snowflakes fell across the sleeve of Pablo's jacket. He looked up but could see nothing. The flakes swirled through the light cast by Juvenal's torch.

"Got to be a hole up in the roof, Victor." Juvenal said.

"How high could that be?"

"I don't know." Juvenal studied the lagoon. A small island in the middle of it, of flat, yellow rock, glowed in the dim light.

"We have to go through the water then?" Pablo said.

"I think so. But let me try first." Juvenal urged Miedo toward the pool. The donkey, nervous about it, held his own and wouldn't move. "Come on, damn you."

Pablo reached out. "Give me the torch."

"Why?"

"So you can use both hands."

Juvenal, surprised by the suggestion, passed the lit torch into Pablo's right hand. "Hold it up high then, so I can see."

Pablo lifted the torch, and its light was strong enough to illuminate the far edge of the lagoon, just barely so. Pablo could understand Miedo's timidity. The water hid itself in obsidian black, and the donkey was seized with fear of it. His eyes gleamed, racing back and forth as he tried to justify to himself doing what Juvenal wished him to do. He snorted twice. He dug in.

"Juvenal, I don't think..."

"*¡Hijo de puta!*" Juvenal grimaced and whipped Miedo's flank with the reins.

"Give me your poncho," Pablo said.

"For what?"

"If you go under, you'll freeze if it gets soaked."

"*Mierda.*" Juvenal quickly removed his wool poncho and threw it at Pablo.

"Give me the other torches."

"Why?"

"The donkey might go under."

"No, not with me..." Juvenal kicked Miedo with the heels of his boots. "Not with me telling him what to do."

Miedo lurched into the lagoon and, with Juvenal, fell from sight.

—

"Take it, Juvenal." Pablo tossed one end of the rope into the pool. Ramada, standing behind him, had wrapped the rope about his waist, cinching it tightly. Victor held the torch above his head. "Grab it!"

Juvenal flailed at the water. Clearly a poor swimmer, he gasped for breath. His shoulders went under. His head floundered. He came back up.

"Take the rope."

He slapped at the rope, finally securing it in his hands. The others pulled him to the edge of the lagoon. But the drop-off was so immediate that he could not pull himself from the water. The sharp, slippery edge of the rock defied him. "Help me."

Pablo went down onto his knees, pulling at the rope. Victor too tried to help, although his ankle had now ceased, really, to function. He sat on the rock behind Pablo, holding the torch in one hand and pulling on the rope with the other, passing it back toward Ramada. Slowly one arm, then the next, then Juvenal's chest and stomach... Finally, as he spat water, gagging on it, his upper body flopped onto the rock. Pablo hoisted him from the pool by the back of his shirt, but Juvenal resisted him, pointing back toward the pool.

"The burro."

Pablo forced Juvenal farther from the lagoon.

"Get him." Juvenal pulled himself from Pablo's grasp, turned on his side and pointed into the darkness. "Miedo." He was too exhausted to move, and he leaned over on both his hands, his head hanging down. "Get Miedo."

Angered, and muttering to himself that the mule could take care of himself, Pablo took the torch from Victor. He stepped back toward the pool and lifted the torch high. Grimacing, he closed his eyes. Opening them, hoping that he had just been having a morbid vision, that what he had seen was just an old log or a flat boulder or something, he found that what he had seen was indeed Miedo. An outline in the dim light far away, the burro floated dead on the surface of the lagoon.

—

Juvenal shivered beneath his coat, his body milky with sweat. He slept, but his dreams were filled with sputtering and grief. Pablo, who could see nothing, tried remaining calm. The deep lagoon had probably been formed when the floor of the tunnel had given way, dropping several feet down into some other cavern to an underground lake, maybe? Some gigantic geologic body of water that rose up through the rock to fill the void? He didn't know. Juvenal had held to the donkey's saddle as Miedo had struggled to get back to shore. But then the donkey had vanished, down into the black water deep, leaving Juvenal to swim on his own.

Now Ramada and Victor, wounded and exhausted, also wandered in dreams, with heavy breathing, their sleep distressed. All the men had bedded down as the single torch had begun losing its light. No one had had the spirit to speak of what had happened, but all had realized that, when they awoke, they would be isolated in total darkness.

Pablo fell into a startling dream. Not of shapes, nor people or events. He saw only colors, every color all at once, as though each element of the spectrum were trying to gain release from the black hole that now sucked the spectrum back in.

—

He awoke. Moonlight fell across him, radiantly so, and illumined an entire side of the cavern. The opening at the top, a hundred and fifty meters up, was quite circular, like the moon itself, and the cavern wall rose to it at an angle. Pablo realized that he could climb up the wall, on all fours probably. Possibly he could reach the opening.

Only he could do it. Even fully awake, not one of the others could make the climb, and it had to be done now. Once the moon moved on, the blindness would return, and who knew when such an opportunity might come back? They would all perish down here in this hole. Pablo stood up and searched the rock near him for his gloves. He could not find them. Swearing, he examined the possible ways to get up the slope, made sure his jacket was secure, and set out toward the moon.

His mind heaved in turmoil, imbued with the pain of his own foolishness. *Why did I have to make that speech in Congress? Why didn't I just go to the concentration camp in Pisagua and spend my days with the guys there, instead of bringing these guys to this perdition here?* Fear forced one hand before the other up the precipitous incline. *"He went alone, himself, a tunnel"*, Pablo recalled. Ironic, that. He grunted, pulling himself further. *When did I write it? "The birds fled from me..." All those paintings, gone now, lost in darkness. "And in me..." How did I come up with it? "Night entered upon its powerful invasion."* A sharp stone cut into the palm of his right hand. *"¡Ay, Jesús Cristo!"* He had to keep his hold on it, so that he wouldn't fall back down the precipice and cause it to cut him even more.

He climbed for an hour, making his way around boulders, up rivulets, across small fields of shale and scree, until his hands were so sore that he could barely grip the rocks that pulled him toward the moonlight. He fell back once, skidding several meters down the slope, his knees scraped and bloodied. He almost gave up altogether when a small boulder gave way and ricocheted down the slope to the bottom. He had come close to rolling with it, and it took him several minutes to rein in the fear that his strength would give out and that he would fall all the way back down and be lost.

"Will I ever get out of here?"

The moon helped him. Thin clouds began passing before it, and the light became a wavering, changing blue, so that the part of the cavern that he could see above and below him resembled the sea moved by tides. He felt like an alien swimming creature in this dry part of the cave, undulating toward the light. He continued up, entirely lit by the moon as he struggled forward on the increasingly steep and rocky slope.

A few meters below the opening, he heard voices. There were others, above, outside. The enormous opening enabled the moonlight to continue its way down into the tunnel even as it passed so quickly overhead. Pablo knew in his heart, though, that there was not anyone else. It was just an illusion, a foolish hope that people awaited him with food and blankets, with a cigar and a bottle of whisky. It was an hallucination imagined entirely. It was nothing at all. Pablo's only true hope lay in getting up through the opening and waiting there until morning when perhaps he would be able to talk Juvenal and the others up. None of the horses would be able to make this climb. They were all condemned. But with light and rage, the men could do it. He would have to talk them into that rage, into anger at death and anger at God for forcing them into such a hole. Rage would pull them up from it.

Aroint thee, God!

Now he climbed almost straight up. Outcroppings of stone helped him, along with holes and cracks in the boulders, finger-holds, concavities in which he could place a knee or an elbow. His left hand took hold of a narrow slice of stone at the very top and, pushing with his right foot, which had found a horizontal crack in the stone, he pulled himself up into the full moonlight.

He was out.

He fell over onto his back. To his shocked surprise, despite the fact that he was surrounded by snow, he felt that he was underwater, sweat everywhere. His mind burned. Physical pain so flamed up in him that he felt that his body would combust. He would be the one dark mark upon all this snow, a splotch of ashen meat.

He drifted to sleep, and then awoke a moment later. The sweat had turned to driven cold, and he knew that he had to stand up and walk in order to get his blood flowing again. He rolled over and brought himself to his hands and knees. His head was riddled with pain. His arms and shoulders could barely hold him up. Before him, piled beneath a dusting of blue-lit snow, lay a half-dozen torches.

He looked over his shoulder, all around. Behind him he saw only forest, dry snow, and the opening in the surface of the earth. But before him, he had a view of an Andean canyon and dozens of full mountains into the distance. The bottom of the canyon was at least a thousand meters below, and the tree growth was so complete that both sides appeared riveted with a blanket of immense blue-white cones, feathered with snow, so many of them that they were uncountable into the distance.

Below the snow line, the trees turned dark blue and, finally, black. Far above, sharp slivers of blue-black rock, some of them a thousand meters high, glittered where the moon lit the snow that rested upon them. The mountain range in the far distance filled Pablo's vision. It was all so unaccountably beautiful to him that he was certain he would never be able to describe it well, if at all. No poem, of few words or many, could be like this. The moonlight dimmed the stars, but by no means all of them. He could see portions of the entire southern sky.

We'll never walk out of here, Pablo thought. *Without horses? Up here? We'll all die.*

"*Don* Pablo."

He looked about.

"Poet." Standing next to his horse, Dominguín held the reins, his shoulders so sloped and beaten down that he appeared hardly alive. Indeed, Pablo knew that he was not alive. A dark ghost, Hamlet's father, King Duncan, poor drowned Ophelia...Dominguín, as dead as the rest of them. "I know your work."

"How could you? Way out here?"

"Yes, but what about '*I write for the people, even when they cannot/read my poems with their rural eyes.*'" Dominguín frowned, letting the reins go. "You wrote that, no?"

Pablo shrugged, nodding his head. "I have it with me now." He pointed toward the hole in the ground. "It's down in the tunnel."

"You were wrong, poet. Those of us out here, we have an eternity for… for reading."

"Dominguín, I'm sorry if I insulted you."

"It *was* an insult. '*Rural eyes*' my ass!"

Pablo grimaced.

"Why do you persist?" Dominguín's *gaucho* clothing was ripped and destroyed even more than it had been in the white meadow. His beard scurried from his face like dying flames. He glowered at Pablo, as though fully wishing to convey what an idiot this poet was. He picked at his teeth with a *gaucho facón* knife, and Pablo saw how there really were no teeth...maybe four or five, but too few to sustain the phantasm through a meal. But he also realized that Dominguín wouldn't ever need a meal. The knotted rope that formed his belt, the *bombacha* pants so soiled that they looked like the death wrappings of an old corpse tossed into a muddy grave, the paltry shirt, itself like folded scars all around him....

Dominguín whispered. "Death is better."

"Than what?"

"Than the few hours of dismal life that will be left to you if you get through these mountains."

"How many hours?"

"Who knows?"

"Enough to get to Paris, Dominguín?"

The *gaucho* reached up and patted the neck of his flea-infested horse, making Pablo wonder whether the fleas too were ghosts. "Where's that?"

"If it's better...if death is better...why did you bring me these torches?"

Dominguín looked about from the corner of his eye, behind him, to the left and right, searching. "The others don't know I'm here."

"What do they say about us?"

"That you are all doomed, and you deserve a fate like the one we have."

"Fate?"

"The one we're living out now. Wandering through these mountains. Surrounded by snow forever. Inundated by snow. Snow running through our very hearts, the anguish...." Dominguín sighed, turning his eyes toward his horse. The horse barely existed. It was difficult to see him, as though his spectral heart had long ago died and left him without strength.

"No one gave me any torches, and I so wanted..." Dominguín lowered his head. "I so wanted to live, poet."

Pablo examined the torches. Larger than those on The Lake of Questions, they had been tied together in a bundle.

"Take them." Dominguín slowly mounted his horse, and there was no sound of any kind of leather creaking, of the horse breathing, of his bit, or the reins adjusting themselves against his flesh. Indeed, there was no flesh. "Don't come back here, poet."

Then there was no Dominguín.

Pablo took up the torches, glanced once more at the canyon's blue emptiness, then up at the vast snow-splendored *cordillera*, and lowered himself back down the hole.

—

Cautious, Tuerto felt for the shelf. Pablo wanted to spur him on, that he be quicker. But he also knew, from their having ridden so far through such danger, that this horse could tell the future, at least that future that was made of molecules, atoms, and substance. Tuerto knew what was down there. He could feel it.

He took a step, then another. The water splashed about his hooves. They followed a narrow shelf around the very edge of the lagoon. One step wrong, and he, Pablo, and Juvenal would be in the black water. Pablo felt Juvenal's steaming face against the back of his neck. He looked back himself and saw that Ramada's pinto Ángel was walking as carefully as was Tuerto, and he wondered if Tuerto's bravery were giving Ángel the nerve to keep on. Victor, slumping with exhaustion, brought up the rear on Pajarita.

Of the two other riders, Ramada was in better shape. The swelling of his knee had subsided, although the bruise and the wound remained as darkly threatening as ever. But he could walk, which meant that he could help Pablo with ropes and with the horses. Victor could barely put weight on his leg, and were Pablo to need any help, Victor could only advise. Anything physical that he once could have done now depended on Ramada and, more important, on Pablo himself.

Pablo depended on Victor nonetheless. The care they had given to Juvenal was due primarily to Victor's terrible experiences on Aconcagua, trying to keep people alive in the worst of hypothermia. "I wouldn't lose you, Pablo, out in that snow, and I won't lose this one either." They had swaddled Juvenal in his jacket and a pair of Pablo's dry pants. The recollection of Victor's loss on that terrible day, the Indian porter dead in his arms, had driven Pablo into a haunted speculation of what real death, not imagined death, could be like.

The worst for him was that, in the end, death was…what was it that Emily Dickinson had said, *"zero to the bone"*? Without Delia, without words to describe it, without a mind and a heart, death was nothing…and that was the worst of all.

It was Victor who had advised Pablo that this shelf around the lagoon was the only possible way out. Pablo had seen a kind of small beachhead to the far right of their encampment, a flat extension of rock that entered the water at a slight angle. When he went to look at it, he saw that a yellow rock shelf, about a half-meter wide, indeed followed the edge of the lagoon twenty centimeters or so beneath the surface. Holding a torch high above his head, he saw that the shelf, sometimes wider, sometimes narrower, appeared to hold to the edge of the lagoon all the way to the other side. It was ephemeral, the yellow shape, and barely visible in the weak light.

"It'll be easier to see ahead when you're on Tuerto," Victor said. "And he'll know, Pablo. Listen to him when you're out there."

—

Halfway to the far side, Tuerto stopped. He would not move, and as Pablo lifted the torch to see what possibly could be ahead of them beneath the surface, Tuerto shook his head violently to both sides. A greasy splash of blood spattered Pablo's face and left shoulder. He attempted wiping it away. He wanted to turn back. But then Pablo realized that he could not turn back. There was no room for Tuerto or any of the horses to turn around. He could not imagine what would happen were the animals to attempt to walk backwards. With no alternative, they had to move ahead.

"Tuerto."

The horse turned his head toward Pablo.

"Juvenal, you can stay on this horse if I get down?"

Juvenal sighed. Words just barely came from him. "Yes, go ahead."

Very carefully, Pablo lowered himself from Tuerto, feeling for the water and the narrow shelf below its surface. He held the torch to the side, above the water, as far from Tuerto's head as possible. Tuerto looked back, as though fearful of what Pablo was about to attempt. Pablo slipped along the horse's left side and lifted the reins over Tuerto's head and ears.

The horse attempted another step. But Pablo wished to examine him before they proceeded. He saw that blood was streaming from somewhere on the front of the horse's head. Tuerto grumbled, but Pablo laid his free hand against the horse's jaw and caressed it. He looked up. Juvenal's eyes were fixed upon him. Pablo realized that Juvenal somehow understood what he was going to do. His eyes like shadows, he was grudgingly giving Pablo permission.

"This way. Follow me." Tuerto's reins in his right hand, Pablo turned and began walking along the black shelf, feeling his way with the front of each boot. The water murmured. Tuerto followed behind, moment by moment. The torch in Pablo's hand lit the path ahead, even though the water simply reflected the light and, so, dazzled Pablo's view of the way. The remnants of the light were taken in by the water and extinguished. Moment by moment, Pablo continued on. The pool to his left, in deepest black, was like hell or death. The other horses followed, and the men on them remained silent, as though they realized that any speech could distract Pablo and drown him. Pablo, straining to keep calm, anguish filling his heart, held tight to Tuerto's reins and slid each foot forward over the invisible rock.

—

An hour later, they came to an auxiliary lava tunnel to the right, as Juvenal had whispered would happen. Pablo brought the horses to a halt and dismounted from Tuerto, handing the torch to Ramada. Taking Tuerto's head between his hands, he saw blood flowing from his nostrils in thick clots black and red. Red blood was streaming from around the horse's eyes. The blind eye sweltered in it. Tuerto had fallen into a paroxysm of shivering.

"*Bestia ciega. Bestia feroz.*" Pablo ran a hand down Tuerto's neck. "Blind beast. Ferocious beast." He placed his forehead against the neck. "I love you, horse."

Descending the tunnel later, Pablo felt the air change. A breeze came up the passage. The footing became easier for the horses. Light shined ahead.

"That's it?" Pablo looked back over his shoulder.

Juvenal looked up. His strength was close to gone. "That's it."

"Where will we be?"

Pablo felt Juvenal's breathing on the back of his neck. While hours earlier, the exhalations had been hot and moist, now his fever had broken. Exhausted, he nonetheless breathed clearly.

"Argentina, *maestro*."

26
THE RADIO ACTRESS

Tuerto led the way.

From this part of the path that bordered El Lago Lácar—an immense body of emerald water surrounded by ridges, sierras, and many summits of the great Argentine Andes *cordillera*—Pablo studied the thousands of ancient fallen trees that had been transported into the lake by rivers and ancillary streams. They were driftwoods of every shape and contortion, leafless ragged branches, and gutted root systems, all settled willy-nilly into a quagmire of grasses and watery lagoons that, to the right of the trail, extended a few kilometers toward the lower skirts of two large forested, snow-covered peaks. The men and horses were all in such ragged condition that they appeared to have emerged from molten volcanic earth. Pablo's clothes were ripped everywhere, the cuffs of his pants shredded and clotted with mud. His wool jacket smelled of sweat and dried water rot. His hair and beard looked like scattered ground slugs. The gear that had been so carefully tied to Tuerto's saddle, and the saddlebags themselves, now hung down with little order. The bags, one of them containing his single moldering copy of *Canto General*, resembled pummeled clods of flesh.

The other horsemen appeared similarly ruined.

The one difficulty for Tuerto was that Juvenal rode on him as well, behind Pablo, holding on with as much strength as he could muster. Victor had suggested tying his hands together before Pablo's stomach, so that it would be much more difficult for Juvenal to fall from the horse. Juvenal had protested at first, but then was ordered to shut up by Pablo, and the cowherd had acquiesced. He realized that the advice could well save his life. As they had descended the rock- and boulder-strewn pass from the end of the lava tunnel, the lake far below, Tuerto had several times stumbled and lost his footing. They descended through steep forest, at first having to negotiate passages through snow-bound narrow canyons, later following various tracks through rolling hills that were covered with dense forest. Without the horse's fine sense of balance and Pablo's ability to stay with him through all the instability of the trail, Juvenal could well have been injured even more.

Finally, after several hours of silent, difficult riding, they entered the town of San Martín de Los Andes.

Holding tight to a rise at one end of Lake Lácar, San Martín was made up of perhaps a hundred buildings. Very little happened here. The structures were made of plank wood or logs. Only a few were painted. Many were cluttered about by ruined boards and bricks, the remains of old wagons, lumbering tools, and farming equipment. An iron plow or an occasional destroyed vehicle that was hopelessly rusted, missing windows or the motor itself, would be invaded by enormous thorned berry bushes and other wildly unkempt weedy detritus. Wood fires burned inside almost all the buildings. Pablo knew of the famed fishing here, so he easily found two *pensiones* where he and the others could rent rooms, get a bath, and a night or two of decent sleep.

It was in one of these that Pablo wooed, or at least hoped that he would woo, the radio actress.

—

They also had to make it through an insulting conversation with Cecil Ardmore.

A servant boy stood behind the counter of *La Pensión Jorge El Quinto* as Pablo passed into the small lobby. Dark-haired, brown-skinned, twelve years old, he was clearly alarmed by the poet's ruggedly frightening appearance. He did not answer when Pablo asked him how many rooms he had available.

"Have you a voice, *chico*?" Pablo's filthy hands lay splayed across the countertop. He glanced back over his shoulder, to see an extremely beautiful young woman sitting in a kind of ersatz pub in an anteroom off the lobby. Two glasses of red wine rested on the small table next to her chair. She held a bouquet of four long-stemmed roses, which rested on the lap of her long wool skirt like a softly painted suggestion of blood. She resembled none other than Evita Perón, her peroxided hair and lovely cheekbones causing Pablo to do a double take. She evidently felt that Pablo was handsome, or at least that was how he interpreted the look of generous interest and fear that she gave him.

Her eyes steadied themselves upon him. An ironic smile graced her large lips. Pablo noted her hands, which caressed the roses as though they were made of soft lace. Her upper legs and hips reclined at an angle to the chair on which she sat. Its red velvet formed a kind of cloud-like cushion for her, although Pablo immediately thought of the delicious, forgiving flames of Purgatory. He had always thought of fleshy sin as a good thing, and this woman's beauty suggested nothing less than that to him.

The passage through the Lilpela behind him, Pablo began to think of softer utterances and quiet intensities.

He removed his wool watch cap and held it in both hands before him. He knew that he was a bear-like, smelly, and beaten man, and worried that she thought him some sort of thief or wandering murderer. His mouth hurried into a smile, which was answered similarly by the woman. He stepped into the pub and nodded to her. "Excuse me, *señorita*, my…" He looked down at himself, thinking that his clothes were made up of as much dirt, errant blood, general sweat, and sludge as anything else. "I'm sorry if my appearance alarms you."

She took up one of the glasses of wine and sipped from it. She wore a fashionable French-inspired cloche, which clung to the side of her head like sleek cobalt. "It does, a bit." She replaced the glass on the table. "But I suppose you've been traveling."

"We have."

"I'd like to hear about it sometime."

Thrilled, Pablo nodded. "I'm certain that could be… May I ask your name."

"María Paula."

"Ay!" Pablo sighed. He smiled once again. "Spaniard? French?"

"María Paula Hoz de Alvear." A brief darkness passed over her eyes, and Pablo worried whether the conversation would continue.

The boy at the counter ran into the room behind.

Pablo heard a scuffle of voices in the back room, one the boy's, the other a man's whose accent in Spanish was barely comprehensible. Pablo excused himself from María Paula and returned to the lobby desk. After a moment, a tall man of bony rigidity, dressed in a proper white shirt and tie, brown slacks and rimless eyeglasses, the fingers of whose hands hung before his stomach like wrinkled earth worms, emerged through the curtain that blocked the view to the back office. His skin resembled a hanging white shroud.

"Yes?" he asked in English.

"You speak Spanish, yes?"

The man's Spanish was serviceable enough, but his accent had all the imperial dismissiveness for which the English were so famous. They were people who, at the moment, were in the process of dismantling almost the entirety of their empire, one of the most rapid descents into capitalist political failure that Pablo had ever enjoyed. India, Pakistan, Southeast Asia, South America…it was all almost gone or quickly going, making ridiculous this fellow's attitude of snippy British disdain.

"What is your name?" Pablo grumbled in English.

"Cecil Ardmore, old boy. And as the Americans would say, what's it to you?"

Pablo did not understand the phrase. He lapsed into Spanish. "I've got three others with me, and we need rooms."

"Yes, well, you can leave, *chico*. We have no room for you."

"Perhaps I should introduce myself."

"Why would that make a difference?" Ardmore's hands remained limp, the ends of the fingers slightly dampening the countertop upon which they rested. He surveyed Pablo down the length of his nose, his lips pursed and downturned at the end.

"I am Pablo Neruda."

"And that is supposed to carry meaning for me?"

A glass fell to the floor in the pub room, with a tinkling of broken shards against wooden planks. Their chat interrupted, Pablo and Ardmore glanced into the room, and for the first time, Pablo realized that María Paula Hoz de Alvear was not alone. A young man stood next to her chair, having just arrived. An Argentine army officer, he was leaning over her as though he had just given her a kiss. He was a very dark-skinned, lavishly good-looking man, a bit smoky and smoldering in the eyes, about thirty years old. He had the self-regarding look of the *compradito* who had lost the fight in *El Farol* twenty-five years ago, except that, where the *gaucho* had been a wind-savaged, roughly hewn, pretty-boy minor criminal, this fellow resembled some sort of prince or perhaps more to the point a tango singer movie star like Carlos Gardel or any of the other now numerous second-rate *gardelianos* that gushed from silver screens all over South America.

He and María Paula stared into the lobby. The officer was especially riveted by what Pablo had just said to the Englishman. The officer's feet were apart, the dark brown leather shoes at an angle to each other. His double-pocketed light brown shirt, long sleeved, appeared in the candlelight to be a blank wall painted with a long sliver of dark brown…his military tie. One hand remained on María Paula's shoulder. The other, which Pablo figured had been holding the now broken glass, clenched before his stomach. Tall and bulky, this man would stand up well in a fight. Pablo turned toward him and leaned on the desk, waiting as the officer approached the lobby counter.

"You're Neruda?" The soldier's jaw fixed itself into a small boulder of disapproval.

"I am."

"We thought you were still in Chile."

"Until today, we were."

A long silence ensued, during which Pablo considered how he would escape. Sadly, the soldier blocked the way to the door, and there appeared no other avenue down which Pablo could bolt.

"This is disturbing news." The soldier let out a long breath.

"So, you're going to take me in?" Pablo's shoulders slumped. *All this way, and it has to end here, at the very edge of freedom. Apprehended in a small hotel at the farthest decline of the Andes mountains, to be run in like a common criminal.*

"Yes." The soldier shrugged, then turned toward Ardmore. He took a few bills from his pants pocket and tossed them onto the counter. "This is for the wine and the glass." He turned toward Pablo. "And now, you come with me."

"Where?"

The soldier glanced once more at the Englishman. "I will not drink in a place in which Pablo Neruda cannot."

"I beg your pardon?" the Englishman grumbled.

"You and your men, *don* Pablo…you come with us. There are plenty of rooms in the other pension, which has the good sense to be run by an Argentine." The soldier retrieved one of the bills from the counter. "I gave you too much, *pelotudo*." A rude Buenos Aires phrase, it suggested that the Englishman's veins ran with boorish stupidity. "Come on." He clapped Pablo on the shoulder, gestured toward María Paula, and the three of them walked out.

—

After Pablo and the others had had a chance to bathe and settle down in *La Pensión Presidente Sarmiento*, the soldier introduced himself. "Carmelo Calderón."

The proprietor, an Argentine named Hugo Schmitt, who was himself from Bariloche and owned the only motorcycle in all of San Martín de Los Andes, had brought a pot of thick, steaming minestrone into the sitting room, with several bowls and spoons. He had a supply of old clothes in a back room, which did little to improve the decrepit look of Pablo and his men. They were still unshaven. They still were wrecked. But this clothing had come freshly washed from a trunk. It was soft against their now soaped and rinsed skins. Enjoying the fire and sipping from the cups of malbec that Carmelo had provided them, they all thanked the soldier, María Paula, and Hugo with considerable gratitude. Juvenal especially appreciated the minestrone, which he said gave warmth to the very bones deep within him that had been frozen now for days. Hugo, pleased by the praise, heaped a second spoonful of shaved parmesan onto Juvenal's soup.

"You serve in the army here?" Pablo and Carmelo stood at a small bar at one end of the pension's sitting room. A few wood-sculpted, painted trout adorned the mantel above the fireplace. The head of a mountain goat stuck out from a wall. María Paula was involved at the moment in a conversation with Ramada. Her legs were crossed, at an extreme angle to the floor. The legs seemed to Pablo excited. The way she gazed at Ramada conveyed immediate and unquestionable attraction. This did not seem to concern Carmelo, although Pablo was mildly worried.

"No, I..." Carmelo gestured toward the woman. "She is a...well, a friend, you might say." He watched the conversation a moment and shrugged. "An actress."

"Like Evita Perón."

"Even more so when you consider that my María Paula..." Carmelo pointed toward his companion. "When you consider that she acts on the radio, like Evita did."

Pablo exhaled. "Those names. Hoz. Alvear. Those are important Argentine families."

"Yes, and she suffers a bit at their hands for exposing herself so brazenly on the air waves."

"And to you, I would imagine."

"Yes. That too.

"But you don't serve here."

"I do. But, *don* Pablo, she and I are here at the *pensión* on a tryst." Carmelo smiled. "We're lovers."

"You're abandoning your post?"

Carmelo looked at the conversation across the room. "For her, I would. But—"

"Why?"

Carmelo's mouth, like a curved suture, turned downward as he considered his answer.

"I expect the Argentine army looks with considerable disfavor," Pablo said, "upon an officer who goes absent without official leave in order to win the affections of a radio actress."

"*Che*, maybe so, but this radio actress…" Carmelo's eyes glowed with spaniel-like sadness. It seemed that he was beginning to notice the turn in attention on María Paula's part, from himself to Ramada. Ramada—stolid, beautiful—was doing little to fan the heat of her emotions, but the heat appeared to be rising nonetheless. "Any soldier would risk himself for this radio actress."

The screen door to the pension flew open and four soldiers hurried in, two of them stationing themselves on either side of the door. The other two, one an officer, approached Carmelo. The officer was unarmed, but the other soldier carried an American M-1 at the ready. Military alert rumbled through the sitting room, and María Paula cried out, bringing a hand to her lips. The soldiers turned toward her, prepared to defend themselves.

The officer confronted Carmelo. "What are you doing here, soldier?"

Carmelo grew immediately restive. He held his hands before him, palms up in a gesture of shrugging cluelessness. "I'm looking for the fugitive, Captain."

The captain was a wide man with a blunt head. "Yes, they've told us that he might be here. But you haven't seen anything, have you?"

"No, sir."

The officer turned to Pablo. "And you, *amigo*? Have you seen a tall man, well-dressed, studious looking? Probably carrying a book. Good talker."

Pablo slurped from his cup of malbec, spilling a bit of it on his shirt-front. His voice grumbled as though a pocket of gravel rested in his throat. He affected a northern Argentina accent of rough words spoken with only partial completion and extreme grammatical sloppiness. "Not me, *amigo*. You lookin' for somebody who killed somebody?"

The captain surveyed Pablo's face, causing the poet to worry a moment about whether he was once again being recognized. The others in the room remained silent. After a moment, the officer broke into a generous grin. "No, *hermano*, nothin' like that." He turned to the other soldiers. "He's not here, *hombres*. Let's go." He strode the few steps to the front door of the pension before gesturing to Carmelo. "You too, soldier. We need you."

"But…but, sir."

"Step lively. We haven't got time for this."

Cowed, under orders, Carmelo followed the captain out the door into the dark.

—

By the time Pablo got to his bed, Ramada had retired to the small room next to his, which was reachable by an open doorway. Judging from his breathing, Ramada was far gone in sleep. Pablo removed his clothing quietly, walked to the door, just as quietly closed it, and then got into bed.

Ten minutes later, a shadow seeped into his room. It was a woman. In the dim light from the hallway, he could see her platinum blonde tresses, shining like bright silver plate from the mines of Potosí. It took him little time to realize that it was María Paula, and the dim light from the hallway also revealed that she wore little, or at least little that covered her.

Pablo gathered himself. The reward for his successful passage through the *cordillera*, María Paula had clearly entered the room in order to smother Pablo's semi-dreaminess with kisses and the certainty of release. He prepared himself.

"Pablito." She touched his shoulder.

"Yes, *mi amor*." He began turning the blankets and sheets aside, to allow her easy ingress to his affections.

"Is Ramada here?"

"I beg your pardon?"

"Excuse me, I must have come into the wrong room. I thought he told me…." María Paula's silhouette blackened against the light from the hallway. Confused, she put a hand to her lips. Pablo made out the ringlets of her hair and the thin gauze of her nightclothes, as well as the curve of her hips and silken flow of her legs.

"He's here." Pablo sighed and gestured toward the closed door to the next room. "That way."

"Oh, thank you, Pablito. You're so sweet." María Paula moved toward the door.

"Yes, *corazón.*"

He listened for the next fifteen minutes or so.

"You are the feminine estuary," Ramada said.

"What are you talking about?"

"You…you are…the feminine—"

"Ramada, kiss me."

"But you—"

"Kiss me!"

Foolish girl, Pablo thought. No imagination.

"Oh God, you're so beautiful." María Paula's whisper sounded almost frantic. "Take me."

"But don't you think that you are—"

"Ramada!"

"You are—"

"No, idiot. Touch me. Here, give me your hand. Touch me there."

"There?"

"Yes. Please. Oh, my God!"

"Like that?"

"Oh…."

Pablo, undone, nonetheless enjoyed the conversation, brief though it was and abrupt, as well as the extensive sighing and declarations of love that followed from the next room.

The poet Ramada, he thought.

27
DELIA IN LOVE

Delia knew that Pablo was alive, even though she had read the reports in the Paris newspapers. The Chilean government was bragging that he had not been found and that, after so much time, he could not possibly be alive, that he had completely disappeared. The Communist, the seditionist, the traitor Neruda. His fate had found him, the government announced, and this criminal deserved whatever that fate was.

Etc.

She believed none of it because she felt his hands caressing her heart and enabling its blood to pass through so joyfully. That was all Delia had to know.

But the dress remained unfinished. She had abandoned the sleeves, as Cocteau had convinced her she must. Picasso was coming again, just this afternoon, with a surprise, he had said, and she had intuited that it must be a design of some sort that he wished to add to the dress. She had enjoyed the conversation when both those men had taken her for a picnic in the *Place des Vosges* week earlier. The glorious wreck that the square now represented had once been the vacation paradise of nobles and aristocrats, their mansion hotels the holders of such sensuous seventeenth century secrets—the summer balls, the risky dalliances, the damp midnight trysts— one mansion after another. Now the *Place des Vosges* had become so run down as to be an abandonment. The lines of its houses modulated up or down depending on the firmness or softness of the earth beneath or the level of ruin of the foundations. Delia loved the *Place des Vosges* because for her it formed a vision of an old Molière play in which sin was still committed, and then laughed at on stage, despite time's slow ruin of the place in which it presented itself.

Picasso and Cocteau had worked together in 1917 in Paris on a Diaghilev ballet called *Parade*, and the two men had shown Delia the drawings for the costumes and sets that they had done. Picasso had also brought along a little pencil sketch he had done of Eric Satie, now long dead, who had composed the music for the ballet. On such a sunny day that the trees in the square glistened like green silver, she had learned about the stitching that those ballet dresses had required, how dancers were so rough on costumes that sometimes the dresses had to be repaired between numbers, and that the repairs were by no means simple. Sometimes an entire costume had to be redone in ten minutes. With the little cups of cold champagne, the delicious warm air, and the designs of the two geniuses, the picnic had been total pleasure for Delia, even though Picasso had insisted on walking her home from the *Place des Vosges*. During the walk to her apartment, she reported to him about her own dress's progress.

Indeed, the dress had provided Delia with something to talk about instead of Picasso's usual hints that they go to bed together. He was rather insistent on that, although he always stopped such talk whenever she asked him to. The request was salacious, but his acquiescence to her refusals was gentlemanly. The trials she had with the dress provided her with something else about which she could converse with the great artist. She wished to disarm Pablo's insistence on the beauties of Delia's skin, his dreams of her breasts, and his barely disguised hunger for her as she would walk across the room with a glass of wine in her hand. What she liked about Picasso were those very things that led to what she had to refuse. His suggestiveness, his rude Catalan manners, his laughter at her playful off-putting gestures. In the end, Delia felt that Pablo Picasso was indeed a man worth loving, but that Pablo Neruda was even more of one. So it was that she had told Picasso so, and consistently turned him down.

Picasso was due in a few minutes with his surprise, and she sat looking out on the Seine and at the street below. A taxi stopped before her apartment building, and the artist emerged from it. Someone inside—the driver, Delia assumed—handed him a portfolio of drawings. Gladdened, Delia quickly stood and walked toward a mirror on the other side of her living room. She straightened her skirt and blouse. She ran a few fingers through her hair, and at the last moment added a touch of color to her lips.

Footsteps came up the stairs, then a loud knocking on the door, in the manner of all Picasso's previous visits. His voice as always sputtered with gravel. "Delia? Open up."

She reached for the door, and Pablo Neruda swept into the room in an overcoat and a felt fedora, carrying a small package in one hand wrapped in English oilcloth. He dropped the package to a chair and took Delia into his arms. *"¡Corazón!"*

His embrace caused in Delia a joy-ridden blinding. Her heart galloped. As she kissed Pablo—*"¡Alfin!"* he murmured. *"¡La neblina se encuentra con su lila!"*—his hat fell behind him to the floor. "Finally!" he had said. Delia threw her arms around his neck, almost faint with surprise and glee. "The mist encounters its lilac!" Just the sort of thing Pablo Neruda would say.

As well, she noticed in a glance toward the doorway how Picasso's grand smile, his teeth gleaming, his eyes brimming with laughter, was ecstatic with joy where he remained on the landing watching the embrace before him.

28
THE POLICE

The next day, Jules Supervielle came to see Pablo. He had phoned him to ask him if he had his passport. Pablo still did, although it was a bit ravaged by recent difficulties, but up to date. "Good. Bring it with you when I come over this morning." Jules, whom Pablo had known for years as a noble Uruguayan poet living in Paris, now was sixty-five years old and in poor health. He seldom went out. Pablo was moved to see Jules as he waited outside Delia's apartment building on the sidewalk. Despite the rain, he stood with obdurate certainty beneath a black umbrella, and the Seine flowed by behind him as though it were made of slow, gray lace.

"I received an important message, Pablo." Jules looked up and down the street. "My son-in-law wants to see you."

"Your son-in-law?" Pablo embraced his old friend.

"Yes. Pierre Bertaux. He's the chief of police here in Paris."

"Oh. Do you know why?"

"I don't."

They crossed the Pont Saint-Louis to the Île de La Cité and walked the streets to the police prefecture. Like all such buildings no matter where, this large, heavy building chilled the heart, although in this case, for Pablo, it did have the fortune of having been designed by some tasteful Napoleonic Frenchman. Nonetheless, he was frightened.

The two men walked up the marble staircase to the office of the chief. While they waited, seated on two wooden chairs in the outer chamber, Pablo noticed that Jules himself was nervous. A thin man, he gave off a sweet odor of frail elderliness. His wool suit, the white shirt and tie that he wore, his overcoat, and his old-fashioned high-top black shoes, even the umbrella dripping onto the marble floor, all seemed from an older time, the First War maybe. Jules's cheeks sagged. A thin bag of skin pouched below his chin. His hair was white and wispy. He spoke perfect French, having lived in Paris for decades as a child and as an adult.

Escorted into the office by a secretary, the two men sat down before a desk laden with telephones, beyond which sat Pierre Bertaux. These were the old French sort of phone that always reminded Pablo of the skeleton of a pterodactyl hung from a brass hanger. Pablo had never seen a desk with more telephones on it, about twenty of them. Pierre's features, which for Pablo were intelligently astute, studied him with doleful glumness from behind this forest of communicative metal and wood. Pablo thought that, here on these dreaded premises, he must be looking at the very end of every secret-carrying wire in all of Paris.

Pierre leaned forward and gathered his hands together on the desk. He was formal, dark-haired, and heavy-featured. "I've read your books."

Pablo sat still.

"You probably wouldn't imagine so, M. Neruda, but I know your work well."

"I…well, I…."

Pierre took up a paper folder. "I've received a petition from the Chilean ambassador, to take your passport away from you. Your ambassador claims that it's a diplomatic passport and is illegal." Pierre fixed Pablo with a dark gaze. "Is this true?"

"*Monsieur,* here it is." Pablo reached into his jacket pocket and removed the passport. Its cover was tattered at the edges and badly stained. He handed it over. "You can see that it's not diplomatic. It's a simple official passport, the one I have as a citizen. And besides, you know, I am a senator."

"The ambassador says you *were* a senator."

"I say I still am. And certainly, it can't be denied that I'm Chilean, no?"

"Having read your work, I have to agree."

"Thank you. So I have a right to that document. You have it in your hand, yes. I can't keep you from looking at it. But you can't take it away because it's my private property."

Pierre thumbed through the passport. Pablo recalled his interview of Leonel Goyeneche, the cork worker, his passport suffering the same degree of ruin as had Leonel's deed of sale. Pierre treated the document with careful delicacy, as though fearing it would soon fall apart. "I see it is up to date, as you say. Who authorized it?"

"Of course it is. But…who authorized it, you ask?"

"Yes."

Pablo glanced toward Jules, who watched the conversation in silence. Looking a moment out the window, Pablo felt his eyes tighten. "I won't tell you."

"Surely, poet, it's simply some functionary, some—"

"My government would destroy the poor fellow who renewed it for me before I left."

"I see." Pierre examined Pablo's photograph. Then he reached for one of the innumerable telephones.

The phone conversation bristled.

"No, *señor* Ambassador. I can't do it. His passport's legal. I don't know who authorized it."

There was shouting in French on the other end of the line.

"Yes, he's right here."

Hearing more shouting, Pablo imagined angry spittle spraying the ambassador's desk.

Pierre put the receiver next to his chest and whispered to Pablo. "You want to talk to this idiot?"

Pablo shook his head.

Pierre brought the phone to his ear. "No, I'm not going to let you speak with him. And let me say it again, *señor* Ambassador. It would be illegal for me to take his papers away."

The voice on the phone buzzed, syllable by syllable, with a ruggedly aimed promise of the highest level diplomatic retribution. Even Pablo heard the words.

"I can't, *señor* Ambassador. I'm sorry."

Irritated in a sort of light-hearted way, Pierre hung up on the ambassador and turned to Pablo. "He seems to be some sort of enemy of yours, Pablo." He handed Pablo his passport. "And mostly because of that, it's my judgment that you can stay in France for as long as you wish."

"Thank you, *monsieur.* It was a great pleasure for me to witness that conversation."

"A poet like you…an inventive lyric angel…I expect it *was* an interesting conversation." Pierre took up another of the many phone receivers and began to dial a number. "I'm sorry that we can't have a glass of wine together, but…" He gestured toward the phone, raising his eyebrows.

"You're busy."

"I am, yes. And I didn't care for your ambassador much. His tone of voice, you know." He continued dialing as Pablo and Jules stood up to take leave. "He reminded me of dealing with the Germans."

"You knew them?"

Pierre completed his dialing. "Intimately."

"You worked with them?"

"No, I killed them. I was in the Resistance, you see." Pierre reached across the desk to take his father-in-law's hand. "Dinner tomorrow, Jules?"

Jules' small, old hand trembled in Pierre's, despite the younger man's affectionate care for his frailty. "Of course. 9:00 o'clock? Maxim's?"

Pierre turned toward Pablo. "Will you join us, maestro?"

"I would love to."

"*Et la madame?*"

"To be sure."

Pierre glanced toward Jules. A quick smile appeared on his lips as he turned back to the telephone. "Yes, I killed them."

29

DON PABLO, INTRODUCED BY *DON PABLO*

"Stay here. And stay hidden." Picasso clapped Pablo's right shoulder, having to reach up to do it. They had known each other for twelve years, having met in Paris where Picasso, commissioned to do so by the Spanish Republican government, had been painting *Guernica* for the 1937 World's Fair. "You'll know when to come out on stage."

In all his life Pablo Picasso had given only one public speech, and in it he had praised the excellence of the poetry of Pablo Neruda. Now on this night, April 25, 1949, he was about to give his second-ever public speech, to the World Congress of Peace Forces at the *Salle Pleyel*. The audience, which represented the entirety of the leftist spectrum, therefore rumbled with unruly intensity. Laughter came from it, with much shouting, slogans, and declarations of every sort. Frédéric Joliot-Curie had come backstage, as had Paul Eluard and Louis Aragon. Both were fans of Pablo's work, as he was of theirs. Pablo also shared a few words with W.E.B. Dubois, who was a quiet man with a small white beard. Pablo had read about his work, enough to know that Dubois was truly a visionary, although not understood in his own country. Indeed, they actively condemned him there…or, rather, ignored him. Pablo felt similarly about himself, although he realized that, because of Dubois's skin color, his problems as an American were deeper than Pablo's as a Chilean.

Most surprising and gratifying for Pablo, though, was the presence of Paul Robeson. "I first heard your voice in Rangoon, *señor* Paul. I was my country's consul there, and I had a lover, my Josie, and we listened to your records."

Robeson took Pablo's hand. He had once written to the poet about how much he had enjoyed *Twenty Poems of Love and One Desperate Song.*

Pablo affected a bass voice. "'*Deep river./My home is over Jordan...*'" His spoken English was heavily accented, and Robeson smiled with the sound of it. Pablo could not remember the rest of the words. But he did remember how Robeson's somber, celebratory singing had pummeled his soul.

"And did you make love to her after listening to my recording?" Robeson was one of the most authoritative men Pablo had ever met. Dressed in a black suit, a blue tie and blood-red kerchief in the breast pocket, he seemed like the president of some vast African nation.

"Actually, while you were singing, *maestro*, many times."

Pleased, Robeson nodded and shook Pablo's hand once more.

A sudden explosion of applause took over the theater. Picasso approached the microphones, so short that the microphones hid his face. But this did not interfere with the artist's brief, gruff announcement.

"Tonight, friends, we have a surprise. I wish to introduce to you one of the best men I have ever met." A ripple of curious whispering hurried through the audience and, as Picasso awaited quiet, he glanced into the wings. Pablo held his arms out to the sides, a manuscript of a few pages in his right hand. He lifted the manuscript to his lips and used it to blow a kiss to Picasso. "Not only the greatest poet in his country, Chile." With this the whispering grew more rabid. Applause broke out. "But also, one of the greatest poets in the Spanish language, one of the greatest in the world." Picasso now extended his arms to the sides and gestured with them into the wings. He leaned toward the microphone. "Friends. Pablo Neruda!"

"He's alive!" The shout came from the audience. Others broke into noisy laughter, declarations of disbelief, and expressions of thanks and joy.

Pablo strode onto the stage and embraced Picasso. Now, applause came on like a clap of thunder, and the audience rose. The ovation grew. The two men stood hand in hand on the stage, their hands raised in a kind of joint salute, until Picasso let go of Pablo and walked to the wings, joining the now deafening roar of approval from the audience.

"My friends!"

The audience would not be quieted. A chant went up. "Neruda! Neruda!"

"Please. Friends. I beg of you."

Delia stood just before the stage, wearing a long green sleeveless gown. For Pablo she resembled a slim lilac arresting in her beauty. She applauded wildly.

"Please… Sit down, please." Pablo repeated himself several times for the next moments until finally the audience agreed to be addressed. Pablo unrolled the manuscript. He flattened it out on the lectern, adjusted the microphones before him, and leaned forward to speak. "Please pardon my little delay in arriving here."

Again, applause.

"But you see there were a few problems I had to deal with." He turned toward the wings and grinned at Picasso, whose face beamed. "And I would like to read to you my poem '*Canto a Bolívar*'."

Generous clapping accompanied the rising of voices.

"Because of what Simón Bolívar accomplished in his efforts to throw the yoke of servitude and oppression from my continent."

As so often happened when he read, the audience quieted immediately. A last few shouts of adulation finally died away. He began, and the sound of his voice justified the glories of the words themselves, as they sang of the great Bolívar and the grand reach of his ideas through the southern American continent. Pablo declaimed the sacrifices Bolívar had made to force the Spanish oppressor into the sea and to deliver the continent into the hands of those who had fought to rid themselves of the Spanish dogs.

He paused a moment, thinking about Gabriel González Videla and whether it was fair that a man like he could possibly become the president of one of Bolívar's grandest achievements. *Such an ignoramous,* Pablo thought. But that was something that could be addressed in the future. Now, Pablo allowed himself simply to revel in the sound of his own words and the humorous irony of the idea that the presumed dead Pablo Neruda could be speaking to González Videla right now, as though he had never left Chile and he were standing in the same presidential chamber with the great leader, thumbing his nose at him.

Pablo arrived at one of his favorite passages in the poem, one that reminded him of the power that Simón Bolívar had to this day and the memory he represented of Latin America's struggles. It came to him that he, Pablo Neruda, had been writing also about himself in these lines, although he had not known it at the time. Pablo's voice caught. He had to gather himself to continue. After a moment, glancing down at Delia in the front row, whose eyes rose to his, luminous with love, he continued on.

"Tus ojos que vigilan más allá de los mares,
más allá de los pueblos oprimidos y heridos,
más allá de las negras ciudades incendiadas,
tu voz nace de nuevo, tu mano otra vez nace."

("Your eyes that keep watch beyond the seas,
beyond the oppressed and wounded peoples,
beyond the black, burning cities,
your voice is born anew, your hand once more is born.")

—

Later that evening, he called it *"el estuario feminino"*, the feminine estuary, and Delia laughed so loudly, her arms flailing above her head with such glee, that Pablo quickly grabbed the opportunity to take her into his arms.

Delia hardly resisted him. "No, tell me, where did you get that phrase? The beauty of it, *poeta*." Delia kissed him once more, placing her right hand on his cheek, and then running its index finger along his right eyelid. "It's just…" She sighed, suddenly so engaged that her excitement almost overwhelmed Pablo. "It's ecstasy."

30
THE SPLENDID CITY

Pablo paused a moment. The Swedish winter moaned in its dreary winds outside the hall. He had little left to say about the Nobel Prize and his gratitude for having won it. There was little that he could say. Death had visited him, tested him, and let him go. The striving for Delia's love had saved him in the middle of the murderous Andean forest. Friendships had determined that he would make it to Paris and to Delia. The friendship of cowherds, sawyers, and a mountain climber, of a reactionary capitalist, a burro, a suffering horse, a ghostly *gauchesco* apparition, an unnervingly beautiful radio actress, a love-smitten army officer, a grand revolutionary Catalan artist, and of course…I almost forgot, he thought…Rimbaud. All these had saved him.

"It is exactly one hundred years since an unhappy and brilliant poet, the most awesome of all despairing souls, wrote down the prophesy." Pablo surveyed his solemn, bankerly Nobel audience. All of them awaited his final words. Each seemed transformed by what he had described. "'*In the dawn*,' Rimbaud said, '*armed with a burning patience, we shall enter the splendid Cities*'."

But perhaps, Pablo thought, smiling inwardly in a moment's silence, *there had been but one splendid city, the Andes cordillera.* He sighed. He waited a moment longer. He could think of little else to say, except to acknowledge the deep happiness that his love for everyone he had met in that *cordillera* had caused him.

"I'm also reminded of a remark by the famous Domingo Faustino Sarmiento, a marvelous writer." Pablo assembled his notes before him on the lectern. He was approaching the end of his remarks. "The president of Argentina a century ago, and a world traveler." He folded the pages twice and secured them in the inside vest pocket of his suit coat. "Who said 'the imposing magnitude in South America suggests scenes so peculiar, so characteristic of South America, and so far outside the circle of ideas in which the European mind has been educated, that the dramatic relations of the two continents would be unrecognized'."

A rumble of humorous interest swirled through the audience.

"And I wish to say to people of good will, to the workers, to the poets, that the whole future has been expressed in the line I mentioned by Rimbaud. Only with a burning patience can we in South America..." Pablo looked the audience over, as though finally to address each member of it personally. "...or anywhere...only with that burning patience can we live in the splendid city that will give light, justice and dignity to all mankind."

He waited, and then sunk into a brief melancholic wish to see the friends who had led him through the mountains twenty-two years previously. He missed them all, so that, tumbling into his soul's happiness, he arrived at the glistening, final circle, the circle of loving memory.

"In this way, the song will not have been sung in vain."

Terence Clarke lives in San Francisco. He is the author of the
trilogy that contains the novels *My Father in The Night,
When Clara Was Twelve, and The Moment Before.*
Available everywhere.